Seagrove Secrets

Seagrove Secrets

Love Along Hwy 30A
Book Three

Melissa Chambers

Copyright 2018 Melissa Chambers. All rights reserved.
First Edition June 2018

Perry Evans Press

ISBN: 978-1-7324156-2-1

Edited by Trish Milburn
Cover image from depositphotos

melissachambers.com

Also by Melissa Chambers

Seaside Sweets (Love Along Hwy 30A #1)

Seacrest Sunsets (Love Along Hwy 30A #2)

The Summer Before Forever (Young Adult)

Falling for Forever (Young Adult)

Chapter One

Chase O'Neil stood in front of the most gorgeous woman he'd ever seen—long, dark hair falling over her chest, intense eyes, and a lean torso that stretched down to hips that curved into one of those asses men only knew about from their dreams. Too bad she was wielding a baseball bat at him.

His friend Bo's dog had gone from barking like the devil was on the other side of the door to wagging his tail and nudging Chase with his nose, looking like he was desperate to jump up on him, but Bo had him too well-trained.

Aware that his size could be intimidating, especially to someone holding a baseball bat looking like she was expecting Freddy Kruger, Chase knelt down and stroked Jake's fur. "Oh, that's such a good boy. Look at that sweet boy. Isn't he a handsome fellow?" He wrapped his arms around his friend's dog in a hug and Jake's long tongue reached out for a wet kiss on Chase's cheek. Chase met the woman's gaze. "Would you hit a man holding a dog?"

The woman looked like she was about to whack one over the fence—that one being Chase's head. She relaxed her swinging stance and moved around Chase, scanning the perimeter of the front yard like a Secret Service agent. She closed the door and ran her hand over the top of her hair, looking like she was catching her breath. It didn't escape him that she was still holding the bat with one hand.

"Can I assume you're Shayla, Bo's sister?" Chase asked.

She exhaled deeply and switched the bat to her left hand. "Yeah." She held out her hand to him, formally. "Shayla Harrison."

"Chase O'Neil."

She looked him up and down. "Yeah, I figured that out."

His ego boosted up a little bit, which didn't take much seeing that she was just ready to take his head off. "Oh yeah?"

"I recognize you from the signs."

"Oh," he said, his cheeks heating. It hadn't been his idea to put his picture on all his signage. That'd been his marketing expert's job, and when they'd initially launched with that plan, Chase's company had been miniscule. Now, his mug was plastered all over signs stretching across the Florida panhandle, proving his smiling face on the signs hadn't been the worst idea. But standing in front of Bo's beautiful, no-nonsense sister, he felt a little silly.

She narrowed her gaze. "What the hell are you

doing with a key to my brother's house?"

"I've had it for years. I've been known to stay here with Jake on occasion when your brother's been out of town. You know how prissy he is about boarding this dog."

Shayla closed her eyes tightly, shaking her head. "Why are you here?"

He was definitely second-guessing his initial intentions, though he could have sworn they were pure. "Well, I was actually coming by to meet you. I've been trying to introduce myself for the past couple of months. I've stopped by the shop, but you've been out on jobs. Bo and I used to go to Alligator Alley quite a bit before he left. I've missed it since he's been gone, so I was heading there this evening, and on a whim thought I'd drop by here and see if you wanted to go with me."

She studied him. "Why did you let yourself into this house?"

"I rang the doorbell, and then I heard a scream and Jake barking like a banshee, and then nobody came to the door, so I was worried about you." He nodded at the bat in her hand. "Any chance I can get you to drop that?"

She looked at the bat like she didn't realize she was still holding it, and then propped it in a corner. "Thanks for checking on me." She exhaled a deep breath looking around. "Do you want to…sit down or something?" she asked, seeming like that was the last thing she wanted.

"No, I'm just heading out. Do you want to come with me?" He hated how wimpy he sounded asking that. Chase had never had trouble communicating with women in a confident but approachable way. He sounded now like he was back in sixth grade asking a girl to *go* with him. Maybe it was the bat.

"No, thanks." She stared at him, waiting for him to make the next move, which she clearly hoped was right out the door.

He nodded, heading in that direction, but a ringing phone somewhere down the hall had him turning his head by instinct. Her face lost all color, and she gravitated toward the bat again.

"Do you need to grab that?" he asked.

"No," she said quickly, stepping away from the bat.

He considered her, trying to gauge what had her so freaked out. "I meant the phone."

"Oh, no." She glanced around the living room scratching her cheek like she was displaced, Jake panting by her side, awaiting her next move.

"You know, I'm a really good listener if you had something you wanted to talk about, not that you do."

"I don't," she said.

"Okay," he said, but he didn't leave.

The phone stopped ringing, and she exhaled. But then it started up again, and she cursed under her breath, holding up a hand. "Just...I'm gonna turn that off." She headed down the hall, Jake following behind her. Chase refrained from sneaking a peak at her ass in those black, skin-tight workout pants. Though it wasn't easy.

He waited for her to come back, not prepared to leave her like this, even if she wanted him gone. She dropped the phone on the table and ran both hands across her hair, staring at it. She faced him, narrowing her gaze. "Would you like a beer?" This time, the question sounded sincere.

"Yeah," he said. "Thanks." He waited while she got the beers out of the fridge and then followed her lead, sitting at the kitchen table, Jake settling at her feet. "So, how are you liking being back home? You moved back from Nashville, right?" Chase asked.

She scraped at the label on the beer bottle with her fingernail. "Yeah. I worked for a healthcare company in Franklin, just south of Nashville."

"What did you do there?"

"Software development."

He was impressed. "Sounds a bit different from taking over Bo's pool cleaning business and shop and all. How has the transition been?"

"I wouldn't say I took it over."

"He says that."

She lifted an eyebrow.

"Not in a bad way. He just told me on the phone that he couldn't have moved to Indianapolis without you in place here. Says you saved his life, dealing with all his stuff while he went off to try to win over a girl."

Something that could almost be considered a smile crossed her lips for a brief moment, and then her brow creased just slightly. "He's coming home, you know."

"For a visit?" he asked.

"For good, actually. With Maya."

He smiled. "Son of a bitch pulled it off. Good for him."

"They'll be home this coming week sometime…temporarily. She's got interviews lined up."

"Really?" Chase smiled, realizing suddenly how much he missed his friend. "How do you feel about that?"

She shrugged. "Glad to have him back." She glanced around the room. "Guess I'll need to give him back his house." She looked down at Jake. "And his dog." Jake looked up at her and wagged his tail. She stroked him with her bare foot a couple of times, and then focused on her beer.

"Do you know where you're gonna live?" Chase asked.

"Not a clue."

"Well, you've come to the right guy."

She gave him a look. "I didn't come to you."

"Of course not. But I'm here. And this is what I do for a living."

She considered him. "Yeah, but you do beach rentals. I need something affordable."

"I've got affordable."

She tilted her head to the side. "I can guarantee you that your idea of affordable and mine are not the same."

"They are. I promise. Give me a chance. I'll just pull some listings and you can take a look. Do you want to stay in PCB?"

She pursed her lips, glancing out the window. "I'd rather get something off 30A if that's possible. I know it's high over there, but do you think there might be something in Seagrove or Seacrest? I want something really small. One bedroom, even an efficiency or studio would work, would actually be preferable."

"I think I can find you something like that in one of those areas. When do you need it?"

"I'd love to have something in place before he gets here. Otherwise he'll go on about how I don't need to leave yet and try to get me to take my time. I'm not interested in living with my brother and his girlfriend."

He bit the inside of his cheek, staring down at his beer as he remembered Bo saying that Shayla had a boyfriend a few months ago, right before she moved back. "What about you? Do you have a boyfriend?"

Her gaze went to the phone like it was the guy in question. "No."

He nodded, waiting for her to elaborate, but she just stared at the phone and then took a drink of beer.

"Was that him who called?" he asked.

She met his gaze, frowning.

"Bo mentioned you were seeing someone, but that was a couple of months ago. The night you were driving back here, actually."

"That's over," she said, staring at him.

"Okay," he said.

She stood up. "Thanks for stopping by."

He followed her lead, wishing he would have kept his mouth shut. "Can I get your email address so I can send you the listings?"

"That's not necessary."

"You need a place to live, don't you?"

She glanced around and then let out a resigned breath. "Yes, I do. Thank you." She held out her hand, and he unlocked his phone and gave it to her. He didn't want to leave. He wanted to tell her whatever was going on with her was going to work out, but that was a lie. He had no idea what she was going through if anything at all. But what he did know was that his buddy Bo was close with his sister, and if she was in some kind of real danger, and Chase just walked away from her like a dumbass when she needed someone, he'd never forgive himself, and Bo wouldn't forgive him either.

She handed him his phone. "Thank you for your help. I appreciate it." She wasn't a smiler. He wasn't used to that. He was flirty, and women were almost always flirty back with him. But this woman wasn't most women. He was figuring that out quickly.

"Have you eaten dinner?" he asked.

"Yeah," she said, but she shook her head slightly as she said it, looking off to the right. She was a terrible liar.

"Are you sure? Alligator Alley has the worst bar food in Panama City Beach."

She hinted at a smile. "That's supposed to sell me on it?"

"I could take you somewhere decent."

"I've got food here," she said. "You don't need to take me anywhere." She must have read the look on his face because she furrowed her brow. "But it's kind of you to offer."

"I just feel bad for rattling you earlier."

"I'm not rattled."

She didn't seem like the kind of woman who got

rattled often, so he imagined whatever did shake her must have been something serious.

He held up both hands. "Got it." He headed toward the door, and then turned back to her. "What are you doing tomorrow?"

She shrugged. "Cleaning, probably."

He glanced around Bo's house which looked as immaculate as the Taj Mahal for once. "Good thing. This place is filthy." He met her gaze with a smile.

She gave him an exhausted look. "Sunbathing."

If only that were true, he'd find out what beach and be there with bells on, but clearly, she wasn't serious.

"Would you like to go house hunting?" he asked.

"Tomorrow's Saturday."

"Last time I checked."

She lowered her chin. "You want to spend your Saturday working?"

"It wouldn't be unheard of. I'm in the property management business. Saturday's our busiest day."

She put her hand on her hip. "Then you don't have time to be carting me around looking for a dinky little apartment."

"Will you please let me gauge what kind of time I have?" he asked.

She pursed her lips. "Okay. Thanks." She pulled the door even farther open.

He walked through the doorway. "Should I pick you up at nine?"

"I'll come to your house since we're looking on that side of town."

He held out his hand for her phone. "Do you want my address?"

9

"I've got it in the system. We clean your pool."

"Ah. That's right. Then I'll see you at my house at nine?"

"Does that give you enough time to find something?" she asked.

"Yeah, it's all in the computer. I just have to put in the parameters. We can actually do that together at my house in the morning if you like. That way we can eliminate some duds from the outset."

"Sounds good." She scratched her forehead, and then scanned the front yard.

"Are you sure you're okay?" he asked.

"Of course I am."

Jake appeared at his feet, tail wagging. Chase reached down and petted his head. "I was going to ask if you had a security system, but I guess you have Jake, huh?"

She looked down at him, her brow furrowed in worry. "For now."

"Want me to find a place that takes dogs?"

She gave him a barely smile. "Beggars can't be choosers."

He smiled at her and held up his hand in a wave. "I'll see you in the morning."

She nodded and closed the door behind her. He walked to his Jeep and got in, but he wasn't ready to back out of the driveway just yet. He pulled up the contact she'd set up in his phone. He smiled when he saw she included her phone number. He texted her.

Hey, it's Chase. Just wanted you to have my number in case you need anything.

He waited a minute and then felt a sigh of relief

when he saw she was typing back.

Thanks.

He tossed his phone in the cup holder. He wasn't sure what to make of Shayla Harrison. She seemed impervious to him, which he wasn't used to. This was the first time in a while he hadn't been able to get a smile out of someone. Chase put on an easy, uncomplicated, fun exterior every day, and people responded to him in kind. Women flirted with him. People smiled at him everywhere he went. Deals were negotiated in his favor.

He was the fun guy. It was his job to plaster on the charm and make everyone feel better, and when he couldn't do that, he wasn't sure what he was good for. When he couldn't make others feel okay, even for a brief moment, he wasn't okay, and he couldn't go back to the place where he wasn't okay...not ever again.

Shayla settled into a spot on the couch and mindless television, because there was no way she was going to sleep after all that had just happened. How fantastic that one of Bo's closest friends got to meet her with a baseball bat in her hands.

She'd overreacted, but not without reason. Chase had rang her doorbell as soon as she'd hung up with Brian. The idea that Brian was waiting at her doorstep to go another round was enough to send her over the edge, and when that door opened, she saw broken ribs, concussions, and hospital rooms...or worse.

When it'd been Chase O'Neil instead, she'd almost kissed him out of sheer relief. There was that face she'd seen on signs covering the PCB and 30A area since she moved back two months ago. She tried not to notice how much better looking he was in person than he was on those signs, not that he didn't look good on the signs. And his height. How tall was he, anyway? She wasn't short. They'd measured her at 5'7 last time she was at the doctor. But she had to lift her chin to look him in the eye. At first, she'd been intimidated, but it didn't take long to figure out he came in peace, or in search of beer at Alligator Alley.

She winced at how rude she must have come off. Why did she have to meet him like that? This was a good friend of Bo's, and she didn't need him running his mouth back to Bo, telling him his sister was a basket case. Bo would want to know what was going on with her, and under no circumstances could Bo find out what had happened to her in Nashville.

The phone rang, but this time she was expecting it. "Hey, Scott," she answered.

"Did I wake you?"

She smiled. Every night he called at nine, and every night he asked if he'd woken her.

"No, I swear that was just that one time. I almost always stay up late. How did your date go? Are you still on it?" she asked.

He hesitated, and she winced, wishing she hadn't asked. First dates usually sucked. "Oh, it was fine. Nonstarter," he said.

"I'm sorry. Did her picture match her profile?"

"Yeah, she was fine. Sweet. Just…no chemistry."

"Mmm," she said, worried again that he was holding out for her. She'd made it perfectly clear that she wasn't interested in a relationship with him or anyone else right now, and he'd sworn he wasn't after her for anything romantic, that he just wanted to be friends. But she wasn't sure she bought it.

"So, my brother's coming back next week," she said.

"That's good, right?"

"Yeah, I'm ready for him to be home. I'll have to move, of course, but that's not a bad thing."

"You can't stay there with him?"

She chuckled. "God, no. He's bringing his girlfriend back. If I had to lay in the bed and listen to the wall thump, I think I'd cringe myself to death."

"I hear you, but Bo can…" He trailed off. They both knew what he was trying to say.

"Protect me?"

"I didn't mean it that way."

"You did, but it's okay. I appreciate your concern. But I can't live the rest of my life hiding in my brother's guest room. I've got to get out sometime."

"He's out of rehab, you know."

She exhaled a deep breath. "I know. He called tonight."

"Do I need to get Travis involved?"

"No, thank you for the offer though. He's done plenty. You have, too. You really have. I appreciate everything so much."

"Stop thanking me, Shayla. I really don't need you to do that again, okay? It kind of makes me uncomfortable. I don't want you to feel like you're indebted to me."

That was exactly how she felt. Scott was the one who helped her get away. Her last day at work, he drove home with her with his cop friend in tow. Travis kept Brian occupied while Shayla gathered what she could. Shayla had refused to press charges. The last thing she wanted was a scene...a public record, pictures, proof that she'd allowed herself to be in an abusive relationship. She just wanted it all to go away.

Two months later, Scott was still calling her daily to make sure she was okay. She wasn't sure how much of that was because he was a concerned friend, and how much was that he wanted more. There was just a feeling she had. Hints he'd dropped about how he'd always wanted to live at the beach. She'd responded with the negatives about the humidity, the traffic in the summer, even telling the story about the time Bo had run over a baby alligator on accident with his truck. He'd back off then, but another hint would come a week or two later.

"So what did Brian say to you?" Scott asked.

"You can probably guess. He wants to talk."

"That's not a good idea."

"I'm not going to, of course," she said.

"Why don't you change your number?"

She turned the sound on the television down another notch. "I was already thinking about it."

"Good. Well, I don't want to keep you."

"Thanks for calling," she said.

"Of course. Text me if you get a new number."

"Of course," she said in return.

"All right. Good night, Shayla."

Scott was a good guy. She wished she secretly had a thing for him, but when he said her name she felt nothing but friendship. She always loved it when a man she was interested in said her name.

"Good night."

Her text alert dinged as she was hanging up. It was Chase sending her a few listings.

Is this your idea of reasonably priced?

They were, surprisingly. Two in Seacrest and one in Seagrove.

Actually yes. You're good.

He texted her back with a picture of Bugs Bunny holding a carrot, all cool. She couldn't help a smile.

She texted him back with a picture of Elmer Fudd holding his shotgun. Was that a stretch? Would he get it?

He texted back.

I deserve that. I promise not to use my key next time. Good night, Shayla.

That time, a tiny flutter knocked at her belly.

Chapter Two

Shayla pulled down Chase's wooded and shaded street which was home to an eclectic mixture of houses of varying shapes, sizes, and ages. His looked a little older but was nothing to sneeze at. Tall like him with a lookout on the roof and painted navy blue and gray, it reminded her of sailing.

She sat in the driveway a minute, studying herself in the mirror and tried a smile. People smiled at handsome guys who were kind and smiling at them. She had to work on that. She looked like a psychopath.

She ran a hand over her forehead, pushing a deep breath out of her mouth. The front door opened, and he stepped out of the house, holding up a hand in a wave. She tried again with the smile, but a glance in the mirror showed her she couldn't get it up to her eyes. She was way too stressed out to smile.

She got out of the car and headed to the front

door, meeting his gaze. He was better looking today than he was last night, if that was possible. Of course, today her heart wasn't beating like an animal being chased by a lion.

"Hey," she said.

He opened the door and stood with his back against it. "Come on in. I've got some places pulled up on my computer."

She stepped into his foyer and hung back to let him lead the way. They walked through to a kitchen that didn't fit the age of the house. It was brand new from top to bottom, modern with sleek sliver, gray, and black lines and an island with a thick glass cutting top. "Did you have this recently remodeled?" she asked.

"I did, last fall. You know Seanna, Blake's wife?"

"Yeah," Shayla said. "We've met a couple of times. Her parents live in the town I lived and worked in back in Tennessee."

"She did it."

Shayla remembered that Seanna said she worked for Chase's company. "It looks good. She works for you, right?"

"Yeah. She did this before I hired her. Hell, it's part of why I hired her. She's a workhorse."

Shayla liked Seanna. She'd taken Shayla out to dinner when she'd come to visit her parents last March. That was when things were starting to head south with Brian. He'd been drinking whiskey while she was gone and by the time she'd gotten home, he'd worked himself into a mood, half-ass joking with Shayla, blaming her for everything from trolling for a new guy to having a lesbian experience. She hadn't found him funny and made sure he knew it. His answer was to say he was joking, but his eyes were no laughing matter. He'd apologized, but the sincerity wasn't there. He'd moved her to the bedroom in a way that almost felt more forceful than passion-filled. She'd acquiesced, trying to keep the dynamic light, for the first time fearing what she saw in his eyes and knowing the mood that whiskey could put him in. But she hadn't enjoyed a second of that sex. Looking back, she should have walked out the door that night. She knew better now.

Seanna had contacted Shayla several times since she'd been back home to get together, but Shayla always had a reason why she couldn't. She was too embarrassed to look her in the eye, even though Seanna knew nothing of what happened when Shayla got home that night.

Chase offered her a seat in front of the computer and pulled up a chair beside her, but not too close. "I've got the first one pulled up. It's in Seagrove."

He was so nice to her, and she'd nearly taken his head off last night. She turned to him. "Can I apologize for last night? You were just stopping by to introduce yourself and…" She wasn't sure how to finish the sentence.

"You swung a bat at my head?"

She dropped her head to the side. "For the record, I didn't swing."

"I was pretty afraid you might for a second there, till Jake welcomed me in, at least."

"Well, anyway, I'm sorry. I'm typically not that

crazed."

He huffed a laugh. "I believe you. Any chance I can get you to tell me what put you in that state?"

She let out a breath, resigning herself to tell him some version of the truth for the sake of damage control. "I'd just hung up with my ex, and I was on edge."

His practically permanent smile faded. "He does that to you, huh?"

"A little bit. It's fine, and it's over. I told him that definitively."

"And I'm guessing he didn't agree."

She sighed and gave him a look. "He's not one to take no for an answer. I'll just say that."

He frowned. "Doesn't sound too respectful."

Shayla thought about that first conversation she'd had on the phone with Brian when she got to Bo's house. Brian had cried like a baby, pleading with her. She hadn't told him she'd gone home, but she knew that would be the first place he'd look. He swore he was going to check himself into rehab, a two-month comprehensive program that included rehabilitation for domestic violence. Scott's cop friend had talked to him about it while she was packing up. She wanted him to do it for the sake of the next woman he would inevitably date, but she was afraid he wouldn't go through with it if he thought there was no hope for them on the other side, so she kept her wording vague, not promising anything but not padlocking any doors either.

"In his defense, we agreed to try something first, before we nailed the coffin shut. He held up his end of the bargain, and I still wanted out."

He narrowed his gaze at her. "That's your right, you know, to change your mind whenever you want. If he's not man enough to accept that and move on, that's his problem, not yours."

She searched his gaze, appreciating his words but feeling a pull to disclose the full truth. She felt inauthentic not to. "What we tried, it was really all on his end. He's the one who did all the work. I didn't do anything."

Chase stared at her in a way that made her feel like he was weeding through her careful words to the core of the truth, and she didn't like it.

She turned to the computer. "Anyway, what did you find?" She scrolled down the page, looking at pictures. "This one's in Seagrove?"

They spent the next half hour looking at what was available. He'd been thorough, presenting her with all possibilities. None offered any sort of security, not in her price range. He'd pulled a few that were a bit out of her range in gated communities, but she knew as well as anyone that a smile and a charismatic personality could get a bad guy into those without issue.

She marked the ones she was interested in. "Is this okay? Going to see these three?"

"Sounds good." He reached for the laptop, aiming it in his direction. "Let me just forward these to my phone and we'll head that way."

She stood up and stretched, glancing out the kitchen window. Bo had mentioned that Chase had a nice pool, and he wasn't kidding. Lagoon style with zero entry at the foot and a waterfall on the far side, semi-private hot tub around the back, all enclosed with a tall, spikey wrought-iron fence. It looked like an eight-footer. This place was as secure as Fort Knox.

A tiny house on the other side of the outdoor kitchen caught her attention. "Is that a pool house?" she asked.

"Yeah. I don't really use it like one though."

She turned back toward him. "Why not?"

He shrugged, still focused on the computer. "The main level guest room has a door that leads out to the pool. If anybody needs to change, they usually do it in there."

"What's in it? Just a room and a bathroom?"

"It's got a little kitchen, too."

"Shower?"

"Yeah."

She moved closer to the window to get a better view. A gate led out to the driveway with a sophisticated lock on it. "You've got this place secure back here, don't you?"

He shut his laptop and stood. "There's some rentals on this street. It took a handful of unwanted visitors before I finally had that fencing put up." He chuckled. "The final straw was a foursome of senior citizens in the hot tub, and they weren't relaxing, I'll tell you that."

She gaped at him. "You're kidding?"

"I'm not. I had Bo drain it while they were putting up the fence. You ready to go?"

She swallowed, nervous about asking the next question, but it was too perfect not to. "Have you ever considered renting it?"

His eyebrows went up. "You want to rent my

pool house?"

She held up both hands. "Just consider it. I'd come in and out that back gate so you wouldn't even know I was here. And if you had a…date back here, you could just text me, and I wouldn't come home till you were back inside, I swear. Or if you didn't want to text, you could just put a sock on the gate and I'd leave."

He crossed his arms over his chest with an amused look on his face. "What are we, in college?"

She closed her eyes tightly, willing this to come through for her. It was too good to be true. The street itself was hidden. She'd never even noticed it before today and she'd grown up in the area. His driveway curved around the back, so she might even be able to hide her car from plain sight. Brian would never find her here. "Please, just consider it. It wouldn't be for long. We could do a six-month lease. Three if you didn't want to commit just yet."

"Shayla, I'm not making you sign a lease."

"Oh, no. I'd want one."

"I mean, if you want to live here, you can just live here. I'll need to get a cleaning crew in there first, but—"

She held up her hand again. "First of all, I would pay to lease it, of course. Secondly, I would clean it myself. I'd actually prefer to."

He scratched his head, glancing around, and then he focused on her. "You really want to live here?"

She bit her lip, trying to think of a way to drive this home. "I don't know you, but I'm asking for this favor. I need this." He stared back at her, his eyes searching again. She cast her glance downward and pulled her hair back out of her face. "Will you just think about it?"

When she garnered the courage to meet his gaze again, a humorless smile played on his lips. "I don't need to think about it."

A breath of relief tumbled out of her. "Thank you. I promise I'll be invisible."

He smiled with his eyes this time. "I'd rather you not be, actually."

His easy smile calmed her in a way she'd craved for months, going on a year if she was honest with herself. She pocketed her hands. "When can I move in?"

"Do you at least want to see it first?"

She smiled. "Sure."

They headed that way, and she started feeling guilty for putting him in a position to pretty much have to say yes. But she couldn't second guess herself. This was what she needed right now, at least until Brian settled down. He just needed time to get past this. Whether that was a few weeks or a few months, she didn't know. But the work he'd done in rehab would have to help with his acceptance. He just needed time to process. She would find a different place when she was sure Brian was contained. Scott was keeping an eye out in Nashville. She just needed to go about her business here like everything was going to be fine, because it was. It'd have to be.

Chase opened the door to the pool house, and a muggy wall of heat assaulted her. He stepped inside and made his way to a thermostat. "I probably don't even have it on." He adjusted it while she gazed at her new place.

It wasn't nearly as bad as he'd made it out to be. A double bed sat in the middle of the place with a TV stand in front of it housing a television bought in this century.

"There's no cable out here. I just never have messed with calling them to get out here and put in an outlet, but I can call them Monday."

"No, please don't," she said. "I read a lot. I don't even care about it."

"It does get the local channels."

"That's all I need."

He looked around. "This is all there is to it. I think it's 300 square feet or something like that."

She narrowed her gaze at him. "Are you sure you don't use this? You've got a bed in here."

"No, I used the kitchen in here last fall when Seanna was redoing the one in the main house, but I haven't been back in here since. I seriously don't think that bed has ever been slept in. I bought it new when I moved in. I thought this would make a good guest house but I overestimated my popularity." She gave him a look, and he shrugged. "People who do visit like to use the guest room so they can be in the main house, near the beer. I can move this bed out if you want to use your own bed."

"No, this is good."

"Where are you storing your furniture?" he asked.

Heat spread up to her cheeks. "I don't really have any." She walked to the bathroom, hoping to avoid more questioning. "You've even got a tub in here."

"Yeah. We should probably check to make sure the water works okay."

With a turn of the handle, the faucet sputtered to life. She looked at him with a smile. "It's not even muddy and gross." Moving past him, she made her way to the kitchen. The water worked fine there, too. She peered into the microwave. "Someone's been using this."

"That was me, back when Seanna was remodeling my kitchen, so that's old food funk there."

She raised her eyebrows. "Yum."

"Well, I would have scraped it out if I'd known it was going to be inspected today."

"Funk scraping is my favorite pastime."

"Glad I can provide you with the funk then."

She smiled at him. He was so easy to be around, and really sort of fun to look at. "Do you care if I get started cleaning this today?"

"Knock yourself out."

She walked over to the door and inspected the flimsy little lock on the door handle. It was secure back there, no doubt, but a bolt lock would make her feel a whole lot better.

"Would you mind if I installed a bolt lock on this?" she asked.

He furrowed his brow. "As opposed to one of my crew doing it?"

"No, I mean, do you mind if I add that to this door, is what I'm asking."

"Of course not. But let me handle that."

"No, I can do it. I'm not trying to put you out with any of this."

"I think adding a bolt lock to a door a tenant is going to be living in is pretty standard landlord stuff."

"I want to do it myself."

"You think I won't do it right?"

She rubbed her forehead. "No. I would just be more comfortable if I knew I was the only one who had a key, and you, of course."

He nodded, but she sensed his concern...and his questions.

She jerked a thumb toward the door. "I'm just gonna run home and grab some grubby clothes and some cleaning stuff."

"I've got cleaning stuff."

"No. I'll get my own." She moved past him toward the main house, hearing him follow behind her.

"Do you need any help? I can come with you and get the lock at least."

"I've got it."

"Let me help you clean then. I can get started while you're gone."

She held up a hand. "Nope. I've got it." She started to open the door to the house, then she remembered that she said she'd leave out the gate, so she stopped short and turned around to find Chase in her face. Instinctively, she pushed him away with both hands knocking him off balance. When it registered in her brain what she'd just done, she covered her mouth with her hand, her heart rate racing. She pulled her hand away from her mouth, shaken as much by her bizarre reaction to a man close to her as her own dramatic hand-to-mouth reflex. Shayla was the collected one, always. Her dad used to tell her she had ice water running through her veins. She liked being a calming presence, not an over-reactor.

"I'm sorry. That was my fault. I just…I said I would go out the gate." She rubbed her knuckle on her forehead. "But my purse is in the kitchen, of course. I'm just going to head out that way."

She tried to force a smile, but his dumbstruck facial expression was enough to make her give up and get out of there. She hurried inside, grabbed her purse, and bolted.

Her stomach sat ill at ease as she drove down 30A. What was wrong with her? She'd never hit anyone before. She was starting now? Was this a side effect of having been hit herself? Whatever it was, she wanted it to stop.

As she passed through Rosemary Beach, her text alert dinged, making her wince. Was that Chase texting to say don't bother coming back? She'd just assaulted her landlord. She was pretty sure that could very easily be a deal breaker. She swallowed hard, rubbing her temple, trying to keep it together as she drove back to Bo's house.

This was supposed to be a happy day. Progress. She still had her house in Franklin to deal with, but during the few moments she thought she had a new home she started to feel human again. She loved her brother, but she'd simply stepped into his life two months ago. Moving into his house and his business while he went to Indianapolis to be with his girlfriend. Hell, she was even driving his truck, but she'd talked him into that. He was living downtown in Indianapolis, and she convinced him it'd be easier to maneuver her car up there than his truck. That way she also could use his truck for the business, so they'd switched. That it also gave Brian one less way to find her was a definite plus.

Two months ago, she'd needed a new life away from Brian and Nashville, but while still paying on her house and bills in Franklin she couldn't afford a new place. Bo's exit had worked out perfectly. But Bo's house and Bo's business weren't her life, not long-term. Moving to her own space that she was paying for herself would be a step in the direction to feeling like a whole person again. And Chase's tiny house could be that first step. They hadn't even discussed a price, but with him saying she could just live there, she was sure they could settle on something reasonable.

But that text waiting for her could change all that.

She made it all the way home without looking. She needed a few moments to dream that this could still happen. The setup was too perfect to be real. Beside the security and privacy, she was tired of being alone. She liked the idea of living a stone's throw from a person, and one who she liked. She had to admit that living next to a guy who was six and a half feet tall didn't hurt matters. He wasn't buff like Brian, but he was in decent shape. He had plenty of muscle—she'd noticed it in his forearms, not that she was looking. But he damn sure looked like he could take care of himself, especially if Brian were to show up at his house.

God, what was she thinking dragging a nice guy

like Chase into her mess? It didn't matter. He had probably just texted her to fuck off, anyway.

She put Bo's truck in park and stared at her phone, afraid to pick it up. When she finally did, she garnered up the courage to swipe his text open.

Bring Jake back with you if you want. Does he do windows?

Relief washed over her and she smiled without even thinking about it. But her smile faded as soon as it came. She definitely didn't need to be dragging him into her shit.

Chapter Three

As Chase sat at his kitchen table working, he tried not to pay attention to the woman in his pool house, but that was about as doable as wrestling a whale. He'd almost felt like he knew her before he ever met her because of how much Bo had talked about her over the years. But this woman's personality didn't match the one Bo had described. Bo had talked of a sister who kept peace between him and his brother with her calm personality and in high school was voted most likely to have Robert De Niro as her sidekick.

The woman he'd spent time with these past two days was on edge. He could see flashes of the personality Bo described when she was wordlessly calling him out on a stupid joke or when she seemed to momentarily forget what was clearly weighing down on her, and he had heavy suspicions of what that might be.

Between the security concerns and the way she shoved him when they almost collided earlier, it didn't take a rocket scientist to figure out that either someone had hurt her or they'd tried. He suspected Bo knew nothing about it or he wouldn't be still up in Indiana in la-la land with Maya. Bo adored Maya, but Chase had never been around him when he didn't either talk to or about his sister. If he had a clue she was in distress, his ass would be down here.

Chase felt a pull in the direction of telling Bo what he was witnessing. Chase would want to know if the tables were turned. Of course, Chase didn't have a sister. But he had brothers, and if he knew one of them was in trouble he'd move the Gulf of Mexico to help them. But Chase didn't know anything for certain, so there was no need for alarming Bo just yet. Besides, Chase could keep his eye on her until Bo moved back, which wouldn't be long.

Chase remembered his trip to Vegas with his investment group this week. He'd have to figure a workaround for that.

The doorbell rang, and Chase went to answer it, letting the grocery delivery guy in. He signed off on the receipt and started unloading food. Blake and Seanna would be there in an hour and a half. He wanted to invite Shayla to stay, but he was half afraid to approach her again. He'd never gotten signals to back off from a woman in a more extreme way. He wasn't one of these alpha males who took a rejection as a challenge to try harder. He only needed to be told no or anything similar to it once.

There were too many women in this world to get hung up on one.

But then again, if she stayed here cleaning and saw Blake and Seanna come in, she might feel weird that he didn't invite her. And it wasn't a date. Shayla knew Blake and Seanna. It was friends hanging out, and she was here. He finished with the groceries and then headed out to the pool house.

Jake wagged his tail from his spot in the sun by the pool. Chase had always wanted a dog but he traveled a lot for work, and he didn't want to be constantly boarding it or having to arrange for someone to come let it out. He also didn't always make it home on a Friday or Saturday night, and he wouldn't let a dog ruin his chances to spend the night with a beautiful woman. Of course, when was the last time he'd done that? Felicity two months ago, for sure. When before that? He probably didn't want to look under that rock.

He knocked on the door, and it opened by itself. It must have been ajar. "Hello?" he said, glancing around.

She poked her head out of the bathroom, wiping her forehead with the back of her arm. "Hey."

Standing there in dirty shorts and a T-shirt holding a toilet brush, her hair up in a loose ponytail/bun thing, wet strands hanging down in her face, she was still one of the most beautiful women he'd ever seen in person, and he'd known a lot of beautiful women in his life. How a man could hurt this woman, any woman, was so far out of his brainstem that he couldn't even fathom it, and the idea caused an ache in his chest.

"The place looks great. I should have asked you to rent much sooner," he said.

She looked over at the bed. "Do you care that I changed the bedding out?"

"Of course not. I'm glad you're making it your own."

"I'm gonna take your old bedding home tonight and wash it."

"You know, I do have a washer and dryer in the house."

"I imagine you do, but no thanks." She glanced around. "It's really perfect. I can't thank you enough." She narrowed her gaze. "We didn't actually talk about rent yet."

"Yeah, I was hoping we wouldn't have to. I'm not out anything by you living here. I just don't see any sense in you paying me."

Her expression turned serious. "I'm paying you or we're not doing this."

He glanced around. "Look at what you've already done. I owe you."

"Chase, I'm not playing."

Damn. She wasn't with that tone. "Okay, what works for you? Fifty bucks a month?"

She rolled her eyes. "That's not funny."

"A hundred, but you're killing me."

She stared at him. "Would five hundred a month work? Plus utilities, of course."

"Including utilities and you've got a deal."

She shook her head, a smile playing on her lips. "That's the most ass-backwards negotiation I've ever been a part of. You say you're a successful businessman?"

"I never said that."

"Your face plastered all over South Walton says differently."

He winced. "You know that wasn't my idea."

"Mmm hmm. Whose idea was it?"

"My marketing team."

"Led by a woman, no doubt."

He scrunched up his face, busted. His neck heated a little bit, wondering if she was insinuating that his was a nice-looking face.

"Mmm hmm," she said again and headed back into the bathroom.

"Wait," he said, scratching his cheek. Why was he nervous? He didn't get nervous around women, especially ones in the process of scrubbing a toilet. "Blake and Seanna are coming over at six. I'm grilling steaks if you'd like to join us."

She blew some stray hairs out of her face. "Thanks for the invite, but I'll head out in just a minute."

He nodded. "Okay." One no was all he needed to hear. He turned to leave, but his feet were heavy like they were muddled down in quicksand. He turned back around and opened his mouth to speak, but she'd already disappeared into the bathroom. He started to leave again, but his desire to know what was going on with her won out. He walked back toward the bathroom. "Are you sure you want to deal with Seanna knowing you left before she got here?" He pushed the door open to find her on the floor with her knees straddling the toilet. Why the hell did he find that sexy?

She dropped her posture. "She knows I'm here

right now?"

"No, but do you want me to not mention you're here?"

She pulled her leg out from under her. "No, don't hide anything. It's not like people aren't going to find out. Just let me call my brother before you tell her I'm here."

"I'm not planning on talking to her before she gets here at six."

"What time is it now?" she asked.

"Four-thirty. Are you gonna run home?"

"I've actually got my clothes from earlier. I just grabbed these when I was at home and changed here."

He paused to take in the fact that she was naked in there earlier, momentarily. What was he, twelve? "You've got a shower right there."

She glanced in there. "I don't have any soap or anything."

"Use my guest room. It's stocked."

She met his gaze. "Really?"

He shrugged. "Yeah."

"I'm crashing your party. This is exactly what I was trying to avoid...you thinking you had to include me in stuff."

"First of all, this isn't stuff. This is two people, both of whom you are friends with, coming to my house to eat steaks. It's mainly so I can see Blake, who I never see anymore outside of work because he's old and married now. But he also never sees his wife which is sort of my fault because she works for me, so we compromise and Seanna and I agree to stomach each other another day of the week for the sake of her husband's and my friendship. But I promise you what will end up happening is they won't be able to keep their hands off each other, and if you're not there, I'll have nobody to roll my eyes at."

A smile played at her lips. "You and Seanna have trouble stomaching each other?"

"Not Monday through Friday, but we're both damn sick of each other by the weekend."

"Why didn't you two get together?" she asked and then winced. "That was a dumb question. Don't answer it."

"Can I if I want?"

She gazed at him with that barely there smile and shrugged.

"Actually, I really don't know. She was remodeling my kitchen, and then I was offering her a job. I guess I saw her as more of a co-worker than a date. Besides that, Blake was nuts over her from the start. Anyone with senses could tell. I didn't want to get my ass kicked."

Her smile deepened, still closed-mouth though. She wasn't easy to impress. Some people would laugh at anything he said, courtesy or otherwise, but Shayla was stingy with her smiles. He could appreciate that.

She tossed a glob of wet paper towels in the wastebasket and stood. "I'll grab a shower if that's okay."

"Be my guest. Or my tenant, I guess."

She moved past him and grabbed a bag off the kitchen table. He closed the door behind them and followed her to the house. "When will you move

36

in?"

"I probably need to stay at Bo's until he gets here because of Jake."

"Jake is welcome here."

She gave him a look as she weaved around the corner of the pool. "You say that now."

"He's been fine all day. He's just been sleeping by the waterfall. It's a good thing, too, because he's got a date coming over tonight."

She opened the door to the house. "Did you tell Blake to bring his dog?"

"Yeah."

She looked at the pantry. "Oh, crap. I need to get him some food for tonight."

"I'm making him a steak."

She shifted her gaze to him. "You're not serious."

"I'm totally serious. He's got to eat."

"Not a steak."

"I've got one marinating for him, Sadie too."

She looked him up and down. "It's a good thing you don't have a dog of your own. You'd spoil it rotten."

"Probably so."

She pointed at the living room. "Your guest room's through there?"

"Yeah, here." He moved past her and headed that way. His cleaning crew always kept it clean and stocked, but he wanted to check it out, just in case. He and Felicity had used that room the week she was here. There was no need for women he wasn't attached to seeing his bedroom or the picture on his nightstand.

He hadn't had a woman back to his house since Felicity was there, the same week Bo met Maya. Felicity had kept him busy for a full week, wore his ass out. He liked her a lot, but he was ready for her to go back to Indianapolis when she did. He wasn't getting attached, but if she would have hung around much longer, he'd start to feel like he was lying to her if he didn't tell her about Sam. Felicity was all about having fun, and so was Chase. The last thing he wanted was to burden her with his personal shit.

They still talked about twice a week, among other things. She'd call him and tell him about a date she'd been on that went well or didn't. He'd make her laugh, and then she'd lower her voice into that breathy register that was as goofy as it was sexy, and the two of them would finish each other off from seven hundred miles apart. He didn't really even hit on other women anymore. That wasn't true. He hit on them, bought them drinks, flirted, and then came home and called Felicity. It was kind of fucked up now that he was thinking about.

He scanned the area around the bed for condom wrappers while Shayla checked out the shower.

"Got everything you need in there?" he asked, peering into the bedside wastebasket, which had been emptied at some point during the past couple of months, thankfully.

"Looks like it. Thanks."

He gave her a nod and left her to it…to get naked in his shower, soapy suds dripping down her breasts and over the curve of her ass. He shook himself back to earth.

"Damn it," he said under his breath as he headed

to the kitchen. "I've got to get laid for real."

Chapter Four

Shayla combed through her hair with a pick. She really needed to get a trim, but she hated messing with it. Maybe she should get it cut short, just in case. She rolled her eyes at herself in the mirror. She wasn't on the run, not really.

She sat on the bed and held her phone in her hand. She needed to talk to Bo so she could tell him she'd found a place. This should be a simple thing, but with as much meddling as her bother did in her life she was bound to get pushback of some kind.

She woke up her phone to multiple text alerts that she had no interest in reading. She didn't even want to see who they were from, because she highly suspected she already knew. She swiped them away and pulled up Bo's contact.

"Hey," he said by way of greeting.

"What's up?"

"I called you earlier," he said.

"I know. I've been cleaning."

"You were cleaning when I called you day before yesterday."

She crossed one leg over the other, ready to break the news. "I wasn't cleaning your house. I've got a new place to live."

"What are you talking about?"

"I've rented an apartment. Well, kind of like a tiny house."

"A tiny house? Where did you find one of those?"

"Actually, it's at your friend Chase's house."

He sat silent for a moment, and she rolled her eyes, readying herself for a potential battle. "Chase's house. When did you meet him?"

"Last night. He came by the house to say hello. Had a beer."

"Did he hit on you?"

"What the fuck, Bo?"

"Look, he's my good friend, but I don't want you dating him."

She huffed a laugh. "Since when have you ever told me who to date?"

"He sleeps around a lot. I've known him going on five years now and he's never had a girlfriend."

"Maybe he's gay," Shayla said, eyeing the door, hoping he couldn't hear her.

"He's not fucking gay. I can promise you that."

"You can straighten out your panties, baby brother. I'm not dating him."

"What are you doing renting his pool house then?"

"Uh, renting his pool house."

41

"I don't like this. You need to stay at my house, at least till Maya and I get home and get settled. I'll help you find somewhere."

That was so typical Bo, trying to run Shayla's life like she was his kid. She guessed that's what she got for agreeing to work for him again, and live in his house, and drive his damn truck.

"Like I said, I've already found a place," she said.

"Well, what about Jake?"

"Oh, he ran away last week."

"Let me talk to him," Bo said, ignoring her.

"I'm not putting that dog on the phone with you again."

"Come on, I miss him."

She hauled herself up off the bed and went out the door leading to the pool and called him. "Jake! Come here, boy. Daddy wants to talk to you."

Shayla put the phone on speaker while Bo carried on in his doggie voice. Jake just panted and stared at Shayla. She put the phone back to her ear. "You finished?"

"What did he do?"

"He flipped you the bird."

"Damn, I miss that dog."

"When will you be here?" she asked.

"This week. Not sure which day yet. I was going to hire movers, but Blake said he'd be pissed if I didn't let him come up and help."

"You two are worse than teenage girls."

"Don't disparage me because I have good friends. So back to this thing with you and Chase."

"There is no thing with Chase and me other than

a rental agreement." The door to the kitchen opened, and Shayla stepped back inside the guest room.

"Before you sign anything, let me get home so we can talk about this," Bo said.

"We've just talked about it."

"What about your house in Franklin? Has it sold yet?"

She shut her eyes tightly. There was nothing on earth she hated worse than lying to her baby brother. "We've had some showings."

"Man, I don't understand that. Seanna told Blake that the market in Nashville was a seller's market right now. Why don't I stop by there on my way down and check it out? I can—"

"No," she said, way more forceful than she intended. "We've got it priced too high. I'm gonna lower the price."

"What do you have it priced at?"

She rubbed her temple. God, she didn't even have a clue what her house was worth. She should know, but she'd been preoccupied these past few months. "I'll check with the real estate agent."

"You okay?"

This is why she didn't want to call him. They were way too damn close. He could tell when she was scratching her ass. How was she supposed to hide something this big from him? "Of course I'm okay."

"You sound weird."

"You sound like an asshole."

He sat quiet for a moment, and then said. "All right then."

She breathed a temporary sigh of relief, but she wasn't off the hook. Just reprieved for the moment. "I'll talk to you tomorrow, okay?"

"Keep your distance from Chase."

"Bye," she said.

She tossed her phone on the bed with her bag of dirty clothes. Now that she'd talked to Bo, she didn't need it for the rest of the night. Her mom was the only other person she really cared to talk to, and she and her dad were expecting her tomorrow night for dinner.

She made her way to the kitchen where she found a warm oven and four potatoes wrapped in aluminum foil on top. She watched Chase as he cleaned his grill with a brush. He didn't seem like the womanizing type, but Bo damn sure seemed to think he was. Bo should know. The two of them were good friends.

Chase flirted, but he wasn't one of those guys who thought a lot of himself. He was a nice guy, too, accommodating. She couldn't imagine him leaving a trail of broken hearts along 30A, but maybe he had.

He closed the grill and headed her way. She stepped back from the window and went to the stove where she pretended to be checking the potatoes. "Should I put these in the oven?" she asked as he came through the doorway.

"Yeah, that'd be great. What do you drink?" he asked. "I've got IPA, pilsner, wheat beer, or do you want wine? I've got that in the dining room."

"You have a wine rack in there?" she asked.

"Yeah, come pick out what you want."

She didn't really want wine, but she did want to see his wine rack, so she followed him in there. Two big, circular racks featuring about twelve bottles each hung on the far wall. The wall next to them was a full bar with cabinets up top, a sink, a stocked wine refrigerator, and what she suspected might be an ice machine. "Is that ice?" she asked.

"Yeah. I'm picky about my ice. This is gourmet style," he said with a grin. She lifted an eyebrow, and he opened it and pulled out a piece. "I'm serious, that's what it's called." He tossed it in the sink.

She didn't understand his kind of money. She made decent money in Franklin, but it wasn't enough to spend on a gourmet ice machine and all those bottles of wine, and she doubted they were in the ten-dollar range.

"Do you drink red or white?" he asked.

She hated that she hadn't been able to bring anything to this, but it was what it was. "I like beer, actually. You said you have pilsner?"

He smiled and headed back into the kitchen. "I should have known. I only keep that here for Bo. It's been in there a few months."

"I'm sure it's fine," she said. "And I'm the one who got him drinking pilsner, not the other way around."

"Damn copycat," he said, pulling a beer out of the refrigerator. He popped the cap on a wall-mounted opener and handed it to her.

She held it up. "Thanks."

He picked up his open beer from the countertop and clinked it against hers. "To roommates."

She lifted an eyebrow. "Ish."

He shrugged. "Ish."

The doorbell rang, and he set his beer down. She rested against the countertop, collecting herself. It was just Blake and Seanna, but it felt like an army descending on her. She hadn't socialized with friends in the longest time, definitely not since she'd been back home, and for months before that as well. She'd become isolated in her own home. The worse things had gotten with Brian, the more she internalized it all. Her main friends were her work friends, and they knew him, too. She didn't want anyone knowing what was happening. Some well-meaning friend would be likely to call in HR and then she'd have a nightmare on her hands. She was fine to handle it herself. The last thing she had wanted was a public stink with her at the center as victim. The idea made her shudder.

Seanna's sweet voice warmed her for the first time in a while. Shayla really should have called her before now, but she was here and ready to enter the land of the living again. Tonight was a step.

Seanna walked into the kitchen with a platter of something in her hand and stopped short when she saw Shayla. "What!" she shouted.

Shayla couldn't stop the smile making its way across her face, and she was even more regretful that she'd waited this long to connect with Seanna.

Seanna set the platter on the table and opened her arms wide. "What in the world? Chase, why didn't you tell me Shayla was coming?" She wrapped her arms around Shayla and hugged her so tightly Shayla had to hold her breath a second. Seanna kissed her on the cheek and then wiped at the spot with her thumb. "Sorry. I'm just so happy to see you. And I had a glass of wine before we left the house."

"It's good to see you, too."

Sadie came in next, leading Blake in by her leash. Blake's eyes widened, and a smile stretched across his face. "Oh, hell yeah." He handed the leash to Seanna and then wrapped his arms around Shayla and picked her up off the ground. "I haven't seen you in like…I don't even know."

"You weren't here last Christmas when I came," she said.

Seanna and Blake exchanged a look, and then Seanna said, "The Kansas City days. We don't speak of those."

"Ah," Shayla said. "I've never actually seen the two of you together."

Seanna put her arm around Blake. "We don't match, do we? He's too traditionally handsome for me."

"Are you nuts, woman?" Blake asked, and Seanna answered with a kiss.

Chase cleared his throat and gave Shayla an *I told you so* look.

Sadie barked, looking out the window, and Seanna let her off the leash and opened the door. She turned back around and looked between Chase and Shayla. "What is this? I didn't even know you guys knew one another."

"We don't," Shayla said, and then seeing the slightly hurt look in Chase's eyes, quickly corrected to say, "Not really. We just met yesterday."

47

"She's moving in," Chase said.

Seanna closed one eye looking at Chase, clearly used to deciphering when he was joking and when he was being serious. Shayla was in just a good enough mood to play along.

"I am," she said.

Seanna shifted her gaze to Shayla, who was not one who joked often. Seanna's eyes widened. "Okay."

Chase raised an eyebrow at Shayla, which she took as a question to see if they could take this a little further. Shayla responded by walking over to him and sliding an arm around his back. What the hell. She was in a good mood for the first time in months.

"I don't know," she said, looking up at him, "It was just sort of magical meeting him yesterday."

Seanna's eyes grew even wider, but Blake's wary expression deepened. Seanna didn't know her as well as Blake did. Blake was like a third brother to her, not that she needed another one. But he was way too clued in to know that *magical* was not a word in Shayla's daily vocabulary.

She looked back up at Chase again, and he met her gaze this time. "Yeah, I've never met anyone like her before. She took me off guard." He furrowed his brow, and his mouth slightly opened. He had unexpected hazel eyes that she hadn't noticed before now, and they were focused on her mouth.

A wave of tingles through her belly caught her completely off guard, and she moved away from him. "I'm just teasing. But I am moving in. I'm renting his pool house."

"Oh," Seanna said, looking more relieved than Shayla was comfortable with. "When do you move in?"

Shayla checked with Chase for confirmation, and he shrugged. "Tomorrow?"

"I'm available tomorrow," Blake said.

"Thanks, but I don't have that much stuff. Chase already has a bed in there and everything."

Seanna tossed up both hands. "Let's go see it."

"Okay," Shayla said.

"I'll help Chase drink his beer in here," Blake said.

"Ooh, give me one," Seanna said.

Chase uncapped one and handed it to her. Shayla didn't miss a significant look exchanged between Seanna and Chase, a warning glance on Seanna's part. What was wrong with these people? Shayla was more than capable of handling herself and every one of them knew it.

"You need another?" Seanna asked Shayla, glancing at her bottle.

"I'm good," Shayla said, and then headed to her place.

"Not bad to get to walk through a path of palm trees and a swimming pool to get home," Seanna said.

"I lucked out," Shayla said, and then opened the door, letting Seanna in.

"Wow, this place is really cute, isn't it? I've never even been in here."

"It's all I need," Shayla said.

Seanna peered out the door at the house, then

shut it behind her and met Shayla's gaze. Shayla had only been around Seanna twice before—on Christmas day at their family's house, when she and Blake were apart in distance and in relationship, when Seanna and her aunt Cassidy had come for dinner, and then when Seanna had visited her parents in Franklin and had taken Shayla out to dinner. Shayla couldn't say she knew Seanna too well, but from what little she did know, she'd figured out that Seanna wasn't one to mince words or leave a stone unturned.

Seanna narrowed her gaze at Shayla, and then had a seat on the bed. Shayla followed suit.

"What's going on here?" she asked, pointing a finger randomly between the house and Shayla.

Shayla shrugged. "He came by the house last night to introduce himself. He was headed to Alligator Alley and wanted me to join."

"And from that you decided to live together?"

Shayla gave her a look. "We're not living together."

"What was that in there?" Seanna asked.

"An attempt at a joke that I shouldn't have tried to pull off, apparently. You know I'm not funny."

"First of all, you're one of the funniest people I know, especially when you're ragging on your brother."

Shayla shrugged. "That comes naturally."

"Secondly, you may have been joking back there, but Chase was not."

Shayla waved her off. "Oh, yeah he was."

"I know that man. I work with that man every day, intimately. That look he had on his face when you had your arm around him and were looking up at him…that was no joke, my friend."

Shayla rolled her eyes and picked at the bedspread. "That's just stupid. I've known him one full day."

Seanna held up both hands, eyebrows raised. "Well, I'm just sayin'. That was weird."

"Excuse me?"

"Not you. Him."

"Why was it weird?"

She pointed at the house. "You don't know him. He doesn't like girls."

"He's gay?" Shayla asked. She'd been joking earlier when she'd said that to Bo.

"No, God no. He just doesn't fall for women. He dates plenty." She rolled her eyes. "Trust me. And he flirts shamelessly. When we go out of town, he always ends the night at the hotel bar when I go to my room. I don't know what he does down there." She held up both hands. "I don't ask."

"You think he gets prostitutes?"

"I didn't say that." But the look on her face indicated it.

Shayla shifted on the bed. Seanna's description of Chase didn't line up with the respectful, caring guy Shayla had been getting to know these past two days, but it did line up with what Bo had said about him. Shayla wasn't altogether sure she liked this version. Being single and thirty-six, she'd had her fair share of partners, but she couldn't help be a little grossed out at the idea of Chase with a slew of women. How many women? Were they talking fifty or five hundred?

Not that it mattered. She had no right getting up in his business. She wasn't his girlfriend and she had no plans to be. She needed this to be a stable place for her to live, nothing more.

"Probably not on the prostitutes," Seanna said. "I just saw him talking to one once. Anyway, I'm not saying he's in love with you. I'm just saying he's interested."

Shayla dropped her head down to the side, giving Seanna an exhausted look. "Anyway."

"So I guess you know your brother's bringing Maya back with him. Is that why you're moving out?" Seanna asked.

"I'm not living there with him and his girlfriend."

"Have you talked to her yet?" Seanna asked.

"A couple of months ago, the week she met Bo."

Seanna grinned. "I heard. She's mortified about that, by the way."

"You heard about it?" Shayla asked.

"Oh yeah. She called me when she got back to Indianapolis to see if I could get your mailing address so she could send you an apology card. I told her to send it to Bo's house. Did you get it?"

"Yeah," Shayla said, remembering the card and the night. Bo had ended things between the two of them, and Maya had gotten wasted and came to Alligator Alley to confront him, only to end up passing out on him, and then puking her guts out later that night at his house. Shayla had been there for cleanup duty.

"She can't believe she met you the morning after she hugged your brother's commode."

Shayla smiled. "I think my memory of meeting her might be different than hers."

"How so?" Seanna asked.

"The night before when she was puking in Bo's toilet, I was cleaning up some that didn't make it all the way to the bathroom, and when she saw me, she said, "Megan Fox is cleaning your floor?" Shayla slurred her words, swaying from side-to-side as she said it.

Seanna died laughing and pointed at Shayla. "You totally do look like Megan Fox."

Shayla rolled her eyes, but smiled. "It's fine. I've been there. Not recently, thank God, but I've been there." She tapped Seanna on the leg. "Hey, how was your wedding, by the way?"

"Oh," Seanna said, waving her off. "It was good. We did it in Nashville. Really small. Just my family, and Bo and Maya came down for it. No fuss whatsoever. I posted the pictures to Facebook." Seanna pointed at her. "This is going to sound weird, but did you unfriend me?"

Shayla scratched her forehead, her ears filling up with heat. "No, of course not."

"Maya tried to find you on there, and she said she couldn't. So I was going to do a friend suggestion, but I couldn't find you in my friends."

Shayla was hoping to get away with simply saying she didn't look on there much anymore, but the cat was out of the bag. "I closed my account."

"Why?"

Shayla shrugged. "I never get on there anymore." She left it at that, and Seanna just nodded but didn't seem satisfied with the answer. Shayla pressed her hands down on her own legs. "Well, that's probably as long as Blake can stand to be away from you."

Seanna laid down on the bed. "He'll live. I may not though. I miss him while I'm at work, like seriously miss him like he's on a different planet. Is that not goofy?"

Shayla gave her a smile.

Seanna pointed at her. "Hey, what happened to that guy you were dating when I saw you in Nashville earlier this year? You worked together, right?"

Shayla's heart rate picked up speed. "We broke up."

"Oh, wow. Really? I'm sorry."

Shayla shook her head. "It's fine."

"When did it happen? When you moved back here?"

"Yeah."

"Mmm," Seanna said, nodding, clearly wanting more info, but Shayla's lips were sealed.

Shayla lay down beside her, settling in. "So, tell me all about the wedding."

Chapter Five

Blake had been satisfied with Chase yapping away about the kickoff of college football season and who was looking good thus far, but as soon as Chase let the conversation lull for a second, Blake pounced on him.

"So," Blake said, holding his beer bottle, eyeing the pool house and then raising his eyebrow at Chase.

Chase stood and went over to the oven, needlessly checking on the potatoes. "So the fuck what?"

"So what's this about?"

"She needs a place to stay."

"Hmm," Blake said. "If only she knew someone who worked in real estate."

Chase rested his ass against the counter. "I offered that. Even looked up a bunch of places for us to go see. But when she saw the pool house that was what she wanted."

"Why?" Blake asked.

Chase held his hands out to the sides. "What am I, chopped liver?"

Blake waggled a finger at him. "None of this is adding up. Are you dating her?"

"No, I'm not screwing her. That's what you mean to ask, isn't it?"

Blake shrugged. "Does Bo know about this?"

"Fuck Bo. I'm not scared of Bo." Blake gave him a look. "All right, I'm a little scared of Bo. But I'm not screwing her."

"Why not find her a place somewhere other than your backyard."

"Do I need to repeat that she is the one who asked if she could live there? Why do you care, anyway? She's not your sister."

Blake pointed at him. "She is for all intents and purposes until Bo gets back as far as you're concerned."

Chase tossed up his hand. "Why is everyone hating on me? I saw that look Seanna gave me earlier. What have I done?"

"You go through women like potato chips. Ninety-nine percent of the time we don't care, but Shayla is a big exception."

"Listen to you...*we*. What, you got married and now you're a plural pronoun?"

Blake shrugged. "It's your ass that's on the line, not mine."

Chase walked over to Blake, hovering over him, using his size for intimidation. "I'm not screwing her. Do you want me to pronounce it in Swahili?"

Blake just gave him a lazy, dismissive look. Chase knew better than to try to act tough. He was so bad at it. Blake loved to fight, and so did Bo. They loved to fight each other like brothers, which Chase thought was idiotic. Chase was the oldest of three brothers, but he wasn't allowed to lay a finger on either of them. His mother was a Buddhist and was all about peace. Chase had grown up soft as a result, despite his size. It usually didn't bother him, but every once in a while he would get the urge to go up to some asshole and say boo just to watch him flinch. But this asshole at his kitchen table knew better.

"You want to put on the steaks?" Blake asked.

"Sure," Chase said, moving toward the refrigerator.

"So why do you think she wants to live here? She doesn't seem into you."

Chase shoved the plastic container with the marinating steaks at Blake. "Thanks."

"Really, why here? Were you trying to rent it?"

Chase closed the refrigerator door and grabbed his beer. "No, I'm telling you, she's the one who brought it up. Started asking me all kinds of questions about it. I couldn't really say no."

Blake pushed through the back door and headed for the grill. "What was she asking?"

"Mainly about the security of the place. That seemed like her primary concern."

Blake set the container down and narrowed his gaze at Chase. "Did she seem overly concerned about security?"

Chase wanted to be careful. He didn't know what

was going on with Shayla, and he hadn't had time to get to the bottom of it. "I don't know. Shouldn't a single woman be concerned about security?" He glanced at the pool house where the two women were lying on the bed, talking. "Especially one who looks like her?"

Blake looked at the pool house and then back at Chase, pursing his lips.

"What? You're so indifferent you can't see she's hot as fuck?"

Blake glared at him. "I can see it."

"That's what I thought." Chase lifted the top of the grill with authority. "And for the record, I'm capable of keeping my dick in my pants even with a beautiful girl living on my property, despite popular opinion."

Blake snarled at him, walking over to the pool house, and went inside.

"She doesn't seem into you," Chase said, attempting Blake's voice, which he sucked at. He chose a steak he would give to Blake and gave it the finger.

Chase raised an eyebrow across the table at Shayla. "How many can you get?"

She looked down at her cards. Her hand sucked just badly enough. "I'm going nil."

"You sure about that?" he asked.

"Have I let you down yet?"

He smiled at her. "All right then. I'm going for seven."

"Well, I think we know whose got all the cards," Seanna said. "We'll go seven, too." Blake gave her a look. "We gotta go out with a bang."

Blake conceded.

They all laid down their cards, Shayla throwing her highest cards on off suits when she could. With each round she sweated it a little harder, but she kept her outer appearance as cool as possible. Chase eyed her. "Will you have some trust in your partner?" she said.

"I trust you," he said with a grin. Was he getting cuter as the night went on, or was that just the beer? Unfortunately, she'd just had the one beer all night, so it was probably him.

She held the last card in her hand. It was an ace, but of a suit that'd been played a few times already, so she crossed her fingers hoping Blake wouldn't lead with hearts. Blake studied her before finally laying down his six of diamonds. She breathed a sigh of relief as they all threw down their cards and waited for her. She winced like it hurt, lowering her head, and then glanced up at Chase, who was holding back a grin. Either he had been counting cards, or she was a terrible actor.

She set her card down, and Blake and Seanna both yelled, "No!" simultaneously. Seanna picked up her empty beer and shook the bottle. "Well, that was fun."

"I'll help you do these dishes before we leave," Blake said.

"No, don't. I'll do them. It's not much," Chase said.

"I'll help him," Shayla said, and Chase didn't argue with that.

"All right," Blake said. "I'll grab Sadie."

They hugged their goodbyes, Shayla promising to meet Seanna for lunch soon. Shayla headed back to the kitchen to get to work.

"Thanks for staying to help me clean," Chase said, following behind her.

She opened the dishwasher. "I helped make the mess."

He walked into the living room. "What kind of music do you like?" he yelled out.

"Different stuff."

"Do you like the Stones?"

"Who doesn't like the Stones?" she yelled back over the rush of the water.

A minute later "Start Me Up" came through the speakers, and he appeared in the kitchen.

"Is this a playlist you made?" she asked.

"It's a CD. Remember those?"

"Vaguely. Is this *Tattoo You*?"

He smiled. "Nice, you know the albums?"

"I had this one, but so did every other redneck girl in PCB."

He dumped scraps into the trash from a platter. "I can't imagine you a redneck."

"Try harder. I drove a '77 Trans Am."

"T-tops?" he asked.

"I wished. It wasn't in good shape either. If I had the money back for every time I had to have it towed home, I could quit my job."

"Repairs must have been expensive," he said.

"Not when you have a brother who's good with cars."

"Bo?"

"No, Dale. He loved that car as much as I did.

He's the one who found it for me. I ended up selling it to him for five hundred bucks."

"What'd you pay for it?"

She laughed. "Five hundred bucks."

He handed her an empty platter, smiling at her in a curious way.

"What?" she asked.

"You're stingy with your smiles."

A rush of warmth came through her chest, and she averted her gaze, focusing on the dishes in the sink. "What's that supposed to mean?"

"Nothing," he said. "I think that's all the dishes. I'm gonna grab the bottles from outside."

She finished up at the sink while he picked up stuff around the pool. The slow, rhythmic "Slave" came through the speakers, which were hooked up all through the house and even outside. Chase did this head bob thing as he scrubbed the grill with a brush. He glanced at her through the window, and then did a horrible little dance with his hips that was too funny not to smile at. He pointed at her with the brush like he caught her doing something.

She turned so he couldn't see her face, but now she was smiling wider than she had in a while. She walked into the living room so he couldn't see her. Windows offered a view of the pool from in there as well, but he couldn't see her from where he was at in the outdoor kitchen. She went through the stack of CDs on the shelf by the stereo. Even though he had speakers in every room of his house, he was old school, with a massive stereo. She couldn't even find where it had Blue Tooth, so it must not have been purchased this decade.

He came into the kitchen, rattled around a minute in there, and then showed up with another beer for her.

"I need to get home," she said, but admittedly, she was stalling. She'd waited until it got dark, stupidly, and now she'd have to go home to a pitch-black-dark house. She couldn't help it. She got lost in the moment of relaxing with friends like she was a normal person again.

He pointed at the pool house. "You are home."

"I don't have anything to sleep in."

"I think I can come up with a T-shirt."

"I don't have a toothbrush."

He pointed with his beer bottle at the guest room. "I've got a package of them in there."

The idea was really tempting. She hadn't left a single light on at Bo's house since she had planned on being home well before this.

"You sure?" she asked.

He proffered the beer. "I'm sure."

She took it. "Thanks." She turned back to the stack. "Do you have any music that was created this century?"

"I'm an old soul. I grew up on my dad's music. That was one thing we had in common."

"Do you have brothers and sisters?" she asked.

"Two younger brothers." He pointed to a framed picture of him with two other guys on a boat. One looked a little like him, just a bit shorter, but the other one had red hair and freckles. She turned back to him. "Were you all adopted?"

"Nope." He walked across the room and came back with a picture of him between a woman with dark hair and features like his and a man with red hair and freckles. "This is my mom and dad."

She couldn't help a smile. "That's amazing. That's your biological father?"

"That's the one. That's just how the genes shook out. People always assumed I was adopted when we were out somewhere on our own without my mom there to put me in perspective."

"Are you close with your parents?"

He frowned, some emotion she couldn't put her finger on crossing his face. "They're not here anymore. I mean, my dad is here, on earth, but my mom passed."

"I'm so sorry," she said, her heart panging for him. She couldn't imagine losing her parents. She knew she'd have to worry about it one day, but they were healthy right now, thankfully. "How did she die?"

He narrowed his gaze, his mouth open but words not coming out. "She died a few years back." He walked across the room to replace the picture on the shelf. She was sure she had asked how and not when, but she certainly wasn't going to ask again.

"Incubus," he said. She took a drink of her beer, watching him curiously. He opened up a cabinet where a ton more CDs were stacked. "They made music this century." He picked up a CD. "Not sure if they made this music this century." He turned the CD over. "2001. Music this century. Here you go."

"I like Incubus," she said, taking the CD.

He opened the CD player and pulled out *Tattoo You*. "Put it in."

She did and waited until the first song played,

"Nice to Know You." He adjusted the volume down. "What does your CD collection look like?" he asked with a hint of a grin.

She shrugged. "Nonexistent."

"You don't have any CDs? Souvenirs from another era?"

"I have a subscription to a streaming service."

He play-glared at her. "It's not the same. You can't hold a streaming service in your hand and look at the artwork."

"You can look at the band's pictures online."

"Don't you want to hold something in your hand though sometimes?"

She shrugged and turned back toward the stereo. "I guess I don't attach to things too easily."

She could feel his eyes on her, but she didn't want to meet his gaze. She needed to keep this thing with him friendly. The last thing she wanted was another relationship, and according to everyone under the sun, he was only interested in one-nighters anyway. There was a day that would have appealed to her, especially with a guy like him. He was fun and easy, damn good-looking. And she'd never been with a guy who was so tall. She'd dated tall guys, but never one this tall. The idea of handing herself over to be dominated by a strong man in bed would once have made her stomach quiver in a good way, but she was nowhere near that headspace these days.

She walked away from him and sat in an armchair across from the couch. She wanted to tuck her leg up under her, but that would mean taking off her shoe and she wasn't ready to be that familiar with him. "Is this where you hang out at night and watch TV?"

"Not really. I'm usually working till late, then I just go on up and watch TV in bed."

"Really?"

"If I don't go out."

"You go out a lot?" she asked, ready to get his reputation out in the open.

He shrugged. "Some."

She smiled. "You entertain a lot?"

He glanced at the pool house and then to her. "Did Seanna say something to you?"

"You could say that."

He rolled his eyes. "What, she warned you about me?"

"She did, and Bo did, too."

He pulled his phone out of his pocket and huffed a laugh. "Yep, there's a text from your brother. I guess I'm gonna hear it from him."

"I already did."

"What'd he say to you?"

"Pretty much the same thing Seanna did." He lifted an eyebrow, and she took a drink of beer and swallowed it down. She looked at the bottle. "They both said you slept around a lot, warned me not to become your next victim." She gave him a hint of a smile so he wouldn't think she was worried about him.

He rolled his eyes, adjusting in his seat. "Jesus. They talk like I'm a damn man whore."

"I think the PC term is simply *whore*, whether you're a man or a woman."

He held up his big hand. "Oh, excuse me. I'm

just a whore then. Jesus, I'm not that bad."

"So what's your number then?" She knew she was treading on thin ice here, but she had to ask.

He averted his gaze. "I don't know. What's yours?"

She huffed a laugh. "I'm not the one on trial here."

"I am?"

"Kind of seems like it."

He rolled his eyes again, biting on his lip and shaking his head.

"You don't have to answer that," she said.

"I don't freaking know."

"You've got a ballpark figure in mind, though."

He looked around like he was really thinking about it, and then shrugged. "I don't know."

She stood up. "Don't worry about it. You say you have toothbrushes in there?" she pointed to the guest room.

"Don't go to bed yet. I don't want this night to end with you thinking I've slept with a thousand women."

She shrugged. "Why do you care what I think?"

He motioned for her to sit down. "Because you matter."

She stared at him, ready to bolt at any moment if this got any more intimate.

"You're Bo's sister. You'd matter even if I didn't like you as a person. Will you please finish your beer?" She hesitated, but then went ahead and sat down. He eyed her, and then stared at his beer bottle. "I'm capable of doing more than sleeping with a woman, you know."

"I'm sure you are," she said.

He met her gaze. "I'm serious."

"So am I. You seem quite capable of doing whatever you set your mind to."

He looked back at his beer bottle. "I was married."

She was not expecting that. "When?"

"I was twenty-five when we married. Thirty-one when we divorced. Thirty-two, maybe."

"How old are you now?" she asked.

"Thirty-seven."

She smiled. "Old man."

"How old are you?" he asked.

"Thirty-six."

"I didn't expect you to tell me. Most women don't like to do that."

She shrugged. "It's my age. It's not like I can change it. Do you have kids from your marriage?"

He frowned down at his beer. "No, I don't have any kids."

She sensed a change in his mood and wondered if that was something he really wanted, a family. If he did, sleeping around wasn't going to get him there. She took a long drink from her beer and then stood. "Thank you for inviting me tonight. I had fun."

He looked up at her like he'd forgotten she was still in the room. "Yeah, sure."

"I'm just going to grab that toothbrush, then I'll head out the guest room door."

He nodded, and then forced a smile. "Good night."

She wondered if he needed to talk about

something, but she didn't know how to ask him or offer an ear without sounding odd. She glanced around in the direction of the kitchen. "Do you need me to help with anything else before I go to bed?"

He hauled himself up off the chair. "No, I'm good. I'll see you tomorrow."

She nodded, still not feeling right about walking away from him just yet. She held out her hands and then brought them back to her sides, quickly, second guessing her hug offer.

He went in though, pulling her to his broad chest. She inhaled the scent of his shirt which had a mix of outdoor cooking and a feint scent of cologne or maybe just men's body wash. It was a smell she wished she could bottle and use as air freshener.

He pulled away first, which was only fair since he was the one who hugged her, but she was still regretful she hadn't made the move initially. She liked to hold the upper hand, always.

He let go of her, his smile rounding out what looked like tired eyes.

"Sleep well," she said, and headed off.

Chapter Six

Chase lay in bed staring at the ceiling. He wasn't sure what had gotten into him. He'd told Shayla he'd been married. That wasn't something he did, ever. He wasn't ashamed of being divorced, but it also wasn't something he advertised—and for good reason.

Do you have any kids? It's a logical question, unassuming even. It could be construed as rude not to ask that question once someone finds out a person has been married for a significant amount of time. Still, it's a question he didn't like answering.

He picked up the picture of Sam and set it on his chest. Sam was Chase's to hold in his own memory. He didn't belong to anyone else, and Chase didn't want to give him to anyone.

He pulled up Facebook and went to Rachel's page. There she was in her profile picture, smile plastered across her face, flanked by her new husband and their beautiful family, a little girl in a yellow dress and a little baby boy in a sailor suit. She'd dressed Sam in something like that for a picture once. God, Chase hated those kinds of clothes. Little boys needed to wear clothes they could move around in, not this prissy crap. But this wasn't his boy.

How could she move on so quickly, like Sam never existed? She'd replaced him, doubly, as if it were that easy to do…as if another child's giggle could be as heartwarming, as if another child's fingers and toes could be as amazing, as if another child's spirit could be as unique and special as their child's had been.

A notification popped up at the top of his screen from Felicity.

You up?

Was he up for talking to Felicity? He knew what she wanted. If memory from earlier in the week served him, she had a date tonight. If she was calling him this early, it must not have gone well. Likely, she was looking to make her own happy ending.

He thought about Shayla in the pool house just outside. He'd have to get used to the idea of having her so close. Could he jack off with her right there? Could he talk to Felicity the way the two of them had come to be with one another, nasty but goofy as hell. It was what worked for them. Anything to keep things light and fun…anything to occupy his mind.

He went to his texts, but pulled up Shayla's contact instead.

Did you make it home okay?

She replied with a smiley face, but not the emoji, just one made from a colon and a parenthesis. He waited to see if she was going to type more, but nothing else showed up. That didn't surprise him. Shayla wasn't one to waste words, spoken or typed he supposed.

He called Felicity.

"Hey," she said, sounding happy to hear from him.

"I take it the date didn't go well?"

"You know, it wasn't terrible."

"Then what are you doing texting me?" he asked.

"He didn't make a move."

"And you didn't either?"

"I didn't have time. He got called in."

He adjusted the phone to his other ear. "That's right. This guy's a doc, isn't he?"

"You don't think he was having a shitty time and had a friend call, do you?"

"With you? Not a chance," he said.

"See, this is why I call you. How'd your night go?"

He glanced at the window. "Good. Seanna and Blake came over."

"She's fun. And he's hot as fuck."

"What am I, canned tuna?"

"You're hot as motherfuck."

"So you're bringing my mother into this now. You're sick."

"Was it just the three of you tonight, or did you have a date over?"

He hesitated, trying to think about how to answer.

"Ooh, must have been good date. Tell me about her."

"It wasn't a date. It was Bo's sister."

"Shayla, right?"

Chase couldn't help feeling a little strange hearing Felicity say Shayla's name. He didn't like his worlds colliding. "You know her?"

"I've talked to her, actually. Remember that last night the week we were there…how drunk Maya got, and she stayed the night over at Bo's, puking her guts out?"

"Kind of hard to forget. I helped haul her to Bo's house from the bar."

"Shayla was at Bo's that next morning. Maya didn't have a phone or anything. I had to talk to Shayla to get her to wake Maya up so we could come pick her ass up and drive back to Indy."

"Did you meet her?"

"Not formally. Maya was out of there like a bolt of lightning. What does Shayla look like? I tried to find her on Facebook but I don't think she's on there."

He had to be careful but honest. "She's got dark hair, dark eyes."

"Is she pretty or what?"

"Um…"

"So she's gorgeous. Figures, if she looks anything like Bo." Chase winced at that idea. Shayla didn't look like Bo, not to him. "So it wasn't a date tonight?" Felicity asked.

"No, she was just…around, so I invited her to stay."

"She was around at your house?" she asked.

"Yeah, she's renting my pool house."

"Oh, you're kidding? That's interesting. Maya didn't mention that."

"I think she just found out today. This all came about today."

"Oh, that's cool. So are you into her?"

That was a loaded question. He was definitely intrigued. He lowered his voice, both to sound sexy, and out of paranoia that Shayla could somehow hear him. "You're the only one that puts my motor in drive, baby."

Felicity rolled a bunch of r's off her tongue and finished with a noise like a chainsaw or something. "Tell me, good-looking, are you wearing those leopard print silk boxers I love so much?"

He smiled. He'd never owned a pair of silk anything to his knowledge. Lifting the sheet, he found himself in his Deadpool boxers. "You know I am, and I've got my hair pulled back in one of those man buns you like so much."

"Mmm, you've been growing it out since I was there a few months ago?"

"Yeah, it grew like twelve inches since then."

"Can you put it in two braids that I can grab onto while I ride you like a mechanical bull?"

"Hang on, give me a sec. Okay, it's all set for you, baby. Don't pull too hard."

"On what?"

He grinned, reaching into his boxers. "I take that back."

The sound of a door opening had him sitting straight up in bed, unhanding his dick. He pulled the covers back and walked over to the window where he peeked through the blinds to see Shayla standing outside with her arms crossed over her chest, waiting while Jake sniffed around.

He stood there with his back to the window, thoughts of Shayla invading his brain.

"Did I lose you already?" Felicity asked. "Damn, someone was ready to roll."

He ran his hand through his hair. "I'm all set if you want to…" His mind searched for words. He was never at a loss for words. "I mean…I'm ready to put my stick shift into…" Jesus Christ, when did he get so bad at this goofy charade? Goofy was his expertise.

"Should I pull up some porn?" Felicity asked.

"No, I've got this. Just give me—"

"I think I've got an erotica novel around here," she said.

"You don't have to read. I've got this."

"Are you sure? Because I just remembered I downloaded this one with three dudes and one woman that looks hot as—"

"No, I've got this. Just relax, okay? Lie down."

"I am lying down."

"Then slide your hand underneath the waistband of your shorts."

"I'm not wearing any shorts."

"Then slide it under the waistband of your underwear."

"You can say panties, you know."

"Panties."

"I'm not wearing any panties."

He separated the blinds again just as Shayla looked up at his window. He snatched his hand away. "Fuck!"

"Fuck? That's what you've got for me?"

He rubbed the hair out of his eyes. "Not you."

"Then who? Are you with someone?"

"No, God no."

"It's Shayla, isn't it? She's there."

"She's not here. She's in the pool house. Well, I mean she's outside of it, letting her dog out...Bo's dog."

"What's she wearing?" Felicity asked.

"I don't know."

"Go look. She might be in a sexy nightgown."

"I'm not going to look."

"You know you want to."

"I was looking a second ago and she caught me."

"Ah, that was what the *fuck* was for." He pursed his lips, even though she couldn't see him. "Go get another look," she said.

He separated the blinds again. "She's wearing what she wore to dinner tonight. Fuck, I was supposed to give her a T-shirt to sleep in."

"You better go do that," Felicity said in sing-song.

"What about you?"

"I've got my novel. Go."

"All right. I'm sorry this didn't turn out...happy."

"Oh, don't you worry. It's getting ready to be in five, four, three..." She trailed off and the call disconnected.

Chase walked over to his dresser and put on a T-shirt and some gym shorts over his boxers, then he found a T-shirt and shorts for Shayla. He headed downstairs, but by the time he got down there she wasn't around. He walked over to the pool house, his heartbeat quickening. It was probably residual effects from his conversation with Felicity. He knocked on the door.

Shayla opened it, the light from the television illuminating the dark room. He proffered the shirt and shorts. "Sorry, I should have given this to you before."

She took it. "Thanks. I hope I didn't wake you up."

"No, I was actually on the phone."

She lifted an eyebrow. "Not with Bo, I hope."

"No, just..." For some reason, he didn't want to say who.

"A woman?" she asked, giving him a little smile, shutting the door a few inches.

"No, I mean, just Felicity. We're just friends. You know her, right? Maya's friend from Indianapolis?"

"I know who she is. You spent the week with her same time Bo spent the week with Maya, right?"

"Pretty much, yeah. Except we didn't fall in love."

"But you're still in touch," she said.

"Yeah, we're just friends. She called to tell me about her date." It wasn't a total lie. They had talked about the date.

"How was it?"

His cheeks warmed as he thought about his conversation with Felicity earlier, and then he realized Shayla was asking about Felicity's date. "It was good. Doctor. He got called away though."

"That's too bad." She closed the door a little farther. "Thanks again for the clothes."

He hated to end the night like this, but he needed to walk away before he made things worse. "Good night." The door shut, and he could hear the bolt lock she'd installed switching over.

When he got back to his bed, he turned on the television and channel surfed, but he couldn't focus on anything. He finally turned the television off and lay in the dark, a million thoughts racing through his brain. Families, exes, doctors, race car drivers, Deadpool, romance novels, but the one that kept occupying the most real estate in his head was of a dark-haired beauty steps outside of his back door, sleeping in his T-shirt and shorts.

Chapter Seven

It didn't take long for Shayla to pack. Most of her stuff was still at her house in Nashville with Brian. When she'd left, she'd done so in a mad rush and had to grab only the essentials. Scott's cop friend was holding Brian while she got her stuff, but she couldn't take all day. Scott helped her as they took what they could fit in her sports car, so she had no trouble getting it all into Bo's truck.

She loaded her clothes into the back seat by the armful, still on the hangers. Her phone buzzed, and she pulled it out of her pocket.

Do you need help moving your stuff?

She looked around the front yard, hating that she was dragging Chase into this.

No, I'm good. Thanks.

I'm kind of bored, actually.

She smiled.

If you're still bored when I get there, you can

help me unload Bo's truck.

Deal.

She didn't doubt that he was bored. He carried an energy around with him. She couldn't envision him lying around with a remote control.

She went back inside and opened the drawer to her bedside table and pulled out her dusty vibrator to pack. She'd felt so asexual since she'd left Brian, like her body was physically rejecting sex. She loved her vibrator and made use of it often until things started going downhill with Brian. Getting off was the last thing she wanted since he'd helped her feel like sex was an obligation and not something to enjoy.

She loaded her lotion, her lip balm, and her headphones, emptying the drawer except for the box of condoms Bo had left. He'd intended her to have them, she was certain of that because he'd put them in the drawer to the guest room she always stayed in. He didn't need them anymore, and she wasn't dead inside. She grabbed them and tossed them into her bag.

She finished loading the truck and then went back through Bo's house to see if she'd forgotten anything. It wasn't like she wouldn't be back there often, but it did feel final. This had been her space for the past three months, her refuge from a place where she'd lived in fear. She still lived that way here, but at her house in Nashville the person she feared was sitting next to her. Somehow, being away from him made him ten times scarier than he ever was in person. Maybe living a life without worry that someone would decide to blow up in a fit of rage had made her soft. God knew she'd had enough of that type of fear growing up. By this age, the feeling should be second nature. But living without it was definitely different. Better.

When she and Jake pulled up in Chase's driveway, Chase was sitting on his front porch scrolling through his phone. He stood and walked her way. She put Jake's leash on and led him out of the truck.

"You're sure you don't mind him being here a few days, just until Bo gets back."

Chase knelt down to pet him. "Jake's always welcome here, aren't you, handsome?"

Jake licked Chase's face like it was a steak lollipop, and Chase finally pulled away.

"I'm gonna take him back there," Shayla said. "Is the gate unlocked?"

Chase handed her a key. "I just texted you the code. I'll go with you and put it in now since you have your hands full with Jake. That's the key to the house. It works all the doors on the main house, bolts and handles."

"I don't need a key to your house," she said.

"Just in case something goes squirrelly with the back gate or something. You never know. Just take it, okay?"

"I won't use it," she said.

"Then humor me. The code for the alarm is the same as the code to the gate I just texted you, and the password if the company calls is Jake. I changed it today so we would both remember. I'd forgotten what I'd set it at originally."

She narrowed her gaze, and then relented.

"You're really okay giving me all this access?"

"Of course."

She cracked the faintest of smiles. "Thanks. Where's a good place for me to park?"

"Around the back by the gate's fine. I don't use that spot anyway. I come in through the garage."

She nodded, and then headed that way. She let Jake off the leash and he sniffed around the yard, finding a place to mark his territory while she got the little house open. It was so nice to come home to one open space that she could see so clearly. She'd just have to check the shower and the closet each time…and maybe under the bed, too.

Chase's footfalls sounded behind her. She couldn't even see his face since he had all her clothes piled up in his arms. "Where do you want these?"

"On the bed, please. Thank you."

He unloaded them and she followed him out. "I'll get it," he said. "You can go ahead and get started putting stuff where you want it." She hesitated, uncomfortable with accepting his help, but reluctantly agreed. Her mother would tell her to graciously accept the help, and then do something nice for the person later. Her mother had always taught her that when people offered to help or do something nice that meant they wanted to. Let them and return the favor, especially when it's their house. Her mother didn't say that part, but Shayla figured she was safe adding it in.

The pool house had a small closet with a couple of boxes in the bottom. She wouldn't mention it to him right now. She didn't want him to think he had to move his stuff because of her. She went to work hanging her clothes up. It would be a tight squeeze, but God knew she wasn't complaining.

Dropping off the last load, Chase glanced around. "What can I do next?"

"I think I'm good, but thanks."

"All right then." He turned to walk out, and she squeezed her eyes tightly.

"Um, can I do something for you?" He lifted his eyebrows, and she shook her head quickly. "Make dinner, maybe? Not tonight, actually. I've got dinner at my parents' house. But tomorrow night?"

He scratched his neck. "I'm leaving to go out of town for a few days."

"Oh," she said, the idea striking her harder than she would have liked for it to. She wasn't here because of him. She was here because of his fortress of security. But the idea of him being here as well didn't hurt. "When are you coming back?"

"Thursday. I was going to talk to you about that. Would it be weird for you if I got a security guard for the nights I'll be gone?"

"A security guard?" she asked. Great. Now he was thinking she was his responsibility.

"Female. I've worked with her before. She's very professional. Just for nighttime."

She stared at him, trying to gauge what he knew. He couldn't know about Brian without her telling him. Scott was the only other person who knew. Chase and Scott didn't even know each other existed.

"Mmm hmm," she said, still trying to figure out what was going on.

"I'm not totally comfortable with this week's renters across the street. That house rents for cheap and it looks like young kids." He chuckled. "God, I sound like my dad."

She scratched her head. "Yeah, of course it's fine. But are you sure that's the reason?"

He shrugged. "Yeah. Should there be another reason?"

She swallowed, not wanting to give herself away. She had a feeling they were playing a game of chicken, and he was going to win this round. "Sounds good. I'll be on the lookout for her."

"Paula is her name. It's her company anyway. I assume she'll come herself. But if it's not her, it'll be another female. She's an all-female company."

"Really," Shayla said, a little impressed that he chose to use them.

"Oh yeah. They're great. I saw Paula take down a three-hundred-pound gorilla at an event in Destin once. Not a strand of hair out of place when she was done."

"Impressive."

"How about Thursday night, for the dinner?" he asked. "My flight gets in mid-afternoon, I think."

"Yeah, great," she said, turning to unpack her basket.

"Okay," he said. "Do you want this open or closed?"

"Closed, please," she said.

He closed the door behind him, and she shut her eyes tightly while pressing down on her shampoo bottle. She'd lost a piece of herself somewhere during her time with Brian. She was someone who she no longer recognized. Since when did she need a security guard to sleep at night? She had a baseball bat and a can of mace. She wouldn't get a gun. It wasn't her thing, though she'd been considering it. Brian had grown up with guns, made it to the shooting range every month or so. He was also fast when he wasn't drinking, of course. She was afraid he would get a gun away from her, and she couldn't run that risk.

She went about assembling her home. Thirty-six years old and living in a one-room pool house. This was not the path she thought her life would have taken. She didn't necessarily expect to have a family—kids weren't a requirement for her—but she did expect to be settled somewhere, whether Nashville or here.

She plopped down on the bed, pulling out the nightstand drawer. She'd left PCB for a clean slate when she broke up with Tony. What a joke. She'd broken up with him because she didn't think he manned up enough, and she'd gone straight into the arms of his polar opposite. At the time, she'd thought Brian was everything she'd ever wanted in a man. Strong, responsible, sexy, kind-hearted and compassionate. That was her perception, and that was the persona he'd kept up for a long time. She'd known going in he didn't drink, but she thought it was because he was into being healthy. She hadn't dreamed it was because he had a problem. How stupid of her. She of all people should have known to be suspicious, given the way she grew up.

She cleaned out the drawer of the nightstand and put her bedside stuff in, including the condoms. She should have left them at Bo's. Who did she think she was going to have sex with?

Lying back on the bed, propping her feet up, she took a minute to imagine Chase having sex in this bed. She wondered if he had. He was attractive, there was no question about that. What did he do in bed? What did he like? She absentmindedly twirled her ring around her finger, staring at the wall, thinking about his long body, so much to work with.

She bit her bottom lip as a sensation flowed through her belly that she hadn't felt since she could remember. It was like turning on a light in a dark closet.

She snuck over to the window and peeked through the blinds. He wasn't anywhere around. Jake was snoozing under his favorite tree. She locked the door and turned off the lights. Making herself comfortable on the bed, she unbuttoned her shorts and ventured downward. She hadn't touched herself in six months, probably. She'd become practically asexual, dressing in baggy clothing, not fixing up her hair. When she looked like that, Brian couldn't accuse her of wanting to find someone else. It just made things easier.

She found herself wet, which made her huff a laugh. She didn't even know she was capable of getting wet anymore, but thinking about Chase's big hands on her thighs, pulling her legs apart had definitely helped. She closed her eyes as the sensations roared inside of her like an old truck starting back up for the first time in years. She pressed down on the mattress as she brought herself alive again, gritting her teeth as she let herself go with a throaty noise she didn't recognize. She relaxed back on the bed, resting her hand on her belly, almost smiling at the ceiling.

The sound of something hitting the pool with a splash woke her back to reality. She walked over to the window to find Chase in the pool shaking out his hair. He pulled himself onto a float shaped like a giant piece of bacon and relaxed back, splashing water onto himself.

He let his leg drag in the pool, the black hair sticking to it. She wondered what his mother's nationality was. She was a beautiful woman with straight, dark hair, not dissimilar to her own. But his mother had a dark complexion that was indicative of something other than Caucasian, which she had passed down to him.

She cleaned up, putting herself back together as if she hadn't just gotten herself off on the bed moments earlier. She got a large cup of water and headed outside. She poured the water into Jake's bowl so it looked like she had a purpose coming out there, other than to gawk at him. She walked over to him. "How are you getting to the airport?"

"I just drive and park."

"I can take you. Are you flying out of the PCB airport?"

He looked up at her through water-sprinkled aviator glasses. "Yep."

"I'm going over there to my mom's house for dinner. I'll take you. What time's your flight?"

"Five-forty, I think."

"That's perfect timing."

He moved his hand through the water to turn his

float to face her. He was in a lot better shape than showed through his big clothes. She had to look away, so she averted her gaze to Jake who was doing nothing.

"Your rent includes use of the pool, by the way," Chase said.

"I need to get back inside."

"That stuff will be there later, you know."

"I don't even know where my bathing suit is." It was a lie. She'd unpacked it earlier. She just wasn't sure that was a good idea at the moment. Especially with her feeling a little empowered from her self-induced orgasm.

"Bathing suits are optional, of course."

She gave him a look and headed back to the pool house. "I'll meet you back out here at three, okay?"

"Works for me."

Chase hauled his garment bag over his shoulder and headed down the stairs. Shayla sat at a table by the pool, flipping through her phone. He really didn't want to go on this trip for a variety of reasons. First of all, he still didn't know what had her so freaked out these past few days. Given, she seemed way more relaxed this afternoon than he'd seen her since he first met her a few days ago. Secondly, he really liked hanging around her. Just her presence nearby gave him a comfort he hadn't known in years.

When he opened the door, she looked up at him and he lost his breath for a second. She was fixed up, her eyelids brushed with makeup, but not too much. Her lips shined with gloss, and her hair hung around her neck and chest in long, soft curls.

"Wow," he said without thinking.

She averted her gaze, glancing over at Jake. "You ready?"

"Yeah," he said.

She held out her hands. "Can I carry something?"

He couldn't help a smile. "No, I got it."

Jake, seeing they were headed to the gate, stood and flopped his way over to them. Shayla pulled something out of her pocket and tossed it across the yard, and he went for it. She nodded at the gate. "We've got about five seconds before that munchie stick is gone." They hustled to the gate and he shut it behind him. She eyed it. "It locks automatically?"

"Yeah. That's another reason I gave you that house key." He opened up the back door of Bo's truck and hauled his luggage inside.

"Did you lock the front door?" she asked.

"Yeah, I think."

She headed that way and pulled on the knob, a few times. He really hated to leave her like this. He supposed it was possible that she was always this paranoid, but there was no way of knowing that for sure without asking.

He stood outside the truck, waiting for her to come back. "Sorry," she said.

"I'm in no rush."

She scooted around the truck, and they both got in. He wanted to open her door for her, but that would feel too much like a date, which this was decidedly not. She made a four-point turnaround and headed up the driveway.

"So, has your ex quit bugging you?" he asked.

She frowned. "Yeah," she said, but he didn't believe it.

"Good. He's still in Nashville?"

"Yeah, as far as I know."

"How did you meet him?"

"We worked together."

"How'd you get up to Nashville to begin with?" he asked.

"I was looking for a change. I'd been in a relationship for a few years, and it was time for it to end." She hit her signal and they turned out onto 30A.

"And you needed to put Alabama between you and the guy?"

She tilted her head in concession. "Pretty much. He wasn't a bad guy. It just wasn't a good relationship."

"What was wrong?" he asked, knowing he was prying, but curious.

She made a little humming noise like she was thinking about it. "It was me. It wasn't him."

"What'd you do?" he asked with a smile, but she didn't return it.

"I was bored. Thought I needed someone exciting." She huffed a laugh like it was a ridiculous thought.

"That's understandable."

She shook her head. "Stupid. He was a good guy."

His heart took a little hit at the wistful look on her face. "Why don't you look him up? Does he still live here?"

"Oh, I don't know. Probably. I'm not interested

in dating anyone."

"Mmm," he said, nodding, glancing out the window, catching a fly-by of his own ugly mug on a sign in front of one of his properties. "Me neither," he said, unnecessarily, unasked.

She glanced over at him. "Where are you going?"

"Las Vegas."

"For business?" she asked.

"Yeah. I'm meeting my investment group there. We have some meetings set up."

She air quoted with her right hand. "*Meetings* in Vegas?"

He smiled. "All right, I'm sure there'll be some drinking, some schmoozing."

"On whose part? Yours or someone else's?"

"I don't know. Maybe mutual schmoozing. Depends on how the week goes." She glanced at him curiously. "What?"

"Nothing," she said.

"Something's on your mind," he said. She let a smile slip through, closed-mouth, of course. "You can't have a look like that on your face and expect me to leave it alone. What?"

She shrugged. "It's just an interesting life you live."

"Going to Vegas?"

She glanced at him and then came to a stop for a couple on bikes at a crosswalk. "Living comfortably."

That was an oxymoron. He hadn't lived comfortably since the day his baby had been born. He'd loved Sam and cared for him more than he could ever have dreamed he would, which brought a vulnerability to him that would one day prove to be ripped open like a zipper, his heart left dangling in the balance.

He looked out the window, Sam's lifeless body engrained in his brain, always. "Who said I was comfortable?"

She drove up a side road to 98, turning up the radio, and neither of them spoke again until they got to the airport.

"You want to check that your flight's on time?" she asked as they got closer.

"I'm sure it's fine."

"Okay," she said, heading toward the departing flights lane.

He pulled out his phone and looked up his flight. How had she known? "It's delayed."

"Till when?"

"Eight."

She glanced at him. "Wanna come to my parents' house with me?"

"No, you can just drop me here."

"You sure? We're grilling."

He lifted his eyebrow at her. "Steaks?"

"Some kind of meat."

"Would you care?"

"If I had a problem with it, I wouldn't have asked."

He pointed at her. "You know, I believe you."

She gave him a curious smile. "What's that supposed to mean?"

He smiled back. "Grilling it is."

Chapter Eight

Shayla had waited eight months before she brought Tony home to meet her parents. Brian had never met her parents. She'd known Chase exactly three days, and there they were.

But she wasn't dating Chase. She was practically living with him, of course, just not dating.

Her heart shot up into her throat at the sight of her own car sitting in her parents' driveway.

"You okay?" Chase asked.

She pointed at it. "That's my car."

"The one Bo has up in Indianapolis?"

"That's the one."

"So he's here, huh?"

"Looks that way." She parked the truck and stared at her car. She had loved that car for three years, but here it was, a representation of her time in Nashville, making her stomach a little sick.

"You want to go in?" he asked.

"Yeah," she said, but she didn't move.

"Are you rethinking inviting me over?"

"No, of course not. Let's go." She hopped down out of the truck and met him around the front where they headed to the door.

"I'd have brought a bottle of wine if I'd have known I was coming," Chase said.

"I don't even know if my family owns a corkscrew."

"Really? They don't drink?"

"Not anymore," she said without looking at him. She opened the screen door and offered him inside. He stepped aside in the entryway while she walked in front of him, leading them both to the kitchen where she'd be sure to find her mother. "Hey, Mama."

Her mother slid a pan of cut-up potatoes into the oven and then turned to meet her gaze. "Hey, sweetie." She came in for a hug but stopped in her tracks when she saw Chase coming up behind Shayla. "Mama, this is Chase O'Neil. He's a friend of mine and Bo's."

"Hello, Chase," she said, doing a good job of not looking taken off guard.

"I apologize that I don't have flowers for you or anything. This was a last-minute invite. Shayla was dropping me at the airport on her way over here but my flight got delayed."

"Well, I don't need flowers, but I'll take a hug." Her mom wrapped her arms around Chase, who smiled, but his brow furrowed a little. Shayla remembered that his mother was dead and her heart ached for him. Her mom pulled away. "Can I get you a glass of iced tea?"

"Yes ma'am, thank you."

"I hope you like it sweet," Shayla said.

He smiled down at her. "Just like me."

Her heart couldn't help a flutter as she gave him a look and then turned to the window where she found Bo outside chasing their nephews around with a red, plastic gun. "Might as well get this over with. Mama, we're going outside."

"I'll bring you both a tea out there."

"Thank you," Chase and Shayla said in unison.

Shayla led them out the back door, and the slamming screen got Bo's attention. He stopped and looked at them both like they were a math problem he was trying to solve. "Hey," he said, and then headed their way. He stopped in front of them, staring them both down, gun still in hand.

"I don't get a hug?" Chase asked.

Bo eyed him and then went for Shayla, wrapping her up in his arms. "What's going on?" he asked, a little bit shy of conversational.

"Just coming for dinner," Shayla said.

Bo looked between the two of them. "Mmm hmm." He held out his hand to Chase and he took it. "I hear you're shacking up with my sister," Bo said.

"That's about the size of it," Chase said.

Bo lowered his chin and pointed at Chase. "We're about to talk."

"I'll talk to you all damn day."

Shayla liked this side of Chase…telling her brother to fuck off, basically. She could get into that.

"Shayla," came a voice from somewhere to her left. She turned to find Maya coming out of the screened-in porch where Shayla's sister-in-law and Dale were sitting with her dad, all holding up a hand in greeting but none bothering to rise.

"Hey," Shayla said, holding out a hand. She probably should have offered a hug.

Maya shook her hand. "So good to see you again."

Shayla turned to Bo. "How are you even here? I talked to you yesterday."

"We were on the road when you called. I wanted to surprise Mama. I'm leaving Maya here for interviews and taking Blake back with me to get everything moved."

"Good luck on your interviews," Shayla said.

"I'll need it. I haven't interviewed in a decade."

"I wanted to grab my truck, give you back that piece of shit," Bo said.

"You think I enjoy hauling that big rig around everywhere I go?"

"You two are fun to be around," Chase said, looking over at Maya, who was smiling like a sixteen-year-old with a crush.

Bo brought her in to him and kissed her while her face turned beet red. "Bo," she whispered, glancing over at the screened-in porch where the rest of the family was sitting.

"You're gonna have to get over that, darlin'. I can't be expected to go a whole night without kissing you."

"Damn," Chase said. "Between the two of you and Blake and Seanna, this town is turning soft."

Bo looked like he wanted to make a joke but Maya's wide eyes stopped him. The only other time

Shayla had been around her brother and Maya was when she was puking her guts out into his commode, and they were supposedly broken up at that point. Shayla had not seen him happy like this since he was in college, before he met Angela who had screwed up his life for the better part of a decade. Maya couldn't be more opposite from that nightmare if she tried.

Bo nudged Maya in the side, and she looked down at her left hand, her smile so big she looked like she'd just won the lottery.

Shayla blinked and met Bo's proud gaze. "You're engaged?" she asked.

Maya nodded, pressing a knuckle against her eye like she was stopping a tear.

Chase absorbed Bo into a hug. "Congratulations, man."

Shayla had been expecting this eventually, but just not right that moment. She shook off the shock and pulled Maya in for a hug, then Bo when he became available.

"When did this happen?" Shayla asked.

"Last night," Maya said. "We stayed at the Opryland Hotel in Nashville on our way down. He did it by the dancing fountains."

Shayla smiled at her cheesy, beaming brother. She guessed one of the two of them needed to be the hopeless romantic.

"When did you get the ring?" Chase asked.

Bo's cheeks turned red.

"He'd had it for weeks," Maya said. "He was waiting for the right moment."

He brought her in to his chest. "I don't know. I

wanted us to be official before we got back here. I wanted to bring her home with me as my fiancée."

The two of them gazed into each other's eyes and then put their foreheads together, closing their eyes like they were physically connecting with one another. Shayla was happy for them, but Jesus Christ, this was a lot to take.

"So when's the wedding?" Shayla asked.

"Three weeks from yesterday?" Maya said like she was asking permission. "Are you available?" Shayla looked at Bo for confirmation and he shrugged. "I know it's soon, but that's the only day we can get the venue for months, and we really didn't want to put it off till next year," Maya said.

"What venue?" Shayla asked.

"Harley West Botanical Gardens," Bo said. He took Maya into his arms. "I took her there on our first official date."

"I was on your first official date, and we didn't go there," Chase said.

"Our first official alone date," Bo said, and then kissed Maya like they were the only two people on the planet. She grinned at him, and then nuzzled her head into his neck. They were about as disgusting as roadkill.

Maya pulled away. "So do you think you have that weekend available?"

Shayla had all her weekends available. "Of course."

"I'm available, too, if it matters to anyone," Chase said.

Maya smiled. "Good. You'll need to be there as well."

Shayla pointed to the fenced-in porch. "I'm going to say hi to Dad and them."

"I'll go help your mom," Chase said, and Shayla loved that he was independent.

"I will, too," Maya said with a smile. "Um, but Shayla, can we talk a little later?"

Shayla gave her an easy smile. "Of course."

Maya nodded and followed Chase to the kitchen.

Shayla started over to the screened-in porch, but Bo grabbed her by the arm. "Hold up." She turned toward him with a warning glance, and he let go. "I want to talk to you a second."

"If it's about me moving into Chase's pool house you can save your breath."

"It's not, really. I just hate that you felt like you had to get out of my house so fast. I hope you didn't leave on Maya's account, because she'd be thrilled to have you there. Hell, she hasn't quit talking about you since I've been up there these past two months. She thinks she's hit the sister-in-law lottery and she doesn't even know you yet."

Shayla exhaled a breath. "That's kind, but I don't need to be living with my baby brother at age thirty-six. It was fine for me to stay there while you were gone and I was in transition, but I honestly don't have a desire to live with you and your fiancée, no offense to Maya. She seems sweet."

He smiled at the kitchen window. "She is."

"Good," Shayla said, and then walked toward the porch.

"Hang on," Bo said, and she turned back to him with an exhausted look. He glanced over at the porch and then tugged on her sleeve. "Take a walk with me to my truck."

"Why?"

"'Cause I want a second of privacy without kids and family around."

"Nobody's listening to us."

He let out a deep breath and then he gave her a serious look. "Is there something you want to tell me?"

Her pulse only picked up slightly. Surely this was something about Chase. "Uh, no?"

He stared her down, and then finally lifted his hand like a stop sign. "All right, don't be pissed."

She immediately got pissed...and afraid. "What?"

"We stopped in Franklin this morning, only because that exit you live off of has lots of good restaurants and we were hungry."

Her heartbeat went faster. "Okay."

He narrowed his gaze. "You've never lied to me before, not about anything important, have you?"

She swallowed hard. "No, of course not."

"Then why did you tell me your house was for sale?"

Her chest constricted as her ears heated up. She pointed at his chest. "I told you not to go by my house."

"I told Maya you lived off that exit, and she asked if we could drive by. I swear to God." He looked her up and down. "I didn't realize I wasn't allowed to drive down your street."

"Did you see anyone there?"

He lifted an eyebrow. "Want to take that walk to my truck now?"

She glanced around, paranoid now. But if Bo knew everything, he would be going through the roof, not acting this relaxed about it all. She glared at him and started walking. He opened the truck door for her just like their mom had always made him do when they were growing up. She'd stick her tongue out at him as a thank you. She'd do it now as a joke if she had any humor in her at all these days.

He got in the driver's side and gripped the wheel. "Goddamn I missed this truck."

He definitely didn't know the whole story, or he wouldn't be focused on his truck. "So?" Shayla said.

He exhaled a deep breath. "So I talked to Brian."

She remained calm. She would have to. "Okay."

"He told me everything, Shayla."

There was no way that was true, but clearly they'd talked and Brian had told him something. "What did he tell you?" she asked through gritted teeth.

"He told me you made him go to rehab."

She breathed again. That was harmless enough, considering. "I didn't make him do anything."

"Poor choice of words on my part. He said you asked him to go." She just looked at him, waiting for his point. "Why didn't you tell me he had a drinking problem?"

"Am I required to tell you everything about guys I date?"

"That particular problem, yeah, you goddamned are, and you know it."

"Well, sorry," she said, and opened the door.

"Will you quit running away from me? What the

fuck is up with that? Since when can we not have a conversation, especially when I haven't seen you in two months?"

She closed the door. "Go on, then."

"You've changed, Shayla."

There was that Sherlock Holmes brother of hers. "Fuck you," she said, because she was mature like that.

"You've been different since the day you came back here, but I've been too caught up in Maya to take the time to see it. I kept telling myself it was because you'd just been through a breakup, which you told me was amicable, by the way."

"It was," she lied.

"Then why did Brian tell me he'd give his left nut to have you back?"

Those were Bo's words, not Brian's. She didn't answer, just bit on her thumbnail.

"You made it sound like the two of you parted ways with no issue, and all the while he was sitting there in rehab. Now you can't tell me the road that led to that was smooth."

"Maybe this was just something I needed to deal with on my own."

"Really? After all we went through with this same exact shit together when we were little. It never occurred to you that I might understand what you were going through?"

She turned away from him, the weight of his words bearing down on her shoulders. They'd protected each other through their father's alcoholic fits of rage as children. He'd never hit either one of them or anyone else in the family as far as Shayla knew, but at least with a hit, you knew the end was near. She knew that now.

"And what about the nine years of Angela that you talked me through? I never hesitated to call you when I was at my limit." He put his hand on her arm. "Shayla, I need to know, did he ever hurt you?"

Her stomach gave a queasy roll, and she swallowed. "No."

"Shayla, look at me."

She forced herself to look into her brother's eyes, so full of honesty all the goddamned time. "I said no." Her own lie stung her like a wasp.

He lifted his chin. "I didn't think so, but I had to ask."

Why didn't he think so? Had Brian won him over, or did he just want so desperately for it not to be so? Because she knew that even though he was four hundred miles away when it was happening, he'd somehow find a way to blame himself for allowing it to happen on his watch. And then he'd also have to drive back to Nashville and kill Brian, and Bo had a wedding to plan.

She looked out the window. "I'm sorry I didn't talk to you."

"I don't need your apology, Shayla. Shit. I just need you to know I'm here. I'm always here. And the fact that I'm getting married doesn't change a goddamn thing. Now listen to me. Maya and I would like for you to stay with us, just for a while."

"Bo—"

"Just please hear me out. There's more going on with you and Brian that I clearly don't know about, and I respect that. But I don't want you to be alone right now. You've been alone for two months dealing with this shit. It's time to let your baby brother do his job and take care of you."

She met his gaze, unable to help a small smile. It must be bad for him to call himself her baby brother. She couldn't remember him ever doing that. That was her name for him. He'd never complained about it, not since they were adults, but he'd also never owned it.

"Thank you, baby brother," she said. "But I'm fine, really."

"Just for a few months. Then you can move into any pool house in South Walton. Let me help you. Do it as a favor to me." She huffed a laugh and rolled her eyes. "And I know I would need to curtail the PDA with Maya. Trust me, she'll be happy to hear that. It drives her nuts when I do that." He nudged her. "So come on. Will you stay with us for a while, just while we get this thing with you and Brian figured out?"

"There's nothing to figure out. It's over."

"If it's over, then what's going on with your house?"

She exhaled a deep breath. "Nothing's going on with the house. I just, I couldn't evict him while he was in rehab. I wanted to give him time to get out and get back to work and find another place. The market is so hot in Nashville right now that I know it will sell as soon as I put it on, especially in that neighborhood. I'm just letting things sit for a minute."

He narrowed his gaze. "Are you sure you're not

leaving the door open for reconciliation?"

"No," she said, probably too quickly.

"I'm not just asking this to be nosy. I need to know if you're going to head back to Nashville, for our business."

"What about the business?" she asked.

"That's another thing I want us to talk about."

"What?"

"I have some ideas, for another time. We've probably left them in there too long. Mama's gonna be pulling out baby pictures if we don't go back inside."

"Can I get a hint?" she asked.

He met her gaze, dead serious. "I want us to be partners."

"In your pool business?"

"Our business."

"The one you built from scratch all by yourself," she said.

"It's more involved than what you think. I want you to help me grow it. I have ideas I've been working on these past few months. Stuff I should have been doing for years. Being with Maya has given me the shot in the pants I've needed these past few years. This business should be a whole lot bigger than it is by this point. I should be to the level Chase is at. Look at him. He's building goddamn hospitals. He's got investment groups and all kinds of shit. I don't have to be small town. I'm ready to take this shit to the next level. But I can't do it alone. And the saddest thing on the planet is for someone like you to be wasting their talents in a shitty little office in PCB."

SEAGROVE SECRETS

"There's nothing wrong with PCB," Shayla said.

"There is something wrong with the shitty little office though."

"It's not shitty at all. It's nice."

"You know what I mean. Come on. Let's go see Dad. I haven't even really said hello to him yet. Just introduced Maya then the boys had me chasing them."

"All right." She considered him. "So did Brian win you over?"

"Fuck no. If he's even got a whiff of alcoholism in him, I don't want you near him. I don't want either of us to relive our childhood through relationships."

She breathed a sigh of relief and nodded, wishing she knew what all they talked about, but she wanted to get off this subject as soon as possible. She needed to know one more thing. "Did you tell him you were getting married?"

"Yeah, it came up."

"You told him when and where?"

He thought about it. "Yeah, I guess we did. I'd actually just hung up with Harley when we pulled off on that exit, so it was fresh on my mind. He was actually the first person we knew to see Maya's ring. You don't think he'd show up without being invited, do you?"

She did her best to hide her sinking stomach. "No, of course not. I was just wondering if he knew."

He eyed her, and she hoped like hell he wouldn't ask more questions. "So you'll move back in?" Bo asked.

Shayla considered him. "Thank you, baby brother. But I'm good."

He let out a defeated breath, and then met her gaze. "Just promise me that you can handle Chase."

"Who do you think you're dealing with here?"

He nodded. "I know. I just don't want to see you get hurt again, not after all this."

"I'm not going to get hurt. Just trust me, okay?"

He nodded, and then got out of the truck. As they walked past the window to the kitchen, Chase smiled at her, his hands covered in dough. It really wasn't fair for her to ask Bo to trust her when she couldn't even trust herself around Chase.

Chapter Nine

"The siblings have emerged," Maya said.

Bo and Shayla's mother, Donna, laughed. "Get used to that, my dear."

Maya smiled, her face turning pink.

Chase rolled another sausage ball out of the dough. "So I take it they've always been secretive."

"Oh, yes. Since they were little. We had Bo and Dale sharing a room since they were boys, and Shayla had her own, but Bo would sneak in there every night and sleep on the floor. Finally we gave up and moved his twin bed in there. Of course that all changed when they went to middle school. We moved Bo back in with Dale, which was a nightmare till Dale moved out the day he turned eighteen."

"How long was that?" Chase asked.

"Too damn long," Donna said with a look that he'd seen Shayla give more than once. "Chase, honey, those go in that oven under the potatoes for twenty-five minutes when you're finished. My grandsons are alone. I'm going to steal a minute with them if you don't mind."

"Of course not," Chase said.

"Flip 'em halfway through now, will ya?" she said, but didn't wait for an answer before heading outside. Maya grinned as she cut tomatoes for the salad.

"You like her, don't you?" Chase said.

"You have no idea. My mom is like her polar opposite in every way, and I couldn't be happier about it." She held out both hands. "Look at this. She's left her two houseguests in her kitchen to do her cooking. My mother would have caterers and the guests wouldn't be allowed to breathe out of order."

Chase smiled and plopped another ball onto the pan. "These are all different sizes."

"You think she's concerned?" Maya slid him a look. "So, I hear you and Felicity have kept in touch all this time."

"Just as friends. I'm sure she's told you that."

"She has. I was just testing you. I love the two of you together, so I was being hopeful."

"Well, that's kind of you."

"Not kind, just selfish. Now that I'm moving down here, I want her to come. But that's not going to happen anyway."

"What's so great about Indianapolis?" Chase asked.

"Her mother."

"She's never mentioned her," Chase said.

Maya nodded with a closed-mouth smile. "She is keeping you in the friend zone, isn't she?"

Chase gave her a curious look, but wasn't sure he should prod for more info.

Maya put the knife down and wiped her forehead with her wrist. "So speaking of Felicity, she's coming down for the wedding."

"Oh. Cool."

"Yeah, so typically she would stay with Sebastian, but he has graciously agreed to host my parents and my sister, Meade, for the weekend, and I love Felicity way too much to do that to her." Knowing where she was leading with this, he started to get a little uneasy. "So, how would you feel about having her stay with you? I mean, if it's a problem, she can totally stay with Bo and me, but I'm not sure who else is coming, and if I can place someone with a person they already know and are comfortable with, it frees up our place for someone who doesn't know anyone, and—"

He turned to her. "Absolutely." There was no other way to answer that question, but even as he said it, his stomach rumbled.

Maya smiled wide. "Thank you. That's one issue down, eight million more to go." The screen door opened, and Bo came in with that look on his face that told Chase he was in for it. Maya's smile increased, if that was possible. "Hello, fiancé."

He took her into his arms and kissed her. "I missed you."

"My God," Chase said, and Bo glared at him.

Bo turned back to Maya. "Darlin', would you mind taking that vegetable plate out to the screened-in porch?"

"I would love to," she said, twirling to pick up the plate. Bo held the door open for her and she finger waved at him as she headed out the door. He watched her until Chase cleared his throat, and then his expression turned ominous.

"If you want to fight me, you're gonna have to let me wash my hands first or else your face is going to be covered with raw sausage dough."

"I don't want to fight your scrawny ass," Bo said.

Bo was maybe the only guy on the planet who could legitimately call Chase scrawny, even being about six inches shorter than him.

Chase ran his hands under the faucet. "Good. I hate to fight. Especially when it's not a fair one."

"You're half a foot taller."

"You've got your brother outside for backup."

"You clearly don't know my brother. If he saw you pounding on me he'd join in."

Chase dried his hands with a dish towel. "I don't get that. I love my brothers."

"And I love my sister, which brings me to—"

"I know where it brings you, and I really don't need to hear it. Stay away. Point taken."

"She's been through a lot lately."

Chase met Bo's gaze. Maybe he did know what was going on with Shayla. Chase had to play it cool to get the info. "I know."

"What'd she tell you?" Bo asked.

Chase crossed his arms over his chest. "What'd she tell you?"

Bo pointed at him. "I'm not fucking around."

"Neither am I."

"Are you sure? Because otherwise, I can't figure out how the two of you went from introducing yourselves to one another to moving in the next day."

"You know it's not like that."

"Then what the fuck?"

"The fuck is she needed a place to rent and I had one."

"She didn't need a place to rent. She can stay with Maya and me."

Chase narrowed his gaze. "Did it ever occur to you a single time that she might not want to live in your little love nest where the two of you can't go five minutes without your tongues down each other's throats? No one wants to be around that shit."

"I told her we would restrain ourselves."

"Ha! I'll give you fifty bucks if you can go the rest of this night without touching your fiancée." The look of panic on Bo's face gave Chase a good laugh.

Bo looked down, defeated. "I just want to help her. I can't believe she never came to me when all that was going on."

Chase hung the dish towel on the oven handle. "I'll tell you what. If you give me a little information, maybe I could be of use."

"What kind of information?"

"What are we dealing with here? Clearly she's a little freaked out."

"What are you talking about?" Bo asked, eyes going wide.

Chase held up both hands. "Not freaked out. Just aware of her surroundings. I just want to know what's going on so I can be sensitive to whatever it is. Can I at least do that?"

Bo lifted his chin. "All right. The guy she just broke up with, he went into rehab."

"Drinking or drugs?" Chase asked.

"Drinking, as far as I know. But it's significant to know that my dad was a fall-down drunk when we were growing up." Chase glanced out at the screened-in porch where they were all talking and smiling. "He's sober now, but he's just been that way about seven or eight years. Life at our house was rough growing up with him drunk. And Shayla had to relive that whole mess."

Chase's heart cinched. "I'm sorry to hear that."

"You have any experience with alcoholism?"

"No, I guess not."

Bo pursed his lips like Chase failed a test. "Just be aware. And keep an eye out for that dude. He's still living in her house in Franklin."

"Why?"

Bo looked out at where she was and then back to Chase. "I don't know. She said she didn't want to kick him out while he was in rehab, but she grew up with my mom making every excuse in the book for my dad's drunken behavior and giving him every concession known to man. I hope she's just being kind and not considering going back to him. I don't want her anywhere near that asshole if he's a drunk, temporarily sober or not."

"We're on the same page there."

Bo furrowed his brow. "Since when do you

care?"

"Since I've gotten to know her a little. Can I care about your sister? Is that up for grabs?"

Bo gave him a look. "You can care, but leave it at that."

"Out of curiosity, what if I did like her? What would be so terrible about me being with your sister?"

"It wouldn't be terrible if I thought you would stay with her, but I've known you a good five years now and I've never seen you with a girl for more than a week."

"I could say the same about you."

"I was with Angela for nine years. You told me you'd never had a long-term relationship, not since college. That's what you said." Chase looked him up and down, not even remembering when he'd said that, but not doubting that he had. He didn't talk about Rachel and that part of his life, and to his knowledge, no one in this town knew her. "Suddenly you're going to change your mind now, with my sister? I'm not taking that risk."

"I think she'd be the one taking the risk," Chase said, just to prod the lion.

"Bullshit. Not after what she's been through. I'm coming back, and I'm going to be watching out for my sister. You better remember that."

"Okay, tough guy. I hear you. Now step off. I've got sausage balls to bake."

"I'm fucking serious, Chase."

Chase turned around, pan full of sausage ball dough in hand. "So am I. Do you mind?"

Bo stepped back, glaring Chase down while he

loaded the oven with the pan. Chase set the timer per Donna's instructions, and then wiped his hands against one another. He pointed at the oven. "Those are going to be the best damned sausage balls you've ever had, guaranteed." Bo lightened his glare, barely. "So, are you really worried about this guy coming around or something? I thought he was in Nashville."

"He is, but he wants her back. There's no doubt about that. I stopped by there this morning. He turned white as a ghost when he saw me, but then when we sat down together, he opened up. I told him he needed to move on, but I'm not sure he heard me. I'd have threatened him, but he started crying. Hell, reminded me of my dad and I softened to him. That's fucked up."

"That's human," Chase said.

Bo met Chase's gaze. "I guess her living in that pool house isn't the worst place in the world. At least I know it's secure back there. You keep that front door of yours locked. And turn on that high-dollar security system."

"I will. I've already been doing that. She has the codes and all."

"Good."

"I should mention that I'm going out of town. That's actually why I'm here. She was taking me to the airport, but my flight got delayed."

"How long are you going to be gone?" Bo asked.

"Till Thursday. But I'm hiring a security guard for nights."

"Really?" Bo asked.

"Yeah, I told her I didn't like the look of the

renters across the street."

"That's gonna cost."

"You know I've got the money."

Bo pursed his lips. "Thanks. Wanna come meet the rest of my family?"

"Since you've spoken so highly of them, sure."

Bo rolled his eyes at Chase, and they headed that way.

Shayla could feel Maya eyeing her from across the porch while she spoke to Dale's wife Cindy. As soon as she found a break in the conversation, she met Maya's gaze. "You want to see Bo's old wrestling trophies?"

"Oh, God yes," Maya said, and they headed toward the house, passing Chase and Bo.

"Where are you all going?" Bo asked.

"None of your business," Shayla said.

"Stay out of my old room."

"Like we want to go in there. Probably still smells like feet."

Maya giggled, as Shayla let her into the house.

Shayla opened the door to Bo's old room, which was a shrine to Bo's high school days only with a bunch of boxes and crap stacked on the floor. "Dumping ground," Shayla said. "My mom turned my room into a sewing room. There's fabric everywhere."

"Do you sew?" Maya asked.

"Outside of a skirt in Home Ec once, no. Do you?"

Maya shook her head. "But I should. Some of the girls at work knit." She looked lost for a second.

"Girls who I used to work with."

"You ready to make this move?" Shayla asked.

"Oh, yes. Definitely. It's just that I didn't expect to be so emotional about it." She tossed up her arms then let them fall against her legs. "But I'm here now for good. I'll be solo until Bo gets back with all our stuff. My boss has agreed for me to work out my notice from home under the stipulation that I'll be available for the next two months."

"Does that work for you?" Shayla asked.

"I'd have agreed to six months if I had to. Once I decided, I was ready to do this."

Shayla nodded, understanding that more than she knew.

"So I'm here if you'd like to have lunch or coffee," Maya said.

"That sounds good. I'll be in PCB for work all week, so I'll text you."

"Great," Maya said, and then picked up a trophy of Bo's but Shayla could tell she wasn't really seeing it. She turned to Shayla. "So, I was hoping I could talk to you, about the wedding."

Shayla sat on the foot of Bo's old bed. "Mmm hmm."

"I want you to know that I care for your brother more than any man, ever."

Shayla nodded, appreciating Maya's need to get this out, but really just wanting to tell her it wasn't necessary.

"I love him like crazy. I just can't believe I'm the one who gets to marry him. I mean, I can't believe I met him and he loves me and it's all so insane."

Shayla smiled, thinking that Maya probably

didn't realize how much she sounded like a teenager. Or maybe it was just being in Bo's old room that conjured that feeling.

"Anyway, I know we don't know each other, but I'm very much looking forward to knowing you. I feel like I know you as it is. Bo talks about you all the time. And he loves you so much."

Shayla gave a sharp inhale. She didn't do emotional or heartfelt well at all. And she knew Bo loved her. She didn't need his new fiancée to tell her that, but she'd keep that to herself.

Maya shook her head like she was resetting. "So I wanted to ask you...Bo and I would both like for you to be a part of the wedding."

Shayla smiled. "Thank you."

"Would it be okay if you stood on my side with my sister and Felicity? Bo's going to have Dale and Blake and Chase, and so it would just sort of even out if you were on my side."

"Sounds perfect."

She gave a smile of relief. "That's great." Shayla stood, but Maya held up a hand. "Actually, I had one more thing to ask. You're Bo's closest friend or sibling, both, I guess, so I'd like you to be my maid of honor to symbolize the importance in—"

Shayla scratched her forehead. "Maya, can I just stop you there? I'm so honored that you'd allow me to stand up with you and help celebrate your wedding to my brother. And I'm happy to. But I don't need to be equal with your sister or in front of Felicity, who I assume you've known a long time."

"Since high school."

"I'm just happy to be up there. Stand me

wherever works based on my height or my hair color or however will make the best pictures. But you don't need to assign any other meaning to it, okay?"

Maya closed her eyes like a huge burden had been lifted. "Thank you."

Shayla stood. "All right, it not only smells like feet now, but there's an added musty mothball stench. Let's get out of here."

They headed toward the backyard where they found Chase and Bo running with the boys, hitting each other with foam bullets and sweeping the boys up into their arms, using them as shields.

Maya covered her heart. "They are so cute."

"Yeah, they both get spoiled rotten."

"I meant Bo and Chase," she said with a smile.

Chase smiled at Shayla's nephew as they played, but as the boys ran off behind the trampoline, Chase's expression dropped and turned into something resembling lonely. Her nephew ran back toward him, and he smiled again, jumping back into the game. He'd said he didn't have any kids, but Shayla wondered if he wanted them. That didn't match with his relationship pattern, or lack of it, but what did she know?

Shayla pulled her car up to departing flights and popped the trunk. She met Chase back there, because it seemed rude not to get out. "Is that everything?" she asked, peering into the trunk.

"Appears so. Thanks for dinner."

"I should have warned you nobody relaxes at my parents' house."

"I loved it. Now I know how to make sausage balls."

That made her smile. "They were good."

"They weren't, but thanks."

"I liked them." She held his gaze, not sure why she was doing it. A car horn honked, and they both turned in its direction.

He threw the suit bag over his shoulder. "So you're okay to hold down the fort while I'm gone?"

"All set," she said with more bravado than she felt. She wasn't sure what to make of the new development of Bo having actually seen and talked with Brian just yesterday. It could mean Brian was feeling safe, like he'd made a friend in Bo, and that Bo was going to help get her back. It could mean he was even more determined now.

"I don't have to go, you know," Chase said.

"Don't be ridiculous. I'll see you here Thursday."

"You're gonna pick me up?"

"How else are you gonna get home? Besides, I'll be here in PCB for work."

"Thanks," he said, and held out his free arm. She wrapped her arm around his waist and inhaled his scent. Sure, it was partially sausage balls and outside air, but that bit that was him was there too. That earthy, man smell that she fell for every time.

She pulled away first. "Do you have any plants I need to water?"

"I have people who do that."

"Are you serious?"

"Landscapers."

She rolled her eyes at him, but gave him a little

smile. "Bye."

"Bye," he said, and she could feel him standing there as she moved around the car and got in. He was still there when she pulled away, and she wondered how quickly Thursday would get there.

Shayla lay on her bed...Chase's bed...petting Jake. She'd have to give him back soon. She'd fed Bo a line of BS about how he better not see Jake this week, because he was just going to leave him again and it'd get him all confused and make him sad all over again. Bo had glared at her, but had reluctantly relented. So she had him until Bo got back later on that week. But sooner rather than later, Bo was going to take him back.

She could get another dog, but Jake was the best dog in the world, for starters, and secondly, she couldn't bring another dog into Chase's home. Jake was perfect. He didn't have accidents in the house, ever, and he was chill and quiet most the time. There was no guarantee another dog would be any one of those important things when it came to renting with the landlord steps away.

Scott wasn't due to call for another hour, so she went ahead and called him, ready to relax, maybe try to watch a movie. She'd brought some DVDs back from her mom's house.

"I see you haven't changed your number yet," he said by way of greeting.

"It's been a busy day. I moved," she said, and then told him about meeting Chase.

"So this guy, you say he's a friend of Bo's?" Scott asked.

"Yeah, a good friend."

"Have you told him about Brian yet?"

"Not everything. I can't run the risk of it getting back to my brother, especially not right here before his wedding. This is supposed to be the happiest time of his life. I'm a little afraid Brian is going to pull something that weekend, knowing Bo will be tied up."

"When's the wedding?"

"Three weeks from yesterday."

"How would Brian even know Bo's getting married that weekend?"

She told him about Bo coming home, stopping by her house and seeing Brian.

"I definitely get why you're nervous," Scott said. "I can come down for it, just to make sure Brian doesn't try to pull something that weekend."

"That's not necessary, Scott."

"I'd like to," he said, and she got the definite feeling it wasn't as much about protecting her as it was about seeing her. "Please, let me help."

She winced, not sure of the right way to handle this. "I really am fine here. Chase has actually hired a security guard for this week. He's in Vegas till Thursday."

"He hired a security guard, for you?"

"He says he's worried about his house getting vandalized because of some sketchy renters across the street, but I'm pretty sure that's a white lie."

Scott was quiet a moment. "So, I guess he'll be around for the wedding, too."

"I'm pretty sure he's going to be in it."

"He's a...good guy?"

Shayla was pretty sure the question he was really asking was more about what her interest in him was. "Yeah. You know Bo wouldn't be friends with him if he wasn't."

"Well, good. It sounds like you landed in the right place."

She closed her eyes. She was not raised Catholic, but with the guilt she carried around with her all the time, one would think she was.

"So is the security guard there now?" Scott asked.

"Yeah, right outside, actually."

"Is that weird? Some guy you don't know lurking around outside your door?"

"It's a woman, actually."

"Oh," he sounded surprised, and maybe a little relieved.

"She looks pretty badass. I wouldn't mess with her."

"Good," he said. "Think about my offer, okay?"

She rubbed her forehead. "Scott, I hope this isn't presumptuous to say, but I just want to make sure you know that—"

"You're not into dating anyone now. Of course you're not. I totally get that. I'm just sort of invested here, you know? I care about you, and I want to see this through to the end, whatever that may be. Can you get that? Besides, I haven't been down to the panhandle in years. I could use a weekend away."

She balanced the phone between her shoulder and her ear and pumped some lotion into her hands. "There are better weekend getaways than having to be on alert for a possible confrontation."

"Yeah, well, I like my travel with an edge."

She smiled. "I'll call you tomorrow night, from my new phone."

"Sounds good. Have a good night."

She let the phone drop onto the bed and exhaled a deep breath, rubbing the lotion into her hands. Why couldn't she find herself attracted to Scott? He was such a great guy. Who knew, maybe she would be if she saw him again.

The time she'd spent with him had been tainted. She met him at work the day after Brian had squeezed her arms a little too tightly. She'd blown it off, but it had bothered her. Scott had been giving a presentation to her team and bumped into her in the cafeteria afterward, asking her if he'd bored her into submission. Her mind had been elsewhere, back in her childhood with her dad when he'd been drinking. She'd offered Scott a seat, and they'd become friends. He was in the process of a divorce, and they talked about that for the next few weeks. Shayla had welcomed the distraction.

Her phone rang again, and she almost slid the bar to answer without checking the name, assuming it was Scott again, but it wasn't. It was Brian.

She didn't know what the right thing to do in this situation was. She didn't want to answer it, but she did want to know what he and Bo had talked about. She also needed to let him know that it was time he start looking for somewhere else to live. This would be their last conversation.

Her stomach went sick as she swiped the call to answer. She didn't say anything. She wasn't in the mood for greetings.

"Shayla?" he asked, his voice sending chills down her spine.

"Yeah."

"How are you?"

"What do you want?"

"I want to have a reasonable conversation with you." She sat, silent. "I guess you've talked to Bo by now. I'm sure you saw him at Sunday dinner."

She hated that he knew these intimate details of her life. Any time she was in PCB, she was expected at Sunday dinner and so was Bo. Hell, if Brian ever wanted to find her, that'd be where to do it. But he knew better than to come around with Bo or Dale there. If anybody thought Bo was tough, they hadn't met Dale. Hell, that was why Bo was as ripped as he was, always competing with his big brother.

"I have," she said.

"He just showed up, Shayla. What was I supposed to say?"

She hated it when he said her name. It was like his claim on her. "What did you say?" she asked.

"He wanted to know where the *For Sale* sign was. I told him the house wasn't for sale."

Shayla winced, imagining the confusion Bo felt at that moment, trying to balance her lie with what he could see with his own two eyes. "What else?"

"I told him I'd started drinking and you didn't like it and asked me to go to rehab."

She rolled her eyes. Like it was that simple. But she was grateful he hadn't told Bo everything. If Bo had known what she had allowed to go on in that house, she'd never be able to look him in the eye again. She could barely look herself in the mirror.

"That's it?" she asked.

"He told me about your father. Why didn't you ever tell me about him?" Shayla rubbed on her forehead. Why did her brother have such a massive mouth? "You're so closed off, Shayla. As long as we've been together, you've never told me your father had a drinking problem? Why wouldn't you tell me that?"

"What would it have changed? You'd have stopped drinking? You wouldn't have shoved me against the wall or squeezed my arms so hard you left bruises in the form of your hands?"

"I've told you a thousand times, I didn't mean to do any of that. I never hurt you when I was sober. You've got to admit that."

Her heartbeat raced, a tear traveling down her cheek that she fucking resented. "You forced yourself on me."

"Don't you dare say that. Don't you dare fucking say I raped you."

"I didn't say that."

"You implied it."

A tidal wave crested inside of her. "Well, what the fuck do you call it when someone throws you over the table and fucks you while you're goddamn crying the whole time?"

Silence sat between them, and she was immediately regretful of her words. She'd never acknowledged his doing that aloud, never let him know how painful it was for her. She hadn't wanted to seem weak. She'd practically talked herself into thinking she'd been okay with it because she'd chosen to take it and not to fight him on it. But fighting him would have been more pain. Fucking meant a release, an end to a buildup. And it had been. He'd pulled out of her and passed out on the couch.

"Shayla, I'm sorry, but I don't remember anything like that."

Her stomach soured, leaving her to be the one to feel empty and questioned, like she'd imagined it. "Well, I fucking do."

"Okay. I'm not doubting you," he said, exactly like he was doubting her. "I'm just wondering if you might have exaggerated some things in your memory."

There it was. And he was so smooth about it. Not loud and accusatory but calm and rational like she was the one teetering on the edge.

"Consider yourself evicted," she said.

"Shayla."

"Quit fucking saying my name. It's not yours to say anymore. I'm calling a real estate agent tomorrow."

"Shayla, you are not kicking me out of our home."

"It's my home." Her words were weak because of her ridiculous guilt. "I know you've paid to live there the past year and a half."

"I wasn't fucking renting from you. I was helping you pay this mortgage with the understanding we'd get married someday and it'd be part mine."

She trembled as she spoke, out of her element. "I

bought that house before I knew you."

"So I've just been throwing my money down the toilet?"

"We'll work something out," she said.

"You better damn well believe we will."

She inhaled a deep breath. "You've got thirty days to vacate."

The silence pierced her ears. "It's gonna be like that?" he asked, his voice ominous.

"Goodbye, Brian."

"Shayla," he said.

She slid the phone to off.

She exhaled a deep breath and ran her hands through her hair. Jake let out a sigh like he was settling in. She stroked her hand over his head. She was talking a big game, telling Brian he had thirty days to vacate. She had no idea if that was how this was done. She needed advice from someone who understood evictions and selling property with someone living there who definitely wouldn't be tidying up for people who wanted to come look. It was possible he would tear up the place in a fit of rage, or even get drunk and fall into a glass shelf or something.

Jake rolled over so she could pet his chest and belly, and she obliged. "I think I'm going to have to ask for help, Jake."

Chapter Ten

Chase had never had a worse time in Las Vegas. The same could not be said for the guys he'd been with. They were supposed to be there to work, and to their credit they had accomplished what they'd gone for, but there'd been way more fun than work. Chase was usually up for it, too, but not this time. He'd opted to stay at the hotel pool when the other guys had gone to the strip club. It wasn't that he objected to seeing naked women, he could pretty much see that at the pool, but he was too old for strip clubs. Or maybe his mind was elsewhere.

Shayla stood by the door, her dark hair falling over her chest. Wearing her standard-issue Harrison Pool Supply polo shirt, khaki shorts, and tennis shoes, there wasn't a showgirl in Vegas who could hold a candle to her.

He smiled like crazy and headed her way. He pulled her into his arms like they were a couple, not meaning to but honestly not able to help himself.

She pressed her hands against his chest and pushed him away gently, a tiny smile tugging at her lips. "Hey," she said, with a huff of a laugh.

"Sorry," he said, "But you have no idea how good it is to see a girl with some clothes on."

She scratched her ear, giving him a little smile. "Mmm hmm. Did you have fun at the brothels?"

"I will pay for just about anything on the planet, but I refuse to pay a woman to have sex with me."

"Come on. I'm in short-term parking. I couldn't handle the stress of arriving flights."

He followed her out the doors and into the bright Florida sunshine. "Damn, it's good to be back home in the humidity."

She cut her eyes at him, that smile still playing on her lips. He couldn't be sure, but he would almost bet that she was happy to see him, which made his stomach do something weird.

"Are you still cooking me dinner tonight?" he asked.

"I was planning on it."

"I could just take us out to dinner and let someone else cook it."

"Aren't you tired of eating out?"

"I never get tired of eating out." He grinned at her and realized his double entendre. She gave him a look, and he held up a hand. "I swear to God I didn't mean anything by that."

"That's too bad," she said with a smile as they mingled with a big group of people rolling suitcases and laughing about something.

Damn. If he'd have known he was coming home

to this, he'd have come home Monday.

She lengthened her stride, pulling ahead of him till they got to her car, which was actually a Harrison Pool Supply truck. "Have you been out on jobs today?" he asked, tossing his luggage in the back where he could find a spot amongst the pool equipment.

"Maya has my car. She was going to keep it until the weekend of the wedding and Felicity was going to drive Maya's car down then, but Bo decided to haul it down behind the truck at the last minute."

"Oh," he said, thinking now might be a good time to mention that Felicity would be staying with him the weekend of the wedding.

"I look forward to meeting Felicity. She's staying with you that weekend, right?" Shayla asked, glancing over at him.

"Uh, yeah," he said, looking out the window, not sure why he was feeling guilty. He hadn't done anything wrong.

"I think my friend Scott is coming in from Nashville for the wedding."

He looked over at her. Who the fuck was Scott? "Oh," he said.

"He's not staying with me though."

"Oh," he said again, sounding highly intelligent. "Is he someone you're seeing, or…"

"Just a friend," she said.

He lifted an eyebrow. "Straight guy?"

She chuckled. "As far as I know."

Just a friend his ass. No straight man was *just friends* with a woman as beautiful as Shayla Harrison. "On your part, I'm sure," he said, against his own better judgement.

"What's that supposed to mean?" she asked.

He looked over at her. "Come on, Shayla."

"Come on, what?" she said with a huff of a laugh.

"Nothing."

She cut her eyes at him and then stared back at the road wordlessly. She didn't look pissed or agitated. Just focused on the road. He'd go out of his mind if she were this girl. She was so aloof, like nothing affected her.

He shook his head at himself. She was driving him crazy, and she wasn't even doing anything.

"I've got stuff to make enchiladas. Is that okay?" she asked.

"That sounds good. Thanks."

She nodded and turned up the radio. He exhaled and looked down at his phone, trying to occupy himself. When they neared his street, she turned down the radio and said, "Do you like to car shop?"

"I think all guys like to car shop," he said.

"I'm thinking of trading in mine for something roomier. Bo wants me more involved in sales and client relationships. I think I'm outgrowing my sports car."

"What do you want?"

She shrugged. "I don't know. What do you suggest for that kind of thing? Something in my price range, not yours."

He thought about it. "Let me do some research."

"I'm not trying to put you to work."

"Oh, no. I love it. Shopping for a new car that I don't have to pay for…it's like car porn."

She put the truck in park. "I had no idea you swung that way." She gave him a smile that swallowed his heart and then got out of the truck.

Shayla stood at the island in Chase's kitchen, layering enchiladas into a slow cooker, smiling like an idiot. She had no idea what had gotten into her when she picked him up from the airport today. She'd not expected to flirt with him like that, but she'd been so damn happy to see him. Being at this place without him had been lonelier than she'd expected.

She'd gotten a new cell phone with a new carrier. She'd been wanting to change anyway. But she hadn't let the other one go yet. It was just a matter of making the switch with the handful of people she talked to regularly. There was something significant about letting go of her old phone, her old life. But she was ready. She'd send out the text tomorrow, letting everyone who mattered to her know.

"That was quick," Chase said, coming into the room, hair wet. "You showered and started dinner faster than I showered and unpacked. You're supposed to take longer. You're a girl." She hoped he'd done that because he felt dirty from travel and not to get some woman's scent from this morning off of him. Not that she'd smelled a woman on him or that it was any of her business who he slept with, but the idea of his hands and mouth on some random Vegas girl didn't sit well with her.

"I didn't put on makeup," she said. "Or do anything to my hair."

"I thought you were intentionally going with the wet look."

She shrugged her response.

"What goes better with enchiladas, red or white?" he asked.

"Green?" she said, and then pulled a bottle out of the refrigerator. "Do you do margaritas?"

"Does a lime grow on a tree?"

"Is on the rocks okay? Or I think you can put this in the blender with ice."

"On the rocks. Extra salt. I've got some in here somewhere," he said, and then pulled a container of margarita salt out of the pantry. "I've got glasses too, I think."

"They're in your dining room buffet."

"How do you know this and I don't?"

"I saw them in there the other day when you were showing me your wine collection." He walked in there and came back with two glasses. She got a little paranoid. "I wasn't in here snooping when you were gone. I only came in here last night to drop off the groceries for tonight."

"I don't care," he said.

"I'm serious," she said.

He poured water into the rim of the container. "I am, too. You want salt?"

"No."

"That's just not right. You have to have salt with a margarita. We need crushed ice with these."

She held a cup up to the refrigerator to get crushed ice. "Your fancy ice won't work with this?"

"Too big for this shallow glass."

She walked over to where he was standing and

poured ice into the two glasses. He didn't move out of the way, so she was right up next to him. She took a whiff of him, freshly out of the shower. He smelled like expensive men's body wash, woodsy and fresh.

She stepped away. "Did you know you had a slow cooker?"

"I vaguely remember my assistant purchasing me one with my own credit card and printing out some recipes for me."

"Have you ever used it?" she asked.

He handed her the salt-free glass with an apologetic look. "Will you hold it against me if I say no?"

She took the glass. "Cheers."

"To what?" he asked.

"New cars, new apartments, new friends."

He smiled. "Cheers." They both sipped. "Damn," he said, looking at the glass. "What brand is that? It's good. Not real sweet."

They both glanced at the bottle. "I took a risk," she said.

He looked down at her. "Worked out well." She bit her lip and went back to the slow cooker, finishing her layering. "It's all in there?" Chase asked.

"Yep. Is that okay? Or are you one of these visual eaters? 'Cause this might come out looking a mess, but I promise it'll taste good."

"I'm not picky...when it comes to food, that is."

She sprinkled cheese on top of her creation. "Where are you picky?"

He stood next to her, keeping a little distance,

resting his ass on the island. "I'm picky about women."

"That's not what I hear."

"I've been unfairly categorized."

"How's it unfair when it's true?" she asked.

"You don't know it's true," he said.

"It doesn't matter what I think anyway."

He tugged on her shorts at the hip. "It does."

A surge of electricity shot through her at his touch. She cut her eyes at him. "Drink your margarita."

"Yes, ma'am."

She turned the slow cooker on high and covered it. "If you're hungry now I've got chips and salsa."

He held up his margarita glass. "I'm good with just this, and your company, of course."

She let out a huff of air and set her gaze on him. "Mmm hmm."

He lifted his margarita to his mouth. "I'm drinking my margarita."

"You're up to no good."

"How do you know?"

She pointed at his mouth. "That smile is how I know."

"You started it."

She widened her eyes. "I did not."

"Yes you did...at the airport."

She picked up the empty cheese pouch and tossed it in the trash can. "I had a momentary lapse of reason."

"You missed me," he said.

She gave him a look. "I don't even know you."

"That's not a denial," he said.

She picked up the empty can of beans and rinsed it out. "Where are your recycle bins?"

"In the pantry."

Of course she knew that, but she was trying to say anything to avoid the mess she'd dug herself into. She walked over there and tossed the can away. When she turned around, he was standing there against his island, rubbing his freshly shaven chin. She rolled her eyes.

"What?" he asked.

"Is this how you do it? Lure women into your kitchen, pump them with alcohol then stand there and look cute?"

He held his hand out to the side. "Hey, you're the one who had the margarita chilling in the fridge. And come to think of it, it was your idea to cook me dinner. So who lured who?"

She shook her head and rolled her eyes. "I'm a real idiot sometimes."

"For doing what?"

"Nothing," she said, picking up her glass.

"I'll have you know that I didn't go to one strip club when I was in Vegas."

She widened her eyes. "Seriously? Not one? Where's this guy's gold star?"

"I'm serious. All the other guys went, and I stayed at the pool."

"Oh, what torture. You, stuck at a Vegas pool. All those bachelorette parties and shot girls walking around. Bless your heart."

"I'm serious about this. They all made fun of me. Said I was pussy whipped and I don't even have a girlfriend. That was hard to explain."

She narrowed her gaze at him. "I hope you didn't hold back in Vegas because of me, because if you did you shouldn't have."

He squinted one eye. "I didn't, but for the sake of argument, let's say I did. What harm did I do? Saved myself from a potential STD?"

She sipped her margarita, looking him in the eye. "I told you I would stay out of your hair here. I don't want you holding back dating someone because of me."

"Maybe I'm tired of dating," he said and then took her glass and set it on the counter. "Maybe I like you."

Her stomach flip-flopped like a fish being reeled in from the ocean. She shook her head. "Not a good idea."

He turned his body toward hers, resting his hand on her hip. "What's not?"

She gave him a look, her heartbeat pounding.

He leaned down. "Me kissing you?" he whispered, and her knees almost gave way.

"Mmm hmm," she said, watching his mouth get closer.

"Should I stop?" he asked, his thumb pressing into her hip.

She opened her mouth, but the word *no* wouldn't form. She closed her eyes as his lips met hers, and her heartbeat soared off the charts. His lips were soft but firm, in control, but she somehow knew she was still in charge. All she had to do was say no, but she couldn't.

Salty and sweet from the margarita, his lips pressed against hers as she ran her fingers through his wavy hair, pushing his head toward her, forcing her own back while he leaned down farther into her. She wanted his tongue, but that was too much, wasn't it? This was a trial kiss. A one-off. A margarita-fueled tryout, though they hadn't even finished their first drink.

The doorbell rang and she ripped herself away from him, her heartrate spiking. And then she remembered.

"Fuck," he said.

She rubbed her forehead. "It might be Bo, coming for Jake."

"Goddamn Bo," Chase said, and she couldn't agree more.

Chase went to answer the door, and when she heard Bo's voice, she headed to the pool house to gather all Jake's stuff. When she got back to the kitchen with the load, Bo walked in, looking around at the margarita glasses.

She went back out to the pool area and called Jake. He came running over, tail wagging. She bent down to pet him, getting his belly like he liked. "I'm going to miss you," she said, and her heart broke a little, even though she could see him anytime she wanted. Jake had helped her through these past couple of months. She wasn't sure what she would have done without him.

She patted the wetness that was starting at the corner of her eye and stood as the back door opened. Could Bo not see she was having a moment with the damn dog?

Jake's tail went nuts when he saw Bo, his tongue all hanging out while Bo knelt down and the two of them had a reunion like long lost brothers. Bo looked up at her. "Thank you for keeping him all this time."

She stuck her hands in her pockets. "Mmm hmm."

Bo narrowed his gaze. "Are you crying?"

"No," she said, scrunching up her face like he was an idiot.

"Did you want to keep him?" The look on his face begged her to say no as Jake nuzzled his head into Bo's chest.

"No. I'm renting here. I can't take on a dog."

Bo just stared at her, stroking Jake's fur like he wasn't sure what to do.

"Go on. Get him home. He's been whining for you every night."

"Really?" Bo asked, smiling down at the stupid dog. She rolled her eyes and shook her head, walking back inside to locate her margarita. "Where's he been sleeping over here?" Bo asked, following her.

This was a question she was not prepared to answer. "He likes a tree outside."

"At night?"

"No, not at night," she said.

"Then where's he been sleeping at night?" She cocked her head to the side, lips pursed. Bo shut his eyes. "Goddammit. You've had him in the bed with you, haven't you? I told you not to do that."

"Not every night," she lied.

Bo knelt down again, taking Jake's cheeks into his hands. "You can't do that at home, buddy. I've got a girl in the bed now."

Shayla looked at Chase for the joke, and he held up both hands. "I didn't say a word."

Bo stood, looking around. "What's this, margarita night?"

"Yep," Shayla said.

Bo looked between the two of them. "I like margaritas."

"I hear they've got good ones at Chili's in PCB," Chase said, and Shayla smiled.

"Is this a date? Am I interrupting?" Bo asked, not sorry.

"Yeah," Chase said, pulling Shayla to his side. "We were just getting ready to take a bubble bath."

Bo shook his head. "I give up on the two of you. I'm going to get him home."

"Make him take you out for a margarita. Have you unloaded the truck yet?" Chase asked, letting go of Shayla.

"Already done."

"Glad I waited to ask," Chase said.

Bo eyed the two of them. "Is this happening, for real?"

"No, you dipwad," Shayla said. "But you're ruining my buzz."

"All right," Bo said, gathering Jake's stuff. Shayla grabbed the bag of food and headed toward the truck with Bo and Jake.

"Hey, thanks again for letting Maya use your car," Bo said.

Shayla had taken it and gotten a Florida tag put on it before she'd passed it to Maya, just in case Brian decided to make a pop-in visit to town. She'd also stuck a plate of a sailing symbol on the front.

She'd never sailed a day in her life. "Sure."

"I'll have it at work for you tomorrow so you can drive it home."

She hauled the bag of food into the truck bed. "When are you coming back to work?"

"Monday. I need to take tomorrow and the weekend to help get Maya settled."

"Sounds good."

He tossed Jake's stuff into the back of the truck. "You ready to have me back or dreading it?"

"Little of both," she said.

He pulled her into his arms and hugged her to him. "I've missed you."

She let him hold her a second, and then pulled away. "You'll be sick of me by Tuesday."

"Probably," he said with a grin, and then his smile faded. "What's been going on this week with the house? Have you let your ex know to find somewhere else to live?"

A quick online search told Shayla she needed to provide written notice via certified mail. She'd do that after the wedding. She didn't want to rock any boats before then. "Yep," she said, because she had told him that on the phone Sunday night. She just hadn't made it official with the letter yet. "I'm giving him thirty days to get out."

"Then you'll list it?" he asked.

"I don't want to risk putting it on the market while he's there, having dirty underwear laying around while people come to see it."

He looked pissed. "That son of a bitch. Blake and I should have stopped by there on our way back here."

"Like a couple of thugs? That sounds productive."

He pointed at her. "If he's not out in thirty days, I'm going back there."

"Fine," she said, knowing she'd never let on if Brian wasn't gone by then. This was her problem and she would work it out on her own.

She headed back inside to Chase, resetting her brain. Nothing like having a really great first kiss interrupted by a brother with an attitude. She supposed she deserved that. She had no right kissing Chase to begin with. She was doing a terrible job of keeping this whole thing cool and friendly.

She walked back into the kitchen to find Chase sitting on a barstool, his back against the island, knees falling out to the sides. Damn he was a lot of man.

"You okay?" he asked.

"Of course. Why wouldn't I be?"

"I saw the way you looked at Jake. You're gonna miss him."

She glanced off to the side, shaking her head like it was nothing.

"You want to go get another one?"

"No," she said with a chuckle. "I'm doing well to take care of myself these days." It was true. She'd been too afraid to take Jake on a walk. She'd just thrown him the ball in the backyard. That wasn't a way for a dog to live. She might get a dog for herself, but not until all this was settled with Brian.

"You gonna be okay to sleep alone?" he asked. She gave him a look, letting him know not to even go there. He smiled, looking down at his margarita. "Well, one thing's for sure, Bo cares about his sister."

She rolled her eyes. "I care about him, too. I just wish he'd back off a little sometimes."

"Why do you think he's so protective?"

She pulled her top lip into her mouth and then let it go, sitting down on the barstool on the other side of the island, putting some space between them. "He's a little more protective than usual. He stopped in and saw my ex on his way down here."

He turned around and faced her. "I heard."

Shayla lifted an eyebrow. "How much?"

"That your ex had been to rehab."

She shook her head. "My mouthy brother."

"I'm glad he told me. I want to help, if that's possible."

"I'm all set," she said.

"So he's still in your house?" Chase asked.

"Damn Bo."

"He thinks you might be considering taking the guy back," Chase said.

"Well he's wrong, I can promise you that."

Chase nodded. "I really didn't think that was the case."

"How come?" she asked.

"Because you seem like a decisive person. Scares me a little, actually."

"Why's that?"

He shrugged. "You seem like you're the one in control of your life, of your relationships. I imagine when you decide one's over, it's over."

She blinked, trying to figure out how to take that

143

comment. She couldn't feel less in control now if she tried.

"Tell me about this house of yours back in Nashville," he said.

"Franklin, it's a suburb of Nashville."

"So it's your house, not his?"

"Yeah, I bought it before I knew him, but he's been helping pay the mortgage since he moved in."

"How long did you have it before he came in the picture?"

She thought about it. "I bought it when I first moved there about four years ago."

"And when did he move in?"

"About a year and a half ago. I don't even care if takes the damn thing. I just want to be separated from him."

"He's not taking your house," Chase said.

Shayla stared down at her glass, trying to understand for the thousandth time how she got herself into this mess.

"Then I'll pay him back for the months he paid."

"Why? He lived there, didn't he?"

"With the assumption that we were going to get married and it'd be his someday, too."

"You were engaged?"

"Not officially. We talked about it a lot at first, much less after he started drinking."

"Look, Shayla, things changed. He didn't hold up his end of the bargain. He turned into a liability for you, not someone who you could build a life with."

She met his gaze, wondering why he hadn't wanted to build a life with anyone else since his divorce. She tabled that thought. "I just can't stand to feel like I owe someone."

His eyebrows went up. "Owe him? You think you owe him?"

She shook her head, standing up. "This is why I don't talk to people about stuff like this. You don't understand."

"Then explain it to me."

"He thinks he held up his end of the bargain. We had a deal that I agreed to because I was…"

She caught herself. What was she doing? She couldn't spill her guts to this guy about how she'd coerced him into going to that specific rehab because she couldn't handle the guilt of turning him over to some other unsuspecting woman who would unknowingly start this whole mad cycle over again. How many women would have to go through the same shit with this same guy? This program was supposed to be effective. If she could offer him the hope of reconciliation if he went through it, then at least he'd go, and there was a chance of ending the cycle.

She held up both hands, backing away. "I'm sorry. I can't do this. I didn't mean to start this with you." He stood and she shook her head. "No." She glanced around his house, a blast of reality overwhelming her. What was she doing moving in with unsuspecting Chase? Was she manipulating him, too? She pointed at the slow cooker. "Um, that will be ready in about an hour and a half. I'm just going to run out for a little while, okay?"

"Shayla," he said, in a gentle voice.

She closed her eyes. "No, it's nothing. It's fine. I

just need some time alone, okay?"

He didn't respond, just stared at her with concern that she couldn't handle. She ran over to the pool house, grabbed her purse, and then headed out the back gate.

Chase watched for lights in his driveway like he was on patrol. This was ridiculous. She was a grown woman, fully able to take care of herself, but he couldn't help how worried he was about her. He wasn't thinking she was going to do anything crazy, but he was worried about her state of mind. She clearly had something she was keeping secret, a thing that was weighing heavy on her mind.

After she finally pulled in, he gave her a half hour to settle in before he grabbed the glass container of enchiladas he'd set aside for her and headed to the pool house.

He knocked. "Shayla, it's me."

A moment later the door opened, and Shayla stood before him in a gray, V-neck T-shirt and a pair of black leggings that hugged her hips in a way that made him twitch in places he hoped she wouldn't notice.

He proffered the container. "I didn't know if you'd eaten."

She took it from him, not meeting his gaze. "Thanks. Did you eat?" she asked.

"Yeah, earlier. I didn't think you wanted me to wait for you."

"No, I didn't."

"It was really good. I ate like half the pot."

She smiled, chancing a quick glance at him.

"Good."

Some music blasted through the television, causing them both to jump. She ran over to the bed, putting the enchiladas down and grabbing the remote.

"Sorry," she said, punching at the remote. "I was messing with this earlier. The sound wasn't working on this DVD player."

It was "God Only Knows" by The Beach Boys. He held out his hand and she gave it over to him. He hit the magic button and got the sound down. "It's this goofy remote. You have to hit this button and then this one." He handed it back to her. "Is that *Big Love*?"

"Yeah, I found the DVD in that cabinet. Is that okay?"

"I forgot I had that. It was going around the office last fall when Seanna was redoing my kitchen. I was too lazy to hook up cable in here, so I brought it home to watch while I ate, but I forgot I had it."

"Well, here. Return it to whoever it belongs to." She went for the DVD player and he touched her arm.

"No, don't. Watch it. I'll return it when you're through."

She stopped and turned toward him, looking up at him like she wanted to say something that had nothing to do with the HBO series. She exhaled and rubbed her fingers down her cheek. "I'm just too antsy to read tonight for some reason."

"Watch your show. Eat your food," he said, and headed toward the door.

Just as he was about to close it behind him, she said, "Have you seen it?"

He inwardly smiled, turning back toward her. "No, I haven't. I think I watched the first five minutes then got distracted. I used to eat over here when Seanna was redoing my kitchen, when I forgot to eat before I came home."

She walked over to the kitchen area and opened the refrigerator. "Do you want to stay and watch it with me?"

She was so nonchalant about it, he wasn't sure if she really wanted him to or not. She pulled out two bottles of water and handed him one, meeting his gaze for real for the first time since he walked in there.

He could get lost in those dark eyes easier than taking his own breaths. "Yeah," he said, taking the bottle of water. "Thanks."

She pulled two forks out of the drawer and walked over to the bed, sitting on the far side. Settling in, she pulled the top off the glass container and stabbed both forks into the food, an invitation to join her.

He walked over and sat on the bed next to her while she hit rewind on the remote, sending the show back to the beginning. Hitting play, she took a bite of food, her eyes glued to the screen. He watched the show, trying not to look at her, but they were so close. He'd bought a double bed for this place since it was so small, but he was second-guessing that choice now. Being so close to her in those clothes that clung to her body was dangerous.

Chapter Eleven

Shayla turned off the alarm on her phone ten minutes before it was set to go off. Lord knew she didn't need it, not with Chase snoozing beside her all night.

He'd fallen asleep somewhere around the second half of episode two, and she'd not done anything to wake him up. He slept like the dead. She'd gotten up, put her dish in the sink, and brushed her teeth, and he'd not moved through any of it. She didn't think he was faking either. She'd watched his chest move up and down with his steady breathing, feeling a little like a stalker.

He'd settled into the bed at some point, which she was glad about. She couldn't imagine the crick that would be in his neck if he'd slept sitting up all night. She wouldn't have let him do that, of course, she didn't think. But it was nice having him there, and she hadn't wanted him to leave. Last night was supposed to have been her first night alone without the company of Jake, but Chase's warm body next to her had been quite the upgrade, she had to admit...no offense to Jake.

Chase was a considerate sleeper. She'd expected his big body to sprawl out over the bed at some point, his long arms having to go somewhere. But he'd kept them crossed over his stomach all night, sort of like a corpse. She lay beside him on her stomach, head turned toward him so she could study his face, but ready to close her eyes if he showed any signs of waking up.

He had such smooth skin. Her fingers itched to trail down his cheek to his lips, which were the perfect size for her. She didn't have a very big mouth or lips, and neither did he, kind of like they were made to work together. She rolled her eyes at herself for that one.

His eyelids were closed, hiding his eyes. He'd been awarded with the best genes from both of his parents, his mother's beautiful skin color and cheekbones, his father's emerald eyes and a little scattering of freckles to give his face even more character than it deserved.

He gave a sharp inhale, and Shayla closed her eyes quickly. She could feel him moving, the sheets rustling.

"Shit," he said under his breath.

She didn't want him to feel bad, so she pretended to wake up, blinking and focusing on him. "Hey."

He put one foot on the floor. "I'm so sorry. I didn't mean to crash here all night. I guess I drifted off when we were watching the show."

"I guess I did, too," she lied.

He pulled the covers back and sat on the side of the bed with his back to her. "Crap."

"Everything okay?" she asked.

"Yep," he said. "I just need...um...a minute."

She grinned, pulling the covers back, and headed to the bathroom. "Happy Friday," she said before closing the door behind her.

Shayla floated through Friday like she was dancing on a cloud. Watching *Big Love* with Chase had been the best thing she'd done in a while. His big body so close to hers...just breathing him in was like inhaling a drug. Watching the show with his quips and commentary had made her smile and laugh out loud more than once. It was like he was prescribed to her by some doctor. *This guy will make you feel better. Take one dose per day, but don't overdo it because you'll become addicted.*

Tracey appeared at her office door. "When do you think you'll have the new schedule posted?"

Shayla hit OK on her screen. "Right this second."

"Cool. Thanks." She started to walk away, and then turned back. "I haven't seen you in this good of a mood since...ever?"

Shayla shrugged. "Glad it's Friday."

Tracey hit her forehead. "Oh, I'm sorry. I totally spaced. That skinny guy that dresses like a Ralph Lauren model was in here earlier. "Sss..."

"Sebastian?" Shayla asked.

Tracey pointed. "That's him. It was when you ran to the bank. He said he tried to text you."

151

"I changed my number."

Tracey reached in her pocket. "He wants you to come to an opening at a wine bar tonight. He invited me, too. Do you think he's serious?"

"I know he is. He's the most inclusive person you'll ever meet."

Tracey laughed. "Like someone like me could mesh with his friends."

"I think you'd be surprised. His friends are all over the place. Bo's one of his close friends if that tells you anything."

"Yeah, I always thought it was weird when he would pop in here to take Bo to lunch. I started wondering if Bo might be gay for a minute, you know, when he hadn't dated anyone in a while."

"Please tell that story at the Christmas party," Shayla said.

Tracey smiled. "Okay, I'm taking off."

"Go ahead and flip the sign. I'm outta here in just a sec." Shayla rummaged through her purse for her old phone to find Sebastian's number. She had thirteen missed calls. She was not superstitious, but even she didn't like that number.

Tracey appeared at her door again. "Speak of the devil. Sebastian is coming to the front door right now."

Shayla exhaled, smiling. "Thanks." She followed Tracey to the front where Sebastian stood like a fish out of water in their pool supply store with his tailored clothes and high-dollar shoes.

When he saw her, he beamed. "How have you been here two months and I'm just now seeing you?" He wrapped his skinny body around hers in a hug. "I've missed you, sister Shayla. Did Tracey tell you I was here earlier?"

Shayla noted that he'd remembered Tracey's name and made a mental note to try to do better about that herself. "Yes. I'm sorry I haven't texted you yet. I was just getting ready to do that."

"I'm not stalking you. Well, maybe a little. After I stopped by earlier, I hit Pier Park for a movie with a friend, and so I was on my way home and thought I'd try you one more time. You haven't been responding to my texts, which isn't like you."

"I changed phones. I'm trying to get my contacts switched."

"Ah. Well, here." He typed into his phone, and then handed it to her. "Input your number and I'll text you hello." She did, and he did. "Perfect. Now, for what I was texting you about. I was hoping you could come to an opening tonight. It's on 30A, so it's close to your new home."

"You know about my new home?" she asked.

"Sweetie, don't insult me."

She rolled her eyes, but lovingly.

"Anyway, it's a happy hour wine bar opening next door to Marigold's shop. We're super excited about it because it means more foot traffic for Mari's place. Tonight we're just trying to get butts in seats, and our group has lots of cute butts, so can I count on yours?" he asked.

She thought about it a second. It was time for her to get back out into the world, and this seemed like a decent next step.

"I've already talked to Chase, and he's coming, so there's that," he said.

"Oh," she said, and then she remembered that Chase and Marigold were close, according to Bo. They had never dated, but Bo always swore that one day they'd surprise them all by showing up to something as a couple.

"That's, cool."

"So you roomies can ride, yes?" But before she could answer, he said. "Come on, I'll make sure you get to your car okay. There was a weirdo across the street a minute ago."

She froze. "What did the weirdo look like?"

"Nappy, blond dreads, super skinny, board shorts. Come to think of it, he was probably just headed to the beach. But I'll walk you to your car nonetheless."

She relaxed.

He dropped her at her car. "I'll see you there in a bit. I assume you're going home to change first?"

"What's wrong with this?" she asked, trying to hide a smile.

"Sweetie, usually I'd say it was unacceptable, but you're so gorgeous you can make a polo shirt stamped with a store logo and khakis look hot."

She rolled her eyes. "You ought to go to work in a women's boutique. You'd outsell everyone."

"Backup plan if the consulting business ever lies dormant."

She slipped in the back gate when she got home, glancing into the house as she made her way to the pool house. Chase wasn't downstairs.

She let herself in and got showered and dressed...in an actual dress. She did own a few.

This was one with small flowers, a little flowy, so she hardened it up with a faux leather jacket she loved but hadn't worn in months. Brian had loved her in that jacket until she put it on one night for an evening out with friends, and one of the guys they were with commented that he liked it on her. Brian had sulked the whole way home and wanted to know why he felt open enough to say that to her right in front of him. She didn't fucking know. The next time she pulled it out to put it on, he glared at it like he wanted to fight it, so she tucked it back in her closet and that was the close of the subject. She was more than happy to don it tonight. Fuck him.

She picked up her new phone and saw that she didn't have any texts, which she was a little bummed about. Had Chase already left? Should she text him?

This was exactly the sort of thing she was trying to avoid. They were supposed to be living separate lives in this house. And this was Marigold's thing. Shayla had met her a time or two and was happy to support her, but what if Chase was really looking forward to seeing Marigold? What if this was the night they wound up together? Shayla's stomach rolled at the idea, but she knew what she needed to do.

She slid her phone into her small purse and locked the door behind her. She glanced into the kitchen where she found Chase talking on the phone. He looked good. His black hair was wet and almost shiny, his jeans fit him just right, with an untucked, black button-up with the sleeves rolled up his arms. He saw her and waved. She returned the wave but kept walking toward the gate, wanting him to call her back. She walked slower than usual, silly girl she was, but made it all the way to the gate without hearing that door open. She settled into the disappointment as she pulled the gate tight and headed toward her car.

She opened the car door, and her heart soared as a door opened and Chase called her name. "Shayla, wait up." She exhaled, feeling every bit the silly girl she was. Chase opened the gate. "You going to the opening?"

"Yeah, Sebastian asked me to." How stupid. Now she just sounded desperate.

"I'll drive us. Let me grab my wallet and keys." She nodded and waited there on the driveway, glancing around. Because when she was out in the open, that's what she did nowadays. He opened the side door to his garage and let her in his Jeep. "You want me to put the top up?" he asked.

She looked at him like he was crazy. "No."

"All right, just asking," he said with a little grin. She'd never been around someone who was so damn happy all the time.

"So, sounds like this is a wine bar opening next to Marigold's shop," she said.

"Mmm hmm. Sounds cool. Good for her business."

"I wonder if she'll start staying open at night," she said.

"I think she will, at least when she doesn't have plans with the group."

Shayla couldn't help herself. "I hear you and her are pretty tight."

"Me and Marigold?" he asked.

"Yeah," she said.

He smiled. "We flirt, but we've never taken it further than that."

"Why not? She's a really pretty girl."

"I don't know. Too much alike, probably. I love her to pieces. I'd do anything for her."

Shayla believed that. She wondered how there were guys out there like Brian when there were ones like Chase. And how did girls end up with one or the other?

He glanced over at her. "Cool jacket."

She smiled, looking away from him. "Thanks."

They arrived at Marigold's shop, which Shayla had admittedly never been to. She'd meant to stop by, but hadn't made it, of course. She'd been holed up over in PCB. That was part of the reason she wanted a place on 30A. It was a drive to get to work every day, but she was tired of her hometown, even having been away from it for four years in Nashville. She needed her distance from her family and the people she would inevitably run into from high school, who were every damn where she went. Being single at thirty-six was tough enough to deal with on her own. She didn't need the pitying looks from her classmates, and in many cases, the self-satisfied expressions of joy when they saw Shayla Harrison's life didn't end up picture perfect after all.

As they walked up to the wine bar, Shayla had to blink as she glanced into what must have been Marigold's shop.

"That's Marigold's place?" she asked Chase.

"Yeah. Have you not seen it?"

"No." It wasn't anything like what she was expecting. Bright colors filled the space with funky art, jewelry, pillows, wall hangings, chairs painted like animals, and Hollywood lights draped across the ceiling. "That looks really cool."

"She'll open it for you and show you around, I'm sure."

"I'd like that."

Chase opened the door to the wine bar and stood there looking so damn handsome as Shayla walked past him. She exhaled a breath, looking around the sleek, cool room with rich leather couches in pockets and a bar that spanned the entire left side.

"Nice," Chase said.

"There they are," came Sebastian's voice from somewhere to her right. She turned and found him with Desiree and Ashe, the three of them looking like a piece of art themselves with their unique styles—Sebastian with his classic prep, Ashe with his sleek look finished with just a touch of eye makeup, and Desiree with her black hair braided intricately and swept up on top of her head. Suddenly, the confidence Shayla felt in her leather jacket waned a bit.

She hugged each of them, Ashe and Sebastian kissing her on the cheek, and Desiree holding onto her for a long time. "I've missed you, sweet friend."

God, these people were nothing like anyone she'd ever known. When Bo had introduced her to them when he first started hanging out with them about three years ago, she'd been baffled at first at how they fit with her redneck brother, but after just one night with them, it all clicked into place. They were genuine and caring, despite their perfect and unique appearances. She'd only met them all a handful of times when she'd been home to visit here and there, but they always made her feel like a part of their circle.

Shayla squeezed her back, wordlessly. Ashe pointed at her. "What happened to you on Facebook? I mean, you never really posted anything but you were always around with your stoically hilarious comments on my pictures. I could just hear you saying them. Then one day, I was like, where's my Shayla love? And I searched for you and you were gone. Now, I know you didn't unfriend me."

"No, of course not. I just got off of there. I got sick of the politics." That was an excuse anyone could believe.

"I just unfriend," Desiree said. "Even if it's someone I liked. I can't take the division."

"I'm a fan of the unfollow," Sebastian said. "That way I don't have to see their crap but I don't have to possibly get confronted by anyone wanting to know why I unfriended them."

"There's my boyfriend!" came a loud, female voice from across the room. Marigold, with her beautiful, flowing blond hair came running across the room on light feet and jumped up into Chase's arms with her legs tucked to her, and he held her there like a human ball.

She kissed him on the cheek with a loud, "M-wuah!" and then hopped down. "I haven't seen you in like a month. Where have you been?"

"I know where he's been this past week," Sebastian said under his breath, and Desiree and Ashe both smiled like they had a secret.

Shayla turned to the group and said in a low voice, "You all know we're not dating, right?"

"Oh, of course," Ashe said, and then exchanged a look with Desiree.

"I'm serious."

Sebastian tapped her on the arm. "We know, sweetie." She rolled her eyes and shook her head at them.

"Oh, my God. Shayla," Marigold said and then swept Shayla into her. She pulled back and squeezed Shayla's arms. "Finally. I've only texted you to come meet us like eight thousand times. Why have you not come to see me?"

"She's not come to see any of us, for the record," Sebastian said. Shayla gave him a look, and he said, "What? You haven't."

"I've been busy with the business with Bo gone and all."

"When are they getting their asses back down here?" Marigold asked. "It was cute, him going up there to win her back, but over two months now? Is she nuts? It's Bo Harrison. He would have had me at *I'm here*."

"Most do," Ashe said, and Marigold shoved him.

"He's back as of yesterday," Shayla said.

"I texted Maya," Sebastian said. "They're still getting settled but will meet us somewhere soon."

Marigold motioned around the room. "What do you all think? Is this not awesome? I'm going to need rehab after a month or two of this."

Chase gave Shayla a closed-mouth smile, and Shayla shook her head discreetly, letting him know she didn't think anything of it.

Marigold looked at Chase and Shayla's empty hands. "You two need vino. Come."

They followed her to the bar, and she turned back to them. "You both like Pinot Noir, right?" They nodded, and she ordered for them. "I'm going to find Fiona. This is her bar. I want you both to meet her." She walked away, and they waited for their wine.

"Your friends are really kind people," Shayla said.

"They're your friends, too."

"Thanks to Bo. How'd you get into this crew?" she asked.

"Shit, I don't know. Through Blake, I guess. He and Seanna should be here," he said, glancing around. The bartender slid two glasses to them and they thanked him. Chase turned back toward her with a look that made her stomach fizz, or maybe that was the wine. "I like *Big Love*."

"Yeah, it's definitely…curious."

He shook his head. "One woman is tough enough, three would do me in." She smiled and took a sip of her wine. "I didn't mean to sleep in your bed like that. I hope you know that," he said.

"It's your bed, actually," she said.

He gave her that little sideways grin that was so cute she could lick it. "I think it's yours now. After having you, it would never take me back solo."

"I thought you'd never slept in it," she said.

"I haven't, actually."

161

"Ah," she said, setting her gaze on the many wine bottles behind the bar.

"Ah, what?"

"You haven't *slept* in it," she said.

He considered her. "Why do you do that?"

She looked down at her wine glass, feeling caught. "What'd I do?" she asked, knowing the answer.

"You bring up me and other women."

She twirled her wine glass. "I don't know. Maybe it helps me establish boundaries with you."

"Why do you need those?" he asked.

She cut her eyes at him. "You know why."

"I really don't, but I'd love for you to tell me."

She took another sip of her wine, staring down at the bar. She finally looked back at him. "What?"

"I'm waiting."

She let out an exhausted breath. "You're really going to make me spell this out for you?"

"I'm not a smart guy, not when it comes to women, clearly."

She gave him a look, and he pinched her hip. "I want to know."

She glanced down at her hip. "Don't do that to me."

"Pinch you?"

"Yeah."

"How come?"

She met his gaze. "'Cause I like it."

He smiled. "Well, if I'd have known that I might have tried to kiss you again last night."

"That's the whole problem."

"What is?"

She shook her head. "Chase."

"Mmm, see, now I like that."

"What?" But she knew.

"When you say my name. You hardly ever do, so when you do, it makes me a little crazy."

"You're so full of shit."

"I'm not. Have I not made it clear that I like you?"

She picked at the beverage napkin her wine glass was sitting on.

"When I saw you standing there at the airport, I couldn't believe how good you looked to me," he said. "I mean, I missed you when I was out in Vegas, but when I saw you, I was like, damn. I don't want to be superficial, but you're one of the most beautiful women I've ever seen."

She closed her eyes and shook her head. "Please don't say that." As the words came out of her mouth, she chastised herself. Change the subject. That was the rule her mother had given her when she was a teenager. *You're an unusually attractive girl, Shayla. People will tell you that. When they do, change the subject. The makeup of your facial features has nothing to do with beauty. That comes from within.*

"I wouldn't tell you that if I thought you already knew it," he said.

She met his gaze, curious.

"You don't seem to be aware of what you look like. Or, I take that back. I think you do know, but I don't think it's important to you," he said.

She didn't know what to make of that. "Why do you say that?"

"You don't carry yourself like a girl who tries too hard. You don't try at all. I've got that big mirror in the living room, I've never seen you check yourself in it. Every girl I've ever had in that house has checked herself in that mirror every chance she's gotten. I love a confident woman, but the second I see them look at themselves in the mirror and pucker up, checking each side of their face, making weird expressions that they think are sexy or interesting, it's a turn off. I'd rather sit and talk to a woman all night with a booger on her nose than have her do that."

She giggled. She hadn't giggled in years.

"I'm serious. I would. A pretty face is nice, but I'd much rather talk to a girl who's focused on the conversation than on her own face."

She narrowed her gaze. "You confuse me."

"How's that?"

"Because when you say something like this, you sound like someone who's interested in women for more than their looks."

He looked offended. "I am."

"No you're not," she said.

He blinked, his body physically moving back from her a bit.

"You go from woman to woman. You don't settle on anyone. You've not had a relationship since your wife, and you two divorced what, five, six years ago?"

His face took on a serious expression, and she knew she'd pushed too far.

"That's why I bring up you with other women. That's why I don't want you to pinch my hip, or kiss me, or tell me you like me. Because one of these days, I'm going to cave. I'm dealing with a lot of shit right now, and quite honestly, the idea of sliding into bed with a guy like you who could make me remember why I used to love sex is tempting as hell. But I'm not a girl who can walk away from that, not with someone I think is a genuinely good and kind person. Not with someone like you."

He stared at her, his brow furrowed, eyes intent.

"Pretty people." Marigold's voice woke her out of the bubble she'd been in with Chase for the past few minutes. She turned to find Marigold with a woman who looked to be in her late twenties or early thirties dressed in all black, her hair cut into a sort of shaggy page boy. She smiled at Shayla with a natural charm that instantly calmed her. "I want you to meet Fiona. This is her fabulous bar."

"Hi," Fiona held out her hand to Shayla, and she shook it.

"I'm Shayla."

Chase held his hand out next. "Chase O'Neil."

Fiona lifted her eyebrow. "I am aware of who you are."

Chase gave a contrite nod and picked up his wine glass.

Marigold snaked her arm around his back. "Everybody wants him but he only has eyes for me."

Fiona smiled. "Well, I can certainly see why."

Marigold squeezed him, narrowing her gaze. "Now, if I could just get him to sleep with me."

Fiona met Shayla's gaze with a smile, a hint of

curiosity in it as she likely tried to figure out who belonged to who. Her guess was as good as Shayla's.

Chase squeezed Marigold and kissed her on top of the head. "You know you're too much woman for me. I could never keep up. Blake just walked in. I'm going to say hi. Nice to meet you, Fiona. This is a great place."

"I hope to see you here again sometime."

"I'm sure you will." He smiled as he exited, but Shayla could tell his heart wasn't in it.

Fiona watched him walk away. "That is what our mothers would call a tall drink of water."

"Oh yeah," Marigold said. "I've been working on him for three long years. He's got so many notches on his bedpost it looks like he's got termites, but he's refused me every time I've tried. And trust me when I say, I've tried plenty."

"I can't imagine why," Fiona said. "You're beautiful."

Marigold waved her off. "I know. I think he doesn't take me seriously, and he probably shouldn't. I'm a mess. If I got with him, I'm sure I'd find a way to fuck it up then I couldn't have him as a friend. And I'm not willing to run that risk. I think if it came down to it and he agreed, I'd back off. I'm all talk."

Shayla took heed of Marigold's wise words. She needed to be thinking along those same exact terms.

Marigold turned to Shayla. "You two aren't together are you?"

"No. I'm renting his pool house. I'm just getting settled back into town."

"Where is it?" Fiona asked.

"Seagrove. It's a beautiful place. I'm really lucky."

"Yeah," Marigold said, "I'm sure it's torture for him having you steps away, floating in his pool in your bikini."

Shayla huffed a laugh. "I haven't worn a bikini since high school. Not with these hips."

"Are you kidding?" Fiona said. "Look at me. I carry my weight in my stomach. I'd love to push it back to my rear."

"I'd love to have a rear," Marigold said.

Shayla smiled at the two of them. They both made her feel at home in this sleek wine bar that didn't suit her redneck heritage. She'd always felt like a fish out of water on 30A, but that was self-inflicted.

"So this is all yours?" Shayla asked.

"Mine and the bank's," Fiona said, looking around. "Some girls choose the family route. I'm choosing wine."

Marigold held up her glass. "Here, here."

A tall woman with a strapless top came up to Fiona and kissed her on the mouth. Shayla had zero gaydar. She found trying to figure people out prematurely never panned out like she thought, so she quit trying.

"Angelica," Fiona said. "This is Shayla."

Shayla nodded at her. "How are you?"

The tall woman lifted an eyebrow. "Much better now. You're a friend of Fiona's?"

Fiona squeezed the woman. "We just met five minutes ago."

The woman looked disappointed. "Oh, damn."

Shayla scratched her forehead, feeling like a fish in a barrel. Marigold must have sensed her unease, because she wrapped her arm around her. "We need to go say hello to friends who just walked in. We'll talk to you all in just a bit."

The women nodded and Marigold and Shayla made their exit.

"I have no gaydar," Shayla said.

"Fiona's fluid. She's harder to shake out. She just broke up with a man. A fucking hot as hell man, too. He was here earlier. They're staying friends. Can you imagine?"

Shayla could not.

Marigold paused by a cocktail table near a couple of forty-something guys. "I'm starting to wonder if it's the worst idea in the world. Fiona's hot. A natural beauty. I have to go through eight beauty regimes a day to look like this. I was thinking about seeing if Fiona would let me take her for a test drive."

Shayla laughed, looking around. "Marigold."

"I'm serious. She's hot. And I'm getting desperate. Do you know that the last guy I went out with said he forgot his wallet and at the end of the night asked me to give him a ride to the airport that following weekend? Who does that?"

Shayla smiled. She'd forgotten how much she liked Marigold.

Marigold leaned in. "How bad could it be? Did you see that show *Episodes* with Matt LeBlanc? Carol did it, and they lived happily ever after, or we were supposed to assume that, anyway."

"I'm not saying don't try it. I'm saying maybe don't with the woman who you have side-by-side businesses with."

Marigold rolled her eyes, glancing around. "I know. You're right. Maybe I'll just keep it a fantasy. Give me and my vibrator something to keep us motivated."

Shayla giggled, again. The giggling was getting out of hand. "That woman Angelica looked like she'd be game."

"You think? I think she might devour me."

They laughed, Marigold putting her forehead to Shayla's. Shayla hadn't felt this free in over a year.

She glanced over at Chase, who was watching them. He held up his wine glass, his smile not all the way there, and her guilt swallowed her. Why did she have to go after him like that earlier? She said too much. But she couldn't help herself. He did things to her that she couldn't control. She winked at him and looked away before she could see his response. She knew when she'd screwed up, and she'd have to apologize. Just not right now. Not when she felt alive.

Chapter Twelve

Chase watched Shayla and Marigold at the bar, two guys in their forties hitting on them. They were probably married, here with their families from Memphis or Birmingham, getting off on two hot, younger girls paying them attention...locals at that. Shayla had opened up her body, leaning against the bar with her elbows up on it, looking chiller than Easy Rider.

Marigold was egging it on as usual. She'd been keeping them all laughing, flirting with both guys shamelessly while Shayla just smiled and watched, the guys watching her. He could only imagine the fantasies these two dads were having about her, what they thought about doing to her body, what they imagined her doing to them while their wives sat back at their rented houses on the beach watching *Magic Mike* with the sound turned down while the kids slept. Every bit of the thought made him sick at his stomach.

"Right Chase?" Desiree said.

"Hmm? Yeah." They all busted out laughing. "What?" he asked looking between his friends.

"She said you liked to wear your tutu when you sing songs from *Annie* on the roof of your house," Ashe said, and they all broke out in laughter.

"Honey," Sebastian said, putting his hand on Chase's back. "I've known you a while now, and I've never seen that look in your eye."

Heat rose up to his ears. "I don't have a look."

Ashe raised his wine glass. "Oh, yeah you do."

"I'm fine. I'm just looking around."

"So what's the scoop with Shayla?" Sebastian asked. "It will not leave this table." Sebastian gave the other two a stern look, and they both pretended to lock their mouths.

"There's no scoop," he said, looking over at her. "In fact, she shut my ass down in no uncertain terms just a little while ago, before the fab forty club honed in over there."

"Oh, man. That's tough," Ashe said.

"How exactly did she shut you down?" Desiree asked, leaning in with her chin resting on her threaded fingers.

Chase scratched his neck. "I don't know."

Desiree lifted an eyebrow.

"All right. Well, she said I was a womanizer, basically."

"Any truth to that?" Ashe asked. "I'm just asking."

Chase let out a huff of air, "It's true I haven't had a relationship in a while."

"How long's a while?" Desiree asked.

Chase met her gaze. "A while."

"Why do you think that is?" she asked without judgement, but still.

He looked around the place. "What is this, a therapy session?"

Sebastian put his hand on the table. "Yes, and it's free. Take advantage."

Chase rolled his eyes. "I've got some issues, I guess."

"Were you hurt before?" Desiree asked.

Chase thought about the night his brother showed up on his doorstep. The desperation that consumed him when he gave them the news. The look of pure horror on Rachel's face.

"Yeah."

"Did she cheat on you?" Ashe asked.

Chase thought about Rachel's Facebook page, her perfect, four-person family, the child she had so soon after they'd lost theirs. The betrayal.

"Yeah."

Desiree walked around the table and took Chase into her arms. This was not the time or the place to let any emotion out. He could do that in his room later on. He hugged her back and then patted her on the shoulder and pulled away. "Thanks, but I'm fine."

Desiree put her fingertips to his chin. "Sweetie, you are anything but fine."

He glanced over at Shayla who was listening to one of the bozos tell a story. He had to get out of there. "I need to leave. Can any of you drop Shayla home when she's ready?"

Sebastian squeezed his arm. "We got it, hun. You go on."

He nodded at Sebastian. "Thank you." He turned to Desiree and Ashe with a half-ass smile, and then headed out the door. He drove down 30A, headed back toward his house, but at the last minute, he turned the car up a side street that led to Highway 98, and eventually to Alligator Alley in PCB. It was the stuffy wine bar that had gotten to him, that was all. He needed to be with a different class of people, ones who didn't judge him or expect a goddamned thing from him. He swung the door open and headed to the bar.

"Hey, Chase," Bobby said. "I haven't seen you in here in months."

"Yep, that's my fault. Give me a Bud on draft. I've been drinking Pinot Noir tonight. I need to grow my balls back."

Bobby smiled. That's right. Chase could do that. He could make people smile. He was good at that.

Chase made eye contact with two girls sitting at the bar across from him, late twenties he guessed. He smiled, and they smiled back. It was so damn easy for him.

Bobby handed him the beer, and he held it up to the girls, and they held up their cocktails. Sunburnt skin, too much makeup, low-cut tops. These two had tourist plastered onto their foreheads. Candy from a baby.

He walked over there and held out his hand. "I'm Chase."

They each shook his hand, the second one holding it and his gaze for a while.

"I was actually just headed to the ladies," the other one said, and the two exchanged a smile.

The girl looked him up and down. "Wow, you're really big." Her eyes slid to his dick and he knew exactly what she was thinking.

Just what he needed. Cliché opening lines and fuck-me gazes. "Yes ma'am, I am."

Shayla waved to Sebastian backing out of the driveway, and then opened the back gate to find Chase sitting slumped down in a chair by the pool, his long legs sprawled out as he studied a beer bottle in his hand.

"There he is," she said, looking him up and down. "Where'd you go?"

"Alligator Alley."

"That's a ways from home just for a drink when there were plenty at the wine bar."

"I wanted a Bud."

She shrugged, walking around the pool on the opposite side from him. "That's your prerogative." She fumbled with her keys, locating the one that opened the door to the pool house. "You're back pretty early to have driven all the way there."

"I just had one beer," he said. "I didn't want you coming home to an empty house with no security guard."

She stared at him, and he finally looked up at her. "I didn't ask you to do that."

"What if I wanted to do that?" he asked.

She gave a huff, eyeing her keys and then him. "Do I need to rewind episode two, or can you catch up if we start in on episode three?"

He gave that grin that made her nuts and then stood. "I thought you fell asleep, too."

Busted. "I may have made it to the end of two. We should probably rewind a little just in case."

He walked over to her, slow and deliberate. She looked down at her keys and then back up at him when he got close. "I'm sorry about what I said earlier," she said.

He shrugged. "You were being honest. You should never be sorry about that."

"I like you, Chase. But I've got some shit going on right now. I can't offer you anything but friendship. Can you accept that?"

"I can."

She unlocked the door but turned back to him before opening it. "Did you meet anyone at Alligator Alley?"

He furrowed his brow, and then gave a resigned breath. "Nobody that mattered, at least to me."

She stared at him, a life with him flashing before her eyes. Everything was wonderful at first. She felt adored and treasured. Then he'd leave for a trip to Vegas or somewhere equally tempting, and she'd be worried about him sleeping with someone else, just how Brian used to worry about that with her for no reason whatsoever.

She shook her head, rattling loose her own psychosis. She nodded at his beer. "Go get us a few more of those, and I'll get changed."

He held up his beer bottle. "Will do."

She dressed for bed, leaving her bra on, though she really wanted it off. That would definitely send signals, and she wasn't trying to do that, though she desperately wanted to.

A knock sounded at the door, and she snuck a peek at herself in the bathroom mirror before heading to it...exactly what Chase had said he didn't like to see a woman do, but now she was paranoid she had a booger hanging out of her nose.

She opened the door to find him in athletic shorts and a red T-shirt which suited him so well. He pulled a bottle out of the six pack he was holding and handed it to her. "Pilsner, I assume."

"You assume right. Are you gonna drink it, too?"

He twirled the box around. "I've got IPA in here for me." She gave a shudder and he headed to the fridge. "There's no accounting for taste."

She plopped down on the bed and aimed the remote at the television. "I can't believe you drove all the way to Alligator Alley for a beer."

He eased his way over to the bed and sat, holding out his hand for her beer. She gave it to him and he popped the top with a bottle opener. "What are you getting at, Harrison?"

She looked at the television. "Nothing."

"What about you with the mid-life crisis club."

She tried to hold back her grin. "Seriously?"

"All right, the soccer dads then. How'd you make out with them?"

"I'd say by the current hour that we both struck out tonight." She glanced down at her phone and winced at Scott's name across her screen. Missed call.

She held her phone face down on her leg. "I've got to make a quick call. I'll be right back." She stepped out to the pool and called Scott.

"Hey, I hope I didn't bother you," he said.

"I'm the one who called you, aren't I?"

"You saw where I called though," he said.

She paced slowly beside the deep end of the pool. "This is true. So, I got the ball started on the eviction notice today."

"He got served?" Scott asked.

"No, not yet. But he will be served the Monday after the wedding."

"That's over two weeks away."

"I know. I just need things to go as smoothly as possible between now and then. This is Bo's time. I don't want Brian freaking out and doing anything to worry him. Right now Bo's biggest worry is that I'm going to get back with him."

Scott huffed a laugh. "He's misinformed."

"Let's keep it that way. If he gets a clue of what really went on, it'll ruin this time for him," she said, watching a little frog hop away into the grass.

"Understood."

"How's work? Is Brian back yet?" she asked.

"Yeah."

She breathed a sigh of relief, glad he was getting back into a routine, as much as she hated it for Scott. "Has he confronted you?"

"Nah. Just a couple of hard stares in the hallway. Nothing I can't handle."

She let out a breath. "Scott, I'm so—"

"Don't, Shayla. It's fine. Have you thought any more about the wedding, about me coming?"

She rested against the short brick wall that framed the outdoor kitchen, scratching her neck. She didn't know how to say no to this request.

She'd tried the approach that she didn't want him to bother himself with it, and the just-friends rigmarole, and he was still asking. She was running out of reasons he couldn't come. And the truth was, she didn't have a date for the wedding. She damn sure wasn't going to go with Chase and stress Bo out. In fact, if she took Scott that would probably ease Bo's stress, her being with someone other than Chase.

"I really do hate to ask you to come all the way down here for this."

"You're not asking. I am."

She glanced over at the pool house, not that she could see in. "It'd be good to see you."

"Great," he said, and she hoped like hell she was doing the right thing.

She hung up with Scott and headed back to the pool house where Chase was lying on her bed, propped up by his pillow, a hand behind his head, beer bottle resting on his lap. His eyes were on the television screen which was playing the last bit of episode two.

"Sorry," she said, stepping in front of the television and then getting in bed next to him.

"Soccer dad?" he asked, still staring at the television.

She supposed she did owe him an explanation, especially after she'd kissed him last night.

"That was my friend Scott from Nashville."

"The one who's coming to the wedding?"

"Yeah, actually, he is."

Chase nodded, gaze trained on the television.

"He's just a friend," she said.

He looked over at her. "Like me?"

That was a loaded question if she'd ever heard one. "Well, I've never kissed him, so not exactly like you."

"Ah, poor bastard."

She gave him a look. "It's not like that," she said, but not sure if it was true or not. "You have no idea how he feels about me."

"I bet I do."

"I'm not that popular, Chase."

He bit on his lip, shaking his head like he was trying not to say something.

"If you have something to say, just freaking say it, okay?" she said, with a little more force than she intended.

He sat up. "Okay, you seem like a pretty perceptive person. Do you really think he's not into you?"

She let a huff of air out of her nose.

He offered a hand. "My point exactly."

"I don't know how he feels. But I do know that I've made it crystal clear that I'm not interested in him for anything other than friendship."

"So he just wants to travel four hundred miles down here for your brother's wedding, why, because he loves weddings?"

"You don't know what you're talking about here, Chase."

"You're damn sure right about that. You don't tell me jack shit even though I'm pretty sure I've made it crystal clear that I care about you and want to help."

She rubbed her forehead, the pressure bearing

down on her. "There's not anything you can help with, not now."

"But there was a few months ago? Before I knew you?"

She scratched her scalp, her throat threatening to close. She nodded, just slightly.

He took the beer from her hand and set it on the nightstand on his side of the bed. Turning back to her, he said in a soft voice, "What happened, Shayla, with your ex?"

"I told you," she said, her voice weak. She cleared her throat and spoke with mustered strength. "He went into rehab."

"What was the catalyst for that?" he asked.

She cut her eyes at him and looked down at her hands which were grabbing the comforter without her even realizing she was doing it. She opened her mouth, but the words wouldn't come. The idea of what had happened was too overwhelmingly humiliating.

"Did he hit you, Shayla?"

She shook her head slightly, an automatic response.

"Did he hit you?" This time Chase's words were distinct and sure.

"No," she said, her voice sounding like a little girl's.

He took her hand in his and she used the back of her other hand to wipe her eye.

"Did he hit you, Shayla," he said again, but he wasn't asking this time. He was telling.

She shook her head, but met his gaze wanting him to understand everything without her having to

SEAGROVE SECRETS

explain it. Wanting him to see that she hated being labeled a victim and that she was not the type of person to be a victim. She wanted him to see that she was strong and independent, not weak and fragile and in need of help from virtual strangers. She wanted him to know she hated running back to PCB, and she hated the fact that she'd done so to be near her brothers and Blake and even certain redneck guys who she'd gone to high school with who she'd never call on for help but would be there in seconds if she ever needed it. She wanted him to know that this was not who she was, and this was not how she saw her life playing out at thirty-six years old...casualty of an abusive relationship, one that would cause her to distrust men and strip her of her own self-worth, her bravery, and her pride.

He took her hand in his, rubbing his thumb over the top of her hand. "This guy who you just talked to, did he help you?" She met Chase's gaze with a nod. Chase nodded back as if in approval or understanding. "Good."

He ran his hand over her hair and then back to her face, pulling the stray hairs away. She closed her eyes, letting his touch permeate her skin. He cupped her face with both hands, and she kept her eyes closed, head down. She couldn't look at him right now, because if she did, she'd let him kiss her, and she couldn't do that.

He kissed the top of her forehead, and she whispered, "Don't tell Bo."

"I won't," he said.

She reached over for the remote, the DVD having gone back to the main menu. She started the next episode and allowed herself to snuggle into his chest to watch it. She wouldn't make a habit of it, but tonight she needed to feel the rise and fall of his chest against hers.

Chapter Thirteen

Season finale tonight. Are you ready to say bye to Bill and the ladies?

Shayla smiled down at Chase's text, having to admit that she wasn't. Today did feel like an ending of sorts. Tomorrow, everything changed.

For the past two weeks, Shayla and Chase had been playing house. One of them would bring home or make dinner, and they would eat it in Shayla's bed in the little pool house while they watched *Big Love*. He'd even snuck a toothbrush over there. He slid it in the toothbrush holder like it belonged there. Neither of them mentioned it, but every time she saw it there she smiled.

Every night, Scott called at nine. Chase would pause the show and say he needed to grab something from the house to give her privacy. Some nights he came back sooner than others, but he never asked her what Scott wanted.

Felicity had called as well, and Shayla had offered the same courtesy, though it killed her. There was no doubt about it. Shayla was falling headfirst for Chase, and she was flat-out jealous of this other girl who knew him more intimately than she did. But what could she say? Not a damn thing.

She brought grilled chicken salads home for dinner. She and Chase had not been discreet with their eating these past two weeks. It was all about comfort food, and she feared she wasn't going to be able to get in the bridesmaid dress she'd been fitted into a week and a half ago.

She texted him when she got home, and he texted back that he was on his way. It was really stupid that they were basically living in this tiny pool house when they had Chase's big, beautiful house steps away. But Shayla was considering everything for the past two weeks a fantasy. She'd get back to real life after the wedding. That's when the eviction notice would be served, and that's when the clock would start on getting Brian out of her house and out of her life.

She left the door ajar for Chase, but he still knocked on it as he came in. He eyed the salads. "Is this a hint?"

"I'm afraid I won't be able to wear that dress hanging in the closet Saturday."

He frowned. "Yeah, I'm sure those tux pants I was fitted for last week will be snug. I guess I should have thought about that before I brought home Chinese food last night."

She raised her eyebrows. "That chicken lo mein was good."

"Damn right it was." He plopped down on the bed beside her and opened his salad.

"You like balsamic, right?" she asked, hoping she remembered that right from last week when they'd had salads with the pasta he brought home.

"Yep. Thanks for getting these."

"Mmm hmm," she mumbled, forking a bite. "I can't believe this is our last episode."

"I think I'm in denial," he said.

She held back a grin as she chewed her salad.

"What are you smiling about?" he asked.

She covered her mouth. "Nothing. I was just wondering something."

"What?"

She nodded at the television. "Those are three very different ladies Bill's married to."

"Mmm hmm," he said, eyebrow up.

"Which one would you pick?"

"I just get one?" She gave him a look, and he grinned. God she loved it when he grinned. "All right, let me think."

He looked like he was really mulling it over hard. She hummed the theme from *Jeopardy*.

"Okay, okay. Nicki."

"Are you serious?" she asked, really thinking he was going to choose Jennifer Goodwin's character.

"I like how she's a little shady. Keeps it interesting."

Shayla cut her eyes at him like she thought he was crazy, but Nicki had been her favorite from the start.

"What about you?" he asked.

"I only have one to pick from."

"I'll let you pick between Bill, the Bruce Dern character, and Roman."

She dropped her hand like she was exhausted since two of the three were old enough to be her grandfather.

"Don't look at me like that," he said, trying not to laugh.

"I pick Roman," she said, deadpan.

He looked back at her in challenge, and she thought for a second he might kiss her, but he knew better, surely.

He shrugged. "He's pretty damn hot."

She grinned. "All right, let's start it."

Chase's phone rang. "Hang on." He pulled it out of his pocket, and she steadied his to-go container.

"It's Felicity. I'm sure this about airport pickup. She keeps forgetting to send me the flight info. Hey," he said, answering without Shayla leaving. Neither Scott nor Felicity had ever called while they were eating. She would feel weird getting up now.

"I thought you said yours was a morning flight? No, it's fine, I'll figure it out."

"I'll pick her up," Shayla said, her heartbeat getting a little faster.

He looked over at her like he was confused.

"I take it you're unavailable," she said.

He covered the receiver. "I thought she had a morning flight. I've got to go with Blake and Bo to pick up our tuxes at three. Her flight's in at three-thirty." He went back to the phone. "No, it's Shayla. Hang on." He looked at her. "Are you sure?"

"Of course," she said, like it was no big deal. "I'll be in PCB anyway for work."

"Are you picking up Scott?" he asked. It was weird hearing him say Scott's name. She wasn't sure she'd even said it to him. But he'd probably seen it on her phone.

"He's coming in at noon, but he's renting a car."

He went back to the phone. "What?" He appeared for a second like he'd seen a ghost. "No, it's…" He looked over at Shayla and then handed her the phone. "She wants to talk to you."

Shayla blinked. She was planning on talking to Felicity tomorrow, of course, but she'd have time to prepare. She wasn't ready right that second, mouth full of salad.

She chewed and swallowed hard. "Hey."

"I can totally cab it back to Chase's," Felicity said like they were old friends.

"No, that would cost you a fortune," Shayla said. "I'll pick you up. I'll be in PC…Panama City anyway."

"Are you absolutely sure? Because if you've got shit going on and don't have time for this, I totally get it."

"It's perfect timing, actually. I'll need to be heading home about that time anyway to get ready for the rehearsal."

"Okay then. I'm totally amped for this weekend, by the way."

Shayla wasn't prepared for Felicity to be so familiar…and nice. "Me, too," she said.

"Hey, so is Chase right there still?" Felicity asked.

"Um, yeah."

"Can you make him go away a sec?"

Shayla looked at Chase, who was staring at her with great interest. She moved her salad and stood up off the bed, heading outside.

She closed the door behind her. "Okay."

"So, I've been double-checking with Chase and Maya, and they both assure me that you are just renting from Chase and you're not with one another, but now that I've got you on the phone, I'd love to get that same assurance directly from you before I haul my ass to his house and make a complete idiot of myself. Trust me, it would not be the first time."

Shayla sat quiet, not sure how to answer.

"Oh, shit. You're with him, aren't you?"

"No," she said quickly. "No." She swallowed hard. "We are not together. Absolutely not. We're just friends."

"Seriously?" Felicity asked.

"Oh, completely. So seriously," she said. Apparently that's what Chase had been assuring Felicity of. No need for Shayla to disagree at this point. Her chest started to heat up.

"Okay," Felicity said, sounding unsure.

Shayla realized she sounded jaded. "I've actually got a date coming in from Nashville. A guy I used to work with."

"Is that the guy Scott that Chase was just talking about? The other airport pickup?"

"Yes, but he's renting a car. He gets in at noon."

"Perfect. He's staying with you?" Felicity asked.

"No, he's at a hotel in PCB."

"Well, that's weird. I mean, not weird. Just, Chase has a couple of guest rooms, right? If you're not ready to sleep with this guy can't he crash in one of those or on the couch?"

"I..." Shayla searched for words. "He's fine at the hotel."

"That's bullshit. Did Chase not offer for him to stay there?"

Shayla tried to remember if he had, but she was pretty positive he had not.

"Put Chase back on," Felicity said.

Shayla walked back inside and met Chase's searching gaze. She handed him the phone, pretty sure what was getting ready to happen but completely unsure how to handle it.

Chase took the phone and put it to his ear. He looked up at Shayla as Felicity talked and Shayla shook her head, waving her hands in front of her chest. "I didn't do this," she mouthed.

"No, it's fine, of course," Chase said, and Shayla wasn't sure if he was talking to her, Felicity, or both of them. "No, there's not. That's not what...it's fine."

Shayla knew she should leave him alone to hash this out with Felicity, but she felt weird to step out and just stand outside.

"Yeah. Okay. Yeah. Me, too. Bye," he said.

Me, too. What was that in response to? Shayla had to figure out how to get through this weekend without trying to analyze everything.

Chase ran his hand through his hair and met Shayla's gaze. He looked off to the side, shaking his head. "I'm sorry I didn't ask if Scott wanted to stay here earlier. I should have."

"He's fine at the hotel."

"No, that's ridiculous. I don't know where my head's been. Please ask him to stay here."

"He's already got the room. It's probably too late to cancel, anyway."

"I'll pay it then. Will you call him?"

Shayla looked off, trying to decide what she wanted this weekend. She didn't even know. Would having Scott here when Felicity was here make things better or worse? Would Scott expect her to stay at the hotel with him? He wouldn't expect something like that, but he might ask.

"Are you sure?" she asked, sounding completely unsure herself.

"Please call him," he said, proffering her phone.

She took it and called Scott. He picked up on the second ring. "Hey, where are you staying this weekend?" she asked.

"Some hotel in Panama City I got a deal on. Hang on." He came back to the phone and told her the name. She winced. Why didn't she think to ask him this before and make sure he was staying somewhere decent?

"That place is a dump, Scott. Will you stay here?"

"Really?"

"In Chase's house. He's got room." She lifted her eyebrows at Chase and he nodded confirmation.

"Is that okay with him?"

"Yeah, he's cool with it." Chase held out his hand and Shayla inwardly winced. "He wants to talk to you."

"Oh, well..."

Shayla handed Chase the phone.

190

"Hi, this is Chase O'Neil. How are you? Good. Stay here with us. Absolutely. My apologies for not asking sooner. It's been a crazy couple of weeks with the wedding planning and all." He shook his head, his face coloring. "Great. I look forward to meeting you. Here's Shayla."

She hung up with Scott, and then met Chase's gaze. "What just happened?"

Chase set his salad on the nightstand. "I don't know." He sat with his back against the bedframe, running both hands through his hair.

They needed to talk about what was happening between them...the fact that they both had people coming in town who either wanted to date them or had dated them. Felicity had slept with Chase for chrissakes, and here she was getting ready to stay in his house...in his bed?

A surge of heat flew through her body at the idea, as she tried to inwardly calm herself. She walked over to the bed, sat down on it, pulled the covers over her legs, and then picked up the remote. "Should we start the finale?"

Chase looked over at her for a long moment before turning back to the television. "Yep."

With the rolling of the closing credits came the fruition of the dread Chase had been feeling the past hour. There was no more binging to be done. He'd stupidly not called the cable company out, so it wasn't like they had anything else to watch. He couldn't fake sleep. He could turn to her and try to talk about what the hell it was they were doing and how they were going to handle the arrival of

Felicity and Scott tomorrow, but she clearly didn't want to do that.

It was so fucked up that they couldn't just be together. He knew she was going through shit with Brian, recovering from him hitting her. Hitting—that's all he knew, all she'd confirmed, and she had only done that after he'd forced the issue. He had no idea of how bad the abuse was. What had he done to her? Chase had lain in this bed with Shayla every night since she'd revealed that bit of information to him, wondering what she'd gone through with that asshole. Where had he hit her? In the face? Had he pushed her against a wall? Punched her? His gut wrenched at the idea, and his face started burning again. He wondered when he'd be able to let it go in his brain, and if he was having this much trouble after just two weeks, what had she been going through these past months? Years?

The unanswered questions left him perpetually helpless. But would knowing the answers, the details, empower him somehow?

Chase had told Shayla that he was going to get Felicity a rental for the weekend, and she'd told him in no uncertain terms not to. She'd become almost obsessed with making sure Bo wasn't worried about anything these past couple of weeks leading up to his wedding. She'd said that if Felicity didn't stay there, he'd think something was up between her and Chase and that would stress him out.

Chase knew Bo would get over it if the two of them became an item. Chase would just have to show him he could do the relationship thing. That was the easy part. But Chase highly suspected that

Shayla was using Bo as an excuse for not jumping into something with him. She wasn't ready, and he could definitely understand that, given what she'd been through. If he could just get a hold of that son of a bitch—

Shayla's movement woke him up from his thoughts and he looked over at her. She stared at him, her expression impassive. He wasn't sure if she was wanting to know what he thought of the finale, if she wanted to know why he was still lying in her bed when the show was clearly over, or if she was ready to finally talk about what the fuck they were doing. They'd been spending every night together, occasionally waking up spooning, eating dinner like a married couple. Flirting, smiling…he had no idea what this was called, not that he was any kind of relationship expert.

She pulled the covers off of both of them and slid over, climbing on top of him, her legs straddling either side of him. He blinked, catching his breath that he'd temporarily lost, his heartbeat skyrocketing to the moon at the idea of this woman he was damn near batty over on top of him.

He opened his mouth to say something, what, he had no fucking idea, but she covered it with her own, her sweet lips on his making his insides turn wobbly. He reached up the soft skin of her back, and she sat up off of him, grabbing his arms and shoving them to the pillow on either side of him.

He wanted to touch her like crazy, but she had his wrists pressed against the pillow, clearly wanting control. She moved down his body, lifting his shirt up and trailing kisses on his chest and his stomach, her hands moving up his sides and over his chest, fuck.

She slid her fingers underneath the waistband of his shorts and boxers and pulled them down, his cock springing up like a jack-in-the-box. Standing at the edge of the bed, she peeled her leggings off of her, but her T-shirt was too damn long, and he couldn't see anything but the tops of her thighs which he wanted to eat like a fucking ice cream cone, but she was on a mission, and he knew better than to try to take control right then.

She climbed back on top of his body, bare except for his shirt, which he wanted off along with hers, but she was running this show. She reached over and opened the drawer to her nightstand and pulled out a box of condoms. She ripped one open and slid it onto him, then before he knew it, she eased herself onto him, her brow furrowing. Instinctively, he reached for her hips, but she took his hands in hers and pressed them back down onto the pillow.

"Shayla," he said out of desperation to touch her.

But she covered his mouth with her kiss as she moved up and down on him. She lifted up again, sitting on him, holding his hands in midair and pressing against them with hers. Her eyes closed, she found a rhythm and moved on him, her tight warmth unleashing those familiar sensations inside of him, but this time, it was Shayla. He'd never wanted a woman as much as he'd wanted her this past month she'd been in his life, and it wasn't just about her looks. It was everything she was, everything he wanted to be when he was with her.

He wanted her close to him. Wanted their

fucking shirts off. He wanted to feel her near him, her nipples brushing his chest as they worked together to bring each other to the brink. But she didn't want that, clearly.

It didn't escape him that this was how he screwed women he didn't care about, with distance between them. He wanted to pull her down to him or turn her over on her back and do this right...the way he'd dreamed of making love to her the first time, but she didn't want that, and she felt so good on him, her body moving in a way he couldn't resist if he tried.

By the expression on her face, she looked like she might be getting ready to lose herself, so he waited her out, though it was hard, especially after not having had sex in months. She slammed his hands down to the pillow and let out a breathy noise that almost made him come all by itself. He took it as a cue to let go himself, and she collapsed around him, letting go of his hands. Her body relaxed on his, her arms damp and warm. What he wouldn't give to feel her chest against his in this state.

She slid off of him and lay on her back for a moment, her eyes closed as she caught her breath. He wanted to say something to her, but he had no idea what. Something sweet and touching was out of the question. He'd just been fucked by her. There hadn't been anything sweet about it.

She sat up, swinging her legs to the side of the bed, not moving to stand. Finally, she walked to the bathroom, tossed him a hand towel, and then closed the door behind her.

He took care of the condom and then waited for

her to come out. But in a minute, the shower came on. He sat on the end of the bed, wondering what to do. Should he leave? He didn't want to. He wanted to sit her down on that bed and find out what the fuck was going on, but he wasn't going to be a forceful prick like the one she'd just gotten away from.

He walked over to the bathroom door and knocked. "Shayla? Are you okay?"

She opened the door, her face flushed. "I'm fine. I'll see you tomorrow, okay?" She barely looked at him, and then closed the door in his face.

He stood there dumbfounded, fucked, and wondering what the hell this weekend was going to be like.

Chapter Fourteen

Shayla sat in her office, diligently working on her computer like nothing else mattered. Reporting was due today. Of course, reporting was due every Friday, and Bo would certainly not be looking at any reporting today, but she wanted it done. Needed it done.

"No, man, don't worry about it," Bo said from his office across the hall. He chuckled. "I hear you. Listen, if I had an opportunity like that I'd blow off your wedding in a heartbeat. Don't think I wouldn't."

He was so damn happy and carefree, just like he needed to be today.

"Shayla." Maya's soft voice at her door got her attention.

"Hey, Maya." She stood and went to hug her. She wouldn't have done that normally, but it felt like she should for some reason and, besides that, she was full of frenetic energy today. After what she'd done last night, her nerves were on edge, and she was starting to feel herself unraveling. "How's it all going?" she asked.

Maya couldn't contain her smile. "So good. I can't believe it's here. Tomorrow. I'm going to be married." She covered her mouth, her eyes going watery.

"Don't start now. There's going to be lots of this tomorrow, I imagine."

Maya nodded, still covering her mouth. She pulled her hand away. "So everything's okay with you?" The look on Maya's face begged Shayla to confirm.

"Absolutely. It's great."

"Oh, good. So, Felicity said you were picking her up from the airport. Are you sure you don't mind doing that?"

"Of course not," Shayla said, swallowing down her lie. "I've got to be here anyway."

"No you don't," Bo said, appearing beside Maya, arm wrapping around her. "I told you to go home."

"I've got an airport pickup," Shayla said, slowly and deliberately.

"All right. I'll stay out of your business. But I'm not keeping you here."

"Have I ever said you were?" she asked.

Bo took Maya's hand. "All right. We're headed out to lunch, but I'll be back."

"I'll have Friday reports ready when you are."

"Oh, don't worry about those this week."

She gave him a look. "They're almost done."

He shook his head. "Sorry. Just, crazy week. I

should have said something earlier."

"Go to lunch," she said, and then sat down.

Not long after Bo was out the door, Tracey appeared at her office door. "Shayla, I have a visitor here for you."

Shayla stood, her heartbeat picking up as Scott rounded the corner. The smile that spread across his lips at the sight of her made her stomach curl into knots. All this time, she'd been hoping that when she finally saw him, there'd be a connection she'd missed before that had been clouded by all the mess with Brian. But he was still just Scott, her friend who helped her get out of the worst situation of her life.

She smiled back and hugged him to her chest. She didn't want to let go, just wanted to stay right there all weekend where she didn't have to face Chase and meet Felicity and act as if everything in her world was just rosy.

He pulled away from her. "What's wrong?"

God, was she that transparent? "Nothing."

"Shayla," he said.

She shook her head. "It's fine. Everything's fine. Just stressed out trying to get everything done before the wedding. I'm hosting the bachelorette party tonight."

"Oh yeah. How's that going?"

"It's fine. Just details, you know?"

"Okay," he said.

Bo reappeared at his office, grabbing something off his desk. He stopped and eyed Scott. "Hey," he said, brow furrowed.

"Bo, this is my friend Scott from Nashville. He

came down for the wedding."

"Oh, yeah." This information seemed to make Bo happy. He held out his hand. "Thanks so much for coming. We're happy to have you."

Scott smiled, looking relieved at Bo's approval. "Thanks, I'm happy to be here."

"Cool," Bo said, looking between Shayla and Scott like he was fitting together a puzzle. "You coming to the rehearsal dinner?"

Scott looked at Shayla.

"Yeah, I R.S.V.P.'d for us both."

Bo waved her off. "Of course. Not my department. Are you going with them afterward?" He pointed at Shayla. Scott looked back at her again.

"For the bachelorette," Shayla said. "It's mostly girls, but Sebastian and Ashe will be there if you want to come with us."

"Come with us," Bo said. "We're going on a craft beer hop, whatever the fuck that is. Anyway, it's guys, so you won't have to deal with all that bachelorette crap if you come with us."

"I'm not doing any of that, Bo," Shayla said, emphasizing his name.

"Come with us," Bo said, and it was decided.

"Okay, thanks," Scott said.

Bo clapped him on the shoulder. "All right. I'll see you tonight." And he was off.

Scott turned back to Shayla. "He was really cool."

"Yeah, if you're not family," Shayla said with a smile.

Scott inspected his hand. "So, that was sort of

strange last night."

"Yeah, I'm so sorry about that," Shayla said.

Scott turned his head to the side. "Sorry that he asked me to stay at his house or…"

"No, it was just all weird. He's got someone coming to stay with him, and when she found out you were coming, she wanted to know why you weren't staying with us, too, and—"

"Us?"

Shayla's defenses went up. "Chase," she said. "At Chase's house."

Scott narrowed his gaze at her. "If the two of you are an *us*, you just need to tell me, Shayla. You've made clear where we stand, so it's not about that. But I need to know what he knows and what I'm walking into this weekend."

She exhaled. "That's fair enough. He knows very little, not nearly as much as you know, but he knows Brian…" She nodded slowly, having a really hard time saying it.

"Mmm hmm," Scott said, letting her off the hook.

"He just knows there was some violence, no specifics, and he knows you helped me. He's grateful for that, I think."

"You think."

"I don't talk about it with him. I've never talked to anyone but you about this."

He smiled and put his hand on her back. "Thank you for trusting me."

She didn't like that look Scott was giving her. She knew that look.

"So, I didn't actually cancel the hotel," he said.

"I felt a little weird."

She smiled. "There's nothing to be weird about. Email them to cancel, or better yet, let's go by there now, and you can see in person why you need to cancel. Trust me, you'll be better off at Chase's. Sight unseen, his pool is nicer, I can promise that."

"Okay, boss. How long do you need to be here?"

"I actually need to stay in PCB for a while. I need to pick up Chase's other houseguest from the airport at three-thirty. But I've got a little while before I need to do that. Do you want to get lunch?"

"Yeah, that's perfect."

She nodded and grabbed her purse.

Shayla left Scott at a Starbucks to work until she got Felicity from the airport. He hadn't wanted to go to Chase's without her, and she didn't blame him. Chase was probably not even home, which would have been even weirder for all involved. So she was thankful he was okay to wait for her.

She collapsed in her office chair completely exhausted from her lack of sleep. She'd gotten zero hours. She pulled up her email, but she couldn't even focus thinking about the mess she made last night. She had no clue what she was thinking. She'd been glazed over the whole time she was watching the finale to *Big Love*, wondering what Chase was thinking, knowing they needed to talk, but desperately not wanting to, not before the wedding. It was like the wedding was the nucleus, and she was circling around it with her arms flailing. After the wedding, all her problems would still be there, she knew that, but it was like she couldn't breathe until it was done and Bo was happily married without a hitch.

She'd have to apologize to Chase, again. She might as well have lifted her leg and peed on him the way she was staking her claim. *Mine. Not Felicity's.* She huffed a laugh. Like the sex they had last night was anything close to as good as what he'd likely had with Felicity. Shayla had not even let him touch her, too afraid she would completely lose herself in him. Last night had been about her claiming him for herself, feeling him inside of her on her terms. She was no better than Brian.

She lay her arms down on her desk, and then rested her forehead on top of them. She was so tired…tired of reassembling her life, tired of doing the wrong thing, tired of…

Chase walked into the pool shop, his heart pounding against his chest. Why was he so afraid of seeing her? She was his friend, the same girl he'd had dinner in bed with every night for the past two weeks and slept beside, more than once waking up with an arm around her waist, which she'd never seemed to have a problem with.

A woman stood behind the counter in a Harrison Pool Supply shirt. "Can I help you find something?" she asked.

"I'm here to see Bo."

She smiled and pointed. "Chase O'Neil, right?"

"Yep," he said, trying to give her a genuine smile back, but he could feel it wasn't working.

"He's on the phone, but he'll be up in just a sec. You're Shayla's landlord, right?"

Landlord. That was all he was. "Yep."

"She's back in her office if you want to say hi to her." She pointed down the hall. "I think she is, at least. I haven't heard a peep from her in like an hour."

"I'll go say hi," he said, and headed that way. Her door was pulled to, but not closed. He peeped inside, and she had her head down on the desk, her face turned toward the door, her eyes closed, her back rising and lowering in a slow, steady, sleep-filled rhythm. He opened the door farther and stood in the doorway.

She blinked awake, looking up at him. She frowned, wiping her mouth with her arm, and he had to smile.

She sat up, glancing around her office like she was placing herself into her situation. Her mouth formed an O like she was trying to ask a question.

"Hey," he said. "Sorry to wake you up."

She looked down at her desk. "I can't believe I fell asleep." She met his gaze. "What are you doing here?"

"I'm meeting Bo. It's almost three."

She pushed her chair back. "I've got to get to the airport."

"You've got a minute. It's ten till."

"I need to go," she said, standing.

He walked into the office and closed the door behind him. "We need to talk."

She shook her head. "No, not now. Open the door. Bo's across the hall."

"And I'm right here, Shayla. And I've got goddamned feelings, in case you didn't realize that."

Her eyes went wide as she recoiled from him. Moving her hair out of her face, she smoothed it down her neck like she was putting it in order. She nodded. "I know. I'm sorry."

"I'm not upset with you. I'm just confused. What was that last night?"

She leaned against her desk. "I don't know."

"You don't? Well, I'll tell you what I know. I've been sleeping in your bed every night for two weeks, waking up with you in my arms half the time, waiting for you to turn around and see me, kiss me, tell me to fuck off, anything. And then last night, I'm getting ready to get up, and you—"

"I know what I did. I'm sorry. I just had a moment of lapsed judgment."

He huffed a laugh, shaking his head. "Lapsed judgment. That's what I am to you? Everything we've shared this month and I'm lapsed judgment? That's fucking fantastic."

She peered behind him, eyes wide.

"Just forget it, Shayla. I don't even know what to say to you."

He opened the door and saw Bo standing in his office with his back to the door, phone to his ear, so Chase closed the door again and turned back to her.

"Actually, I do know what to say. I've wanted to make love to you since the first day I met you, but I've abided by your wishes and left you the fuck alone, letting you make the call. And then when you finally decide it's time, I'm not even allowed to be a part of it. That's bullshit, Shayla. Did it ever occur to you that I wanted to touch you…taste your skin, hold your body against mine, and not through goddamned T-shirts? I wanted to be with you, not get fucked by you and then discarded like an old rag." He started to walk out then turned back around. "Don't ever do that to me again. I don't want you like that. I don't want you again until you're ready to be with me, not use me to get off."

He opened the door just as Bo was turning off his phone. "Hey, man. What's up?" Bo asked. He nodded at Shayla's office with a grin. "Did you see Shayla? She's out like a light."

Chase ran his hand through his hair and plastered on a smile. "Yeah, I woke her up. Told her she slept through the wedding."

Bo chuckled. "Blake's gonna meet us there. You ready?"

"Yep."

He let Bo go first, glancing at Shayla who stood in her office, staring at him, her expression impassive, but a tear rolling down her face. He winced, wanting like hell to go to her but knowing he couldn't, not without Bo knowing something was up and making everything ten times worse...if that was possible.

Chapter Fifteen

Shayla stood at the airport waiting for Felicity, her stomach a wreck. She'd bagged up some clothes to change into along with her makeup bag, but of course, she'd left those things sitting on the bed at home. So here she stood wearing her Harrison Pool Supply polo, khakis, and tennis shoes, ready to meet the woman who fucked Chase senseless multiple times a few months ago.

A girl with shoulder-length hair, a deep auburn dye job but a good one, walked toward the exit in a pair of high, strappy wedges and a tight skirt with a flowery, flowy top. Shayla's gut wrenched at the idea of this beautiful, feminine woman staying with Chase steps away from her this weekend. Would they sleep together in the same bed? Was that the plan? Shayla had very particularly not discussed the details of the visit with Chase, not wanting to know.

Felicity glanced at Shayla and then kept walking,

no recognition setting in. They'd texted pictures of themselves to one another, but, admittedly, Shayla hadn't had a good one to send her. She wasn't someone who thought to take pictures often, and she hated selfies with a passion.

Shayla stepped in front of her. "Felicity?"

She stopped, blinking Shayla into focus, looking her up and down. "Oh my God, Shayla?" Shayla nodded. Felicity put her hand to her chest. "I'm so sorry. I thought you worked here or something."

Shayla cursed herself for leaving her change of clothes at home. She raised her eyebrows, forcing a smile. "All set? Nothing in baggage claim?"

"No, I fit everything in this little guy, if you can believe it. I hope it's warm. I brought all slutty clothes." She smiled at Shayla, genuinely, and Shayla's stomach soured. She really didn't want to like her.

"Well, our bridesmaid dresses lean a little more conservative."

She rolled her eyes. "I know. I've seen. I had to send my measurements. I fibbed a little on them so at least it'd fit tight."

She put her hand on her slim waist. Her body was as close to perfect as Shayla could imagine. No big hips, no belly fat, slim, toned legs, perfectly proportioned C-cup. This was not helping matters.

Felicity stared at Shayla, searching her eyes. "Maya was not exaggerating about you. You may be the most beautiful creature I've ever seen."

Shayla's chest sizzled. The word FRAUD might as well be plastered across her forehead. She could not have felt uglier at that moment if she tried, inside and out. She took Felicity's suitcase from her. "You ready?" she asked, and then headed out the door.

"So thank you for letting me crash at your place this weekend."

Shayla frowned. "It's not my place."

"Oh, sure," Felicity said. "But, you know."

"I just rent the pool house," Shayla said, wanting to make the boundaries clear, despite marking her territory last night. If Chase wanted Felicity this weekend, he should be free to have her. It was what was best all-around, anyway.

"Mmm hmm," Felicity said, sounding like she didn't believe her. Shayla met her gaze, and Felicity nodded, eyebrows raised, but Shayla knew that tone.

Shayla stopped walking and faced Felicity, not particularly looking her in the eye though. "Listen, I just want to make it crystal clear that Chase and I are not dating or anything like that. I know you and he have dated or maybe you are dating now, or whatever, and I don't intend to get in your way at all this weekend. So please, make yourself at home when we get there, and…that's it."

Felicity's mouth twitched like she was trying to smile.

Shayla blinked. "Okay?"

"Oh, yes. Sure. Of course."

Shayla put her hand on her hip. "What?" She usually didn't talk to perfect strangers like that, but this girl was laughing at her.

"Oh nothing." She held up her hand. "I'm crystal clear. All set, and ready to eat bon bons on the couch naked." Shayla gauged this girl, trying to figure out if she was joking or jabbing at her. Felicity closed her eyes. "Sorry. You don't know me yet. I'm kidding. You'll learn how to read me before the weekend's over."

"Okay," Shayla said, and then tentatively started walking again. "We have to stop by Starbucks for my friend Scott. He's been waiting for us there, working."

"Working? In Panama City? Why?"

"He's just waiting for us. He didn't want to go to Chase's alone, I think."

"Yeah, I imagine that'd be a little awkward." Shayla didn't respond to that. "So he's just a friend?" Felicity asked.

"Yeah. We worked together in Nashville. I just moved back home from there about three months ago."

"Yes, yes, I know all about your life, Shayla Harrison. Maya's told me everything. She's very excited about being your sister-in-law, in case you haven't already picked up on that."

"She seems really kind," Shayla said.

Felicity tapped into her phone, and Shayla was happy for the break. They arrived at the truck, and Shayla opened the passenger door, sliding Felicity's suitcase behind the seat.

They both got in, and Felicity viewed the dash. "This is a nice truck."

Shayla had ditched her car for the weekend, just in case. "It's Bo's. Belongs to his company."

"So you work for him, right? Running the business while he's been in Indy?"

"Yeah," she said, backing out of the space.

Felicity shook her head, staring at Shayla. "I bet your parents are gorgeous. Those are some damn good genes running through your family."

Shayla put the truck in gear, looking for a subject change, trying to figure out how she was going to make it through this weekend without puking. She glanced over at Felicity's smooth legs, buttered in some sort of shimmery lotion. This was a girl who took care of herself from her manicured nails, to her flawless skin to her fat-free body. Shayla imagined she was not someone who'd spent her twenties in the sun cleaning pools.

How could Chase be attracted to both Felicity and her? They couldn't be more different if they tried. Felicity represented everything feminine and elegant about a woman, and Shayla had never owned a pair of high heels or set foot in a spa. Her idea of a haircut was whichever walk-in place didn't have a line, if she didn't cut it herself.

Shayla tucked hair behind her ear out of nervousness. She realized that's what Maya did. She was not turning into Maya. Not that there was anything wrong with Maya, but Shayla had never carried around a nervous energy, not until lately.

Shayla let out a deep breath. "I think I need a drink."

"Did someone say happy hour?" Felicity asked.

Shayla smiled over at her, and Felicity gave her a warm smile in return. Yep, Shayla was doomed to liking this woman. "Have you seen Chase's wine selection?"

"Have you seen his stocked bar?" Felicity asked.

"High quality stuff, too. Shame for it to go to waste." Felicity's phone rang. "Do you care if I take this?"

"No," Shayla said, relief flooding her. "Please."

"Hi, Mom," Felicity said, her mood changing.

They pulled up at Starbucks, and Felicity told her mother she had to go. "I'll come in with you," she said. "I'm going to grab a latte. A little caffeine to pep me up from that flight and all that sitting. I might need to run around the block to wake up."

Scott stood and started packing up his stuff when he saw Shayla and Felicity walk in. "That's him?" Felicity asked under her breath.

"Mmm hmm."

Felicity rolled R's over her tongue, causing Shayla's cheeks to heat.

Shayla walked over to him. "Scott, this is Felicity."

He blinked when he saw Felicity, holding out his hand to her, his face brightening. "Hi."

"She's staying with us this weekend."

"Oh, great," he said, seeming to mean it.

Felicity smiled back in a way only a charming movie star who knows everyone wants her could. She took his hand. "Hello, Scott, roomie."

Scott blushed, looking at Shayla like he was caught. Shayla didn't know whether to be thrilled at this possible love connection or jealous. One thing was for sure. Felicity knew how to attract a man.

"So, I guess I'll follow you to the house?" Scott asked.

When Shayla had left him, he'd still been

considering whether or not he was going to stay at the hotel. She guessed Felicity changed that. Shayla couldn't help a little smile.

"Yep. I'll text you the address in case we get separated."

"I'm going to grab my latte. I'll be out in a sec," Felicity said with a wink.

They walked to their cars, and Scott put his stuff in the back seat. He turned to Shayla. "So that's Chase's girlfriend?"

Shayla shrugged. "That's a good question."

"Oh," Scott said, scratching his eyebrow.

"She seems really cool," Shayla said.

"Yeah, definitely," he said, looking at her through the window as she gave a little wave. He turned back to Shayla and focused on her. "Are you okay? You look a little rattled."

"Yeah, I'm fine. I'm just having a weird day."

"Is this about Bo getting married?"

She waved him off. "Oh, God no. I'm happy for him. Seriously."

"Anything with Brian?"

"Not that I know of. He doesn't have my new number and I haven't checked the old phone. Was he at work yesterday?"

"Yeah, and he's on email today. Someone sent a group email that he responded to. But that really doesn't mean anything." He motioned toward Starbucks, where he'd just been working. Shayla nodded, glancing around, paranoid now. Scott brushed her arm. "I'm here so you can enjoy this weekend. I'm watching for him okay? If he shows up here, I promise you won't even see him."

She smiled at him. "I really don't deserve you as a friend."

"I'm the one who's lucky, Shayla."

The door opened and Felicity came out with her cup. "All caffeinated and ready to go." She headed toward the passenger door of Shayla's truck, and Scott looked down at his keys.

"Why don't you ride with Scott, Felicity, in case we get separated," Shayla said. "You know your way, right?"

"Yep," she said, changing direction.

Scott looked at Shayla like he was in trouble and she gave him assured smile.

Shayla got in her truck and pulled out to the exit, waiting for them. That was an idea she could get on board with. Felicity and Scott. God knew he deserved a good lay. Unless he'd been lying to her, he hadn't had one in months. None of his dates worked out and he always called her at nine o'clock. She doubted there was a woman lying next to him during those times, though there could have been.

But more importantly, it'd keep Felicity away from Chase. Shayla rolled her eyes at herself, hating what she was turning into.

Chase had just pulled in when Shayla's truck and a car he didn't recognize pulled down the driveway. Trouble headed his way in the form of two women he'd slept with in the past few months and a guy who wanted one of them. Chase narrowed his gaze to find Felicity in the car with the guy. Hell, after a car ride from PCB with Felicity, Scott probably wanted her, too.

Shayla got out of the truck and walked around to the passenger side where she pulled Felicity's suitcase out of the back. Chase went to her. "Let me get that."

"I've got it," she said.

"Let me," he said.

She met his gaze with a look so serious he took a step back. "I said I had it."

He held up both hands and backed away, wanting nothing in the world but to take her inside, straight up to his bed where he'd show her what a real night of making love with him was supposed to be like.

Chase glanced over at Felicity, who was watching their exchange with interest. A smile slid across her face and she walked toward him with her arms open, her purse balancing on one of them. "Chase O'Neil. You are a sight for wide open eyes." Felicity wrapped her arms around him, and he hugged her, glancing at Shayla, who was looking down at the suitcase and adjusting the handle on it. Felicity pulled away and pointed a finger at him. "You're a big fat liar," she said in a low voice. Chase gave her a curious look, but she stepped aside.

He turned to see Scott walking toward him, and he instinctively stood taller. The guy was better looking than Chase had hoped he'd be, in good shape, too. Better than Chase was, probably. Chase's gym visits were sporadic due to his schedule, though he did force himself to get there at least once a week.

"Scott Stover," the guy said as he held out his hand to Chase.

"Chase O'Neil. Good to meet you."

"I hope this isn't odd, me staying here, a complete stranger. I promise not to steal your silverware."

"Well, you're welcome to it, but I don't think you'd get much for it. Come on in."

He took them in through the garage and then pointed to the guest room on the left. "Felicity, you can stay in there."

Felicity stopped, looking between Shayla and him like she was confused. "This is your bedroom."

"No, that's the guest room," Chase said.

"Oh." She looked surprised, and maybe even a little offended. He winced. That room was where he and she had slept, or not slept, actually, when she was there a few months prior. He'd never said it was his room, but he'd never said otherwise either. Shayla rolled her suitcase in there.

"Scott, I've got you upstairs. You can follow me, or we can all have a drink first?" Chase asked, glancing between all three of them.

"I'm going to grab a shower," Shayla said. "We probably need to leave around five for the rehearsal."

Chase got out his phone to text the limo company. He'd told them five-thirty.

Felicity stepped into the room. "I better skip the drink, too, if I'm going to transform this look into my bachelorette bling. See you squirrels in a bit." She shut the door behind her.

Chase led Shayla and Scott down the hallway

and to the staircase. Shayla stepped to the side. "Text me if you need anything," she said, looking at Scott.

The idea that the two of them shared this bond of him helping her get away from a monster didn't sit well at all with Chase. "I'm right down the hall, too," he said, looking at her in challenge.

She held his gaze long enough to prove something, and then headed through the kitchen.

Chase turned back to Scott, who was looking at him curiously, and he forced himself to relax, realizing he was wound tighter than a yo-yo. He pointed up the staircase with an easy smile. "Just up the way."

Scott let Chase pass at the top of the stairs, and he took him to the guest room at the end of the hall, the farthest one from his room. He wasn't wild about Scott staying there, but if he had to, Chase wanted him upstairs with him where he could keep an eye on him, or on Shayla coming and going from his room, more so.

"Smells like the cleaning crew were here earlier," Chase said. "I told them to rewash the towels in the closet there. Nobody's used this room in a while."

"This is great. Better than the shithole I was going to stay in. I should have checked with Shayla before I booked it."

Chase nodded, unease creeping up his chest at the idea of this guy's relationship with Shayla. Chase knew he called her every night…almost appreciated that he was still looking out for her after whatever it was she'd gone through with her ex. But he hated the fact that this guy knew more than he did. This guy had the details Chase's imagination had run wild with.

"Well, let me know if you need anything. I'm the first room at the top of the stairs. There's a rec room right around the corner, too, if you want to just hang and watch television or whatever."

"Thanks, man," Scott said, giving him a closed mouth smile with a look in his eye that told Chase he wasn't the only one of the two of them uneasy with the other's relationship with the girl in the pool house. Good.

Chase shut himself in his room and picked up the picture of Sam, staring at it like he was seeing it for the first time. He did that sometimes when he felt like he was losing control of what was circling around him. Sam grounded him. Reminded him that he was human and that the worst thing in the world had already happened to him. He could deal with anything else thrown his way.

He needed to put the picture up. Too many people floating around his house this weekend, and one right down the hallway. His phone buzzed and he lay the picture down on his bed.

It was the limo company confirming the times for the limos, but by the look of the text, they had the address wrong. He texted them back. One limo to his house at five, the other to Maya and Bo's house at five. Then he had to text Bo to let him know the limo would be there at five and not five-thirty. Then it became a whole thing with picking up Maya's parents at Sebastian's first and swinging by to get Blake and Seanna, and Chase was caught up in a frenzy of logistics. Tonight's limos were part of his contribution for the weekend. No good deed went unpunished.

Chase headed downstairs, showered and dressed, but feeling somehow shittier than he had before he'd cleaned up. He'd also cut himself shaving and had a bloody gash on his cheek, which was guaranteed to turn on the ladies.

He caught a glimpse of Scott sitting at the kitchen table, typing into an iPad. Chase headed on to Felicity's room, wanting to know why she called him a big fat liar earlier. He knocked on the door.

She opened it, standing in front of him with nothing on but her bra and thong underwear. He glanced out the window at the pool house, which was sitting undisturbed at the moment, and then in the direction of the kitchen. He put his gaze back on her. "What if I were Scott just now?" he whispered.

She waved him off and walked back into the room. "He's hot. I wouldn't kick him out of bed. I haven't been with anyone since you if you can believe that. This may be a record for me."

"You're not bothered by the fact that he's here for Shayla?" Chase asked.

Felicity stood in front of the mirror, fluffing her hair. "He may be here for her, but she's not here for him, I can promise you that."

He sat down on the bed. "Why, did she say something?"

"Didn't have to. Now you, on the other hand, are an entirely different story." She turned to him. "Why didn't you just tell me?"

"Tell you what?"

"That the two of you are madly in love with one another."

Heat rose up through his chest to his neck. "What are you talking about?"

She picked up a tube of lip something and smoothed it onto her lips. "Don't be obtuse, Chase, it's annoying."

"I'm not being obtuse," he said, not entirely sure what it meant.

She turned to him with an exhausted look. "Please. You couldn't hack through the sexual tension between the two of you with a machete."

"How can you tell something like that after being around us together five seconds?"

"I have eyes, Chase. Actually, I have a blind friend who could have sensed that chemistry."

He adjusted himself on the bed, not sure what to say.

She put the lipstick down and walked over to him. "Don't worry. I'm going to stay out of your way this weekend."

"You don't need to do that. You're welcome here, of course."

"What's the deal, anyway?" she asked. "Did you two have a fight? Not about me staying here, I hope."

"No, nothing like that."

"About Scott staying here? About me basically making you have him stay here?"

He looked up at her, a couple of feet away, still in her bra and panties. "Will you please put some clothes on?"

"Chase O'Neil, I could strip naked and you wouldn't see me right now. You certainly wouldn't appreciate it."

He exhaled a deep breath, meeting her gaze. "Were you expecting for the two of us…" He looked down at the bed and then back to her.

She shrugged. "Not necessarily expecting. I did get waxed, just in case. It may not go to waste though. I hope not. No woman should have to go through that torture unrewarded."

He stood. "Thanks for understanding."

"Sure." She walked over to him and wrapped her arms around him in a hug. He wasn't sure he'd ever had a lover go to a friend like that, not genuinely. "I am going to miss our phone sex. That's some of the best sex I've ever had." She pulled away. "That's pretty sad." She smiled at him. "It's worth it though for you to be happy. You deserve it."

He glanced in the direction of the pool house. "Nobody's happy right now, I can promise you that."

"This is a stressful weekend. A lot going on. Once you get through this and you get rid of your pesky houseguests, all will clear away."

He smiled at her. "Here's hoping."

"Hang on before you leave. You can zip me up." She walked over to her closet and took off her bra, her back to him, before pulling something off the rack. He glanced around, feeling like he was about to get caught, but it wasn't like he hadn't seen her back and ass before. She stepped into the outfit which was all one piece. He zipped it up and waited for her to turn around. "Go on," she said. "I'll make my entrance."

"I know you will," he said, and headed into the kitchen where Scott was still on his iPad. "I hope you found the beer," Chase said, opening the refrigerator.

"I could use one. You can leave the state, but you can never truly get away from work, you know?"

"I definitely do." Chase handed him an IPA. He couldn't stand it if he found out Scott preferred pilsner like Shayla.

"Thanks," Scott said, shoving his iPad away. "It'll still be there tomorrow, right?"

Chase could tell he was trying to convince himself with that statement. "What you're doing there and more, I imagine."

Scott frowned at the iPad. "You're right about that." He picked it up and went back to work on it.

Chase sat down at the table and scrolled through his phone. A few minutes later Felicity walked into the room, making an entrance worthy of an actress at the Oscars. Her green silky outfit had a V-neck that plunged all the way down between her boobs, with sky-high heels to top it off.

Scott suddenly had no interest in whatever he'd been doing on his iPad. "Hey," he said, drool practically running down his chin.

Felicity twirled. "I like to make an entrance."

"That you did," Chase said. "You look great."

She put her hands on her hips, tapping her fingers. "Great? That's all you've got?"

"Stunningly gorgeous?" Chase asked.

She shrugged. "I'll accept that."

She walked over to Scott and took his beer from him, but Chase imagined she just wanted him to have a better look at her tits. "What's this? IPA?" She turned to Chase. "You got a whiskey sour somewhere?"

"I think I can come up with one." He walked over to the bar in the dining room and pulled a bottle of sweet and sour mix out of the refrigerator, aware of Felicity teasing Scott about something. In another life, he may have felt territorial about a woman he'd slept with flirting so shamelessly with another man in front of him, but at the moment, he couldn't have cared less. He just wanted to see Shayla.

He came back in the kitchen and handed her the drink. "Let me know if it's too strong."

She gave him a look. "Do I look like I'm going easy tonight?"

He smiled back at his friend, happy to know her, the week they spent in bed together feeling like a decade ago.

The door to the pool house opened, and Chase's jaw dropped as he laid eyes on Shayla, who was turned around locking her door. She wore skin-tight, faux leather black pants and cowboy boots with a red, long-sleeved top that draped down her back just far enough to reveal that she might not be wearing a bra. She turned around, dropping her keys into a small purse, and walked toward the house brushing big, soft curls out of her face, revealing red-painted lips.

"Holy fuck," Felicity said. She and Scott both stood beside him, mouths agape as Shayla neared the house. "Why the hell did I even try?"

Shayla opened the door and blinked as the three of them stared at her. "What?" She looked down at herself, craning her neck to see her ass. "Do I have something on me?"

"You look stunningly gorgeous," Scott said.

Chase shot him a glare for stealing his line, and Scott cut his eyes at Chase, his lip curling up just slightly in victory.

Felicity offered a hand toward Shayla, looking back at Chase. "How am I supposed to attract a man with that standing next to me all night?"

Shayla frowned, glancing around. "Are we having a drink?"

"Yeah," Chase said, finally able to form words again. "Pilsner?"

"I'll just take a vodka rocks, please."

He headed to the dining room and got two glasses out of the cabinet. The speed of his heartbeat indicated her presence in the room with him. He opened the ice freezer and scooped ice in the glasses like nothing was wrong.

She moved in close to him, and his chest ignited. "Can we call a truce for the evening?" she said in a low voice.

He pulled a bottle of vodka off the shelf. "I'm not pissed at you."

She gave him a look and he poured the vodka and then handed her a glass, holding her gaze, his cock twitching at the sight of her. She was nothing short of breathtaking dolled up like that, her eyes all dark and smoky. She didn't even seem like the same person. The idea of this mysterious side of her ran scenarios through this brain that were fit for a *Fifty Shades of Gray* movie.

Her hand brushed his as she took the glass from him. "Bullshit." Her fingers wrapped around the glass with her short nails painted black made his breaths come quicker, and he thought about her hand wrapped around his cock last night as she guided him into her.

He cleared his throat, trying to collect himself, but wishing like fuck that two other people were not one room away and the lights of the limo were not illuminating his house right at that moment.

He inspected his glass. "I'm willing to table any further discussions for the sake of the group, and Bo and Maya." He held his glass up near hers.

"Thank you." She clinked her glass against his, and they both drank their vodka, watching each other as they drained their glasses. They both set their glasses down on the bar, and Shayla walked into the kitchen. "I think our ride's here."

"Did you order an Uber?" Scott asked.

"Limo," Chase said. "Special night."

"Ooh la la," Felicity said. "I'll grab my purse."

Scott's face colored a little, and Chase wasn't sure if he was embarrassed or pissed. Chase thought he should probably ease up on him...he'd keep thinking on that.

The girls piled into the limo, and Chase waited for Scott to get in. Scott motioned at the door. "After you."

"No, you go ahead," Chase said.

Scott eyed him and then got in...and sat next to Shayla.

Chapter Sixteen

Shayla had opted to watch her drinking closely. This was a long night, and they had a big day ahead of them, so she'd purposefully waited until the end of the dinner to have another drink. The one she'd had at Chase's house was out of pure survival, especially after having seen Felicity in that J-Lo dress. Scott's gaze was permanently attached to Felicity's breasts, which was fine with Shayla. Chase hadn't looked at it the whole night thus far that Shayla had noticed, which made her feel bad. What if the two of them had planned to relive their past this weekend, and Shayla had thrown a bomb in that plan last night? Shayla was a train wreck this weekend. She'd have to spend the next week apologizing.

Shayla got a beer at the bar and headed back to the room where all of their friends and family were gathered full of smiles and laughter. Bo had his hand on Maya's waist as they stood with Felicity, Scott, Dale, and Cindy. Maya swiped at her eye with her cocktail napkin, and Bo pulled her in closer to him with a look of satisfaction Shayla had never seen from him. How the two of them found each other in this huge world was beyond Shayla, but she couldn't imagine Bo with anyone else. He'd spent his twenties in misery with his ex Angela, who dragged him to hell and back. If anyone deserved a woman as sweet, responsible, and adoring as Maya, it was her brother. Now Shayla was starting to tear up, dammit.

Blake sidled up to Shayla. "Do you think there's a chance Maya won't cry tomorrow during the ceremony?"

Shayla gave him a look. "During? She'll be at it before it even starts."

Blake smiled. "I'm guessing Bo will at some point, too."

"That would be a sight. I haven't seen him cry since we were little. And I really don't remember him doing it much then."

"It's a rite of passage for a man to cry tears of joy for the woman he loves."

She turned to him slowly, looking him up and down. "God, you people down here are hopeless."

Blake stared at Seanna who stood with Chase across the room, looking like they were talking business or something else that required no smiling. "What about you?" he asked.

"What about me?"

"Are you hopeless yet?" He took a drink of his beer, staring at Chase and Seanna.

"No. Of course not." Blake slid her a look, and her neck heated. "Don't look at me like that."

"It's fairly obvious, Shayla. The two of you can't keep your eyes off one another, and Chase has shown zero interest in Felicity in that dress."

Shayla pursed her lips. "It's not a dress. It's a jumpsuit."

"It's hot, whatever it is, and he hasn't even noticed it. He's only got eyes for you. Given, if I wasn't a pseudo brother of yours, I'd probably think you looked pretty hot tonight, too." She gave him a look and he smiled back then looked at Seanna. "But I only have eyes for my wife, of course."

"Of course," she said with a smile. "Where are you all headed tonight for the bachelor party?"

"Craft beer bar hop. But after talking to Bo's co-workers, I'm thinking we should probably have done the whole thing at Alligator Alley."

Shayla nodded. "Yep."

"I would, but Chase has a thing set up at Amberjack."

She froze. "I have a thing set up at Amberjack. The one on 30A?"

"Is there more than one?"

She rolled her eyes. "Not that I know of. What's Chase's thing?"

"He knows the owner. He set up a tasting or something. I don't know. It's a bunch of free beer. Who doesn't want that? What's your thing?"

"Lingerie shower in their private room. Where's your beer thing?"

"I don't know. Maybe they have more than one private room. Or maybe they've got us in one of the little living room areas or on the back deck. There's not as many of us as there are of y'all."

She rubbed her forehead.

"Don't stress it," he said. "We'll stay out of your hair."

Shayla motioned at Maya and Bo, who were even closer together than they were before. "You think those two can be apart from one another, knowing they're in the same bar?"

Blake smiled. "It'll be a co-bachelor/bachelorette thing. We'll be breaking ground."

She glared at Chase. "If I don't break something else first."

"So the two of you never discussed what you were planning for tonight? Aren't you living together?"

Her cheeks warmed. "We're not living together. I'm renting his pool house."

"But you have to bump into one another once in a while."

When she was taking off his pants, sure. "I see him from time to time. This just didn't come up this week."

Seanna and Chase made eye contact with the two of them. Seanna smiled and nudged her boss, and they headed toward them, Chase looking like he'd rather be heading to the dentist's office.

"Everyone having fun?" Seanna asked.

"Blake!" Bo shouted. "Come here. Bring your wife. Settle a bet."

Blake smiled at Shayla. "See you soon."

Chase stood there next to Shayla, looking down at her. "What was that about?"

She looked up at him. "Amberjack?"

"Yeah."

"I've got Maya's shower set up there."

"Are you serious?" he asked.

"Yeah. Where's your beer tasting? We have the private room at nine."

"They've reserved one of the living room areas for us."

She shook her head, glancing around, her body on fire just from his proximity.

"Is that the end of the world? All our friends together in one place?" he asked.

"I guess not," she said. "I just hope Sebastian doesn't shame me. You know how he likes things like he likes them. It was all I could do to make him let me do this for Maya. He was itching to get his hands on this party."

"I'll take care of Sebastian," Chase said.

She met his gaze. "No, I'll take care of him."

He shook his head at her. "Fine. Have at it."

"I will."

They stood side by side, her insides twirling. She sipped her beer.

"You look good tonight," he said. "I mean, you always look good, but...never mind."

She looked him up and down in his dress pants and vest. "You look good, too."

He looked down at his chest. "Thanks."

Felicity grabbed Scott's arm, laughing about something and he smiled back at her.

"Does that bother you?" Chase asked.

"No, of course not. Does it bother you?"

He held her gaze, staring hard into her eyes with

his emerald green ones. "No."

She had to blink, looking away from him. Bo looked over at her with a curious glance, and she smiled, holding up her glass. He did the same thing as Dale tapped him on the arm and got his attention.

"You think he knows?" Chase asked.

She glanced at him quickly. Her heartbeat in a frenzy "Knows what?"

"That we'll all be together at Amberjack."

She relaxed, knowing that's not what he was thinking. "I'm damn sure not telling him."

He raised his eyebrows. "You think I'm telling him?" Bo looked at them again, and then stepped away from the group. "Here we go," Chase said. He waited until Bo got into earshot and then said, "Act natural."

"You two are antisocial," Bo said, gauging the two of them.

"I'm saving my voice for cat calling the stripper later," Chase said.

Bo pointed at him. "I said I didn't want a stripper."

"Relax, Virgin Mary. I'm joking. Have you met me?" Chase asked.

Shayla had to hide her grin. She loved how Chase took on her brother.

Bo rolled his eyes, his face red. "I just don't want anything fucking up this weekend, you got it?"

Shayla swallowed hard, her guilt bearing down.

"It's going to go smoother than your lily white ass, I promise you that," Chase said.

Bo eyed Shayla, and then turned his gaze to Scott and Felicity. "I'm confused. I thought he was your date this weekend."

"He is," Shayla said, feeling Chase's stare on her.

"If you're not careful, Felicity's going to walk away with him," Bo said and then looked at Chase. "Aren't you supposed to be with her this weekend?"

"The four of us are one big happy family this weekend. We're having an orgy later if you want to stop by."

Bo glanced between the two of them. "Something up between the two of you?" he asked, ignoring Chase. "Are you together?"

"We're standing together," Shayla said.

"You know what I mean."

Chase tossed up his hands. "Okay, you know what. We fucked up."

There went Shayla's heartbeat again.

"Oh yeah?" Bo asked, looking at Shayla.

Chase nudged her. "Tell him what happened. Tell him what you did."

She stared at him hard, him keeping his expression even. Bo stared at her, too, waiting to hear about how she'd fucked up.

"All right, I'll tell it," Chase said. "Last night, Shayla forgot to tell me she'd booked the same damn place for Maya's bachelorette as I booked for your bachelor party."

Bo looked between them, landing on Shayla. "That's it?"

"Sebastian's going to kill me," she said, her voice monotone.

Bo smiled, looking back at Maya who was in conversation with Cindy. "I can deal with that.

Where is it?"

"Amberjack. But we can find another spot," Chase said.

"No, no," Bo said, holding up a hand. "I like Amberjack."

"We're gonna be separated in our private room from nine to ten," Shayla said.

"For what?" Bo asked.

"The stripper," Shayla said like he was stupid for even asking.

Chase played along, nodding. God, she wanted him.

Bo smiled. "Even you two can't ruin this night for me."

"We'll try harder," Chase said.

Maya walked up and put her hand on Bo's arm. "My parents are ready to leave. We should—"

"Yep," Bo said and then turned back to Shayla and Chase. "Drink up, and let's go." He met Chase's gaze. "Thanks, by the way, for the limos. They're a big hit."

"No problem."

They walked off and Shayla looked up at Chase.

"What?" he asked. "Oh, did you think I was going to tell him about…"

She held back a smile.

"I don't even feel bad about that." He leaned down into her ear. "The next time I make love to you, there's gonna be a lot more to feel sinful about."

He walked away and joined a conversation with Shayla's parents like he'd known them for years, leaving her in a puddle on the restaurant floor.

Chapter Seventeen

Maya opened the last gift, the one from Sebastian, of course, and the group roared at the items she pulled out of the basket. She picked up a vibrator and then tossed it back in. "Sebastian," she said, her face coloring even worse than it had been the past hour. She grinned and picked it back up. "Would any of you ladies like this? I don't need one anymore."

The group oohed and ahhed.

"It's not for you, sweetie," Sebastian said with a waggle of an eyebrow, and then Maya looked back at the vibrator, which Shayla had to admit was shaped a bit differently from the ones she'd seen.

Maya covered her mouth. "Oh, my God, Sebastian!"

They were all laughing so hard she was afraid they would get themselves kicked out.

She tossed it back in the basket. "You guys,

thank you so much," she said, glancing around the room, her gaze landing on Shayla's. She mouthed another thank you while pressing her hand against her chest.

They all flooded Maya with hugs, swooping into a big huddle around her.

Maya hugged the vibrator to her chest once they all backed off. "Can we please go see the boys now?"

"Only if I get to see Bo's face when you show that to him," Ashe said.

Maya grinned while tossing it back in the basket. Shayla went to her. "I'm going to go ahead and load up the limo with this stuff, okay?"

"I'll help," Maya said.

"We got it," Felicity said. "Go see your man."

"Thank you," Maya said, and then Desiree was whisking her off to the main room.

Seanna picked up several bags. "Don't let Blake see any of this stuff. He'll be pissed I insisted on keeping our wedding so private."

Felicity held up a pink negligee. "Here, sneak this one into your purse. I know her. She'll never wear it."

Seanna eyed it. "I couldn't get my left nipple into that."

Felicity held it up to her own chest. "Yeah, me neither."

"Yes you could," Shayla said, stuffing tissue into a bag.

"On weeks I don't eat, maybe."

"You go weeks without eating?" Seanna asked.

"How else do you think I could wear something

like this?"

Seanna smiled and glanced at Shayla quickly like she was uncomfortable, and then headed out with the bags.

"You look fantastic in that, by the way," Shayla said.

Felicity looked Shayla up and down. "Not as good as you. Where did you find that top?"

Shayla waved her off and picked up some boxes.

"It's okay to look fabulous, you know," Felicity said.

Shayla blinked.

"You seem uncomfortable when I comment on your looks. Do I make you uncomfortable? When I make those comments, I mean."

Shayla furrowed her brow, picking up Sebastian's basket. "No, I just...no."

Everyone had cleared out of the room, Felicity stood in front of the door. "You're beautiful, and you should own that. That's all I'm saying." Felicity stared at her, almost in challenge.

"Well, I think you're beautiful," Shayla said, her words shaky but honest.

Felicity smiled at her, turning her head. "I'm a pretty girl. I make myself beautiful with potions and spa visits. You're naturally beautiful."

Shayla looked down at her clothes. "Not tonight."

"It's more than your looks. You're considerate and kind, and you seem to care more about everyone else's comfort than your own. Do you ever take care of yourself?"

Shayla couldn't believe how blunt this girl was.

"Yes, of course I do."

"Don't forget to do that," Felicity said, turning around and walking out.

Shayla stood there, wondering what kind of vibes she was putting out in the world. Or maybe it was just this one nutty weekend.

Shayla picked up the remnants of what was left in the room, and then headed out to the limo. When she got back inside, she found her crew of friends on the back deck, the night ocean set as their backdrop. She realized she hadn't been to the beach in months...years? She certainly hadn't been since she'd been back in town. She walked up to the railing and stood and stared at it a minute, realizing how much she'd missed the mesmerizing rhythm of the waves washing up to shore.

Sebastian sidled up beside her. "Fantastic shower. I couldn't have done better myself."

"Yeah you could have," she said.

"I'm serious. Maya was aglow. I think what she loved most was that you did this for her."

Shayla waved him off.

"Will you take a compliment, please?"

She glanced over at Felicity, who was flirting with some random guy. Maybe she did have a problem with accepting praise of any kind. "Thanks for saying that, about Maya," she said.

"You're welcome."

Shayla looked around and saw Scott sitting at the outside bar by himself. "I better go check on my date."

"Oh, Chase is fine," Sebastian said, and then looked at her all innocent. "Oh, did you mean...oh

of course." He gave her guilty smile, and she
lovingly rolled her eyes at him.

She went over to Scott. "Want some company?"

"Yeah...if your boyfriend won't try to knife me
in my sleep."

She looked around and found Chase talking to
Blake and Seanna, glancing at her, forcing a smile.

"He's not my boyfriend," she said. It sounded
like a lie, but it clearly wasn't.

"If that guy isn't into you, then I must be a way
bigger asshole than I realize."

"You're not an asshole."

"I think your friend would disagree."

They both looked over at Chase, who was
glaring at Scott. Chase quickly morphed his features
into a smile and held up his beer in greeting.

"I'm staying at the shitty hotel tomorrow night,"
he said.

A stool came open right beside Shayla, so she sat
in it. "Please don't."

He met her gaze. "I don't think I'm needed here
as much as I hoped I would be."

She frowned, unsure what to say.

"I knew you said you'd moved in with a guy,
and I knew he'd be into you, no matter who he was
because you're you. You're beautiful and lovely,
and completely irresistible. But I thought you might
not be into him in return because of everything with
Brian and because," he exhaled a deep breath, "I'd
talked myself into thinking you weren't into me
because you needed time to get over everything that
happened with Brian, but you're so clearly into
Chase. You've never once looked at me the way

238

you look at him."

"Scott," she said, looking down at her lap.

"It's fine, Shayla. I'm glad I came. I'd been hanging on, thinking when the time was right, you'd see me as someone who you could be with, and I would have given you all the time in the world to come to that conclusion. But that guy's got something I don't, at least in your eyes."

She glanced over at Chase, who said something that made Blake and Seanna laugh. "I'm so sorry."

"Don't be. You can't help it. He can't help it either. He's just being himself. I'm glad I'm seeing him with you. I can go back to Nashville knowing he's taking good care of you, because I believe he will."

She smiled at him. "I can take care of myself, you know."

He waved her off. "I know you can."

She glanced at Chase and then back to Scott. "You know I was swinging a baseball bat at him the first time I met him."

He chuckled. "That's right. You told me. That's perfect."

She took his hand and squeezed it. "I do love you, you know."

He gave her a resigned smile. "I believe that you do. I love you, too, Shayla."

She winced, realizing he didn't mean the words in the same way she did. She stood and wrapped her arms around him, hating that she was losing someone she truly cared about but knowing it was for the best. She pulled back. "Will you head home tomorrow?"

"No, I'm going to stay for the wedding if you'll still have me." He glanced over at Felicity, who had moved on from the one guy she'd been talking to and was with another.

Shayla smiled. "Mmm hmm."

"Would that piss you off…if I got with her?"

"Of course not."

"Damn." He smiled at her. "Now that's all sorted out, if you'll excuse me, I'm gonna go make my move."

"While she's talking to that guy?"

He shrugged. "I guess I better make it a good one." He headed that way.

"Have fun," she said.

He turned around. "Oh, I plan on it."

Shayla huffed a laugh and leaned against the bar, elbows up on it. Chase watched Scott walk over to Felicity and then put his gaze on Shayla. She gave a shrug like she'd lost out, and then turned around and ordered a beer from the bartender.

Chase appeared next to her. "How did the panty shower go?"

"Good. Nothing better than spending an hour seeing your future sister-in-law open lingerie and sex toys all for use on your brother."

He chuckled. "Sex toys? Bo? In what alternate universe is that going to happen?"

"One far, far away, I hope."

"Everything okay with Scott?" he asked.

"What would be wrong?"

He shrugged. "I don't know. You were looking pretty cozy with him, but now he's over there with Felicity."

She gave him a look. "I know you don't think he and I are romantic."

"I don't know. You were holding his hand and then hugging up on him. But it's not my business, I guess."

She just stared at him, trying to hold back her smile.

"What?" he asked. "Were you not?"

"Are you jealous?"

"No. I love seeing a man with his hands all over the woman I've spent the past two weeks in bed with."

She couldn't help letting the smile through now. "We haven't been sleeping together."

"Oh, I beg to differ. I've slept better in that bed with you than I have in my own high-dollar bed in a year. Of course, that doesn't have much to do with the mattress." He brushed her knee with the backs of his fingers. She glanced over at Bo. "He's fine. He's over there arguing with Blake about who gets custody of the butt plugs."

She stifled a laugh, his smile making her heart so warm. The bartender handed her the beer she ordered. "Put that on my tab," Chase said to him, and he nodded.

"Thank you, but for future reference I can buy my own."

"I know you can, but I can buy your own, too."

"I know you can." She smiled at him and then sipped her beer.

"Are you flirting with me? You'll have to let me know because it's not something I'm used to from you."

She cocked her head to the side, giving him a lazy stare. "I flirt."

"Bullshit."

"I do."

"With Scott, sure. You were practically in his lap over here earlier."

She rolled her eyes and shook her head. "You're so goofy."

"I take that as a compliment." He looked over at Scott, who had successfully gotten Felicity away from the guy she was talking to. "Look at him. He's off to another woman. Are you heartbroken?"

"Torn up."

"Aww, well, if you need someone to comfort you tonight, I could give you a cuddle."

She lifted her eyebrows. "A cuddle? Is that what the kids are calling it these days?"

He shrugged. "Just the cool ones, like me."

Blake sidled up to them. "So it looks like the Harrison Pool Supply guys are done with craft beer." Blake looked in the direction of Shayla and Bo's co-workers, who looked bored to tears in this high-end bar.

"Think we need to head to PCB?" Chase asked.

"Quick, before we lose them."

"Is Bo okay with that?"

"Yeah, he's been worried about them all night. Just wants to make sure they feel comfortable."

"I'm more comfortable at Alligator Alley myself," Chase said. "You ready now?"

"Yeah, I'll grab Bo. You grab them."

"Will do," Chase said and then turned to Shayla. "My offer stands no matter how late the hour."

She nodded, running her hand over the cold beer glass. "I'll keep it in mind."

He looked around at their friends. "You'll all stay together? You and Felicity will go home together and all?"

"Mmm hmm," Shayla said, knowing damn well she wouldn't hold Felicity to being her babysitter.

He patted the bar with his hand. "Have a good rest of your night. Don't get too out of hand." Chase glanced around like he was surveying the place.

"You're leaving me with Felicity. Are you sure that's possible?"

He gave a resigned sigh. "I guess I've brought this on myself." He pointed at Scott, who was laying it on thick with Felicity. "I'm taking him with me, by the way."

"Leaving Felicity to find us a whole new set of men, huh?"

He rolled his eyes at her. "Just be good, okay?"

"Me? I'm the one who needs to be worried. You're going to Alligator Alley."

He leaned in to her ear. "There's nobody else in the world I'd rather give a cuddle to." He squeezed her knee and then headed over to the guys.

Her chest ached at his absence, even though he was just steps away. She tried to recalibrate her brain to friend mode, focus on Maya and the reason they were here tonight. She took her beer and walked over to where Desiree stood with Ashe. "Anywhere we want to go next? We've got a limo, we might as well use it."

"We've been conjuring some ideas. Just trying to get rid of the guys," Ashe said.

"They're going. Chase is gathering them now."

"You gonna survive?" Desiree asked.

Shayla didn't answer that. She was being too obvious. Everyone could see how she felt about Chase, and she hadn't even decided on anything herself.

Marigold came outside from the main bar. "Where have you been?" Ashe asked.

She waved him off, taking his drink. "I thought I'd met a guy, but he turned out to be a dud." She sipped his drink and then handed it back to him. "That's good." She looked at the bar.

"Save it for the next place. We're heading out," Desiree said.

Marigold shrugged. "Sounds good to me."

Sebastian walked up with Felicity and Seanna. "I think we're good. Everyone ready?"

"I need to settle up the tab," Shayla said, and started to walk off.

"I already tried," Sebastian said. "Chase beat me to it."

Shayla let her posture drop. "Are you serious?"

"Yep. And there they go," Sebastian said. Chase held up a hand in a wave and then headed toward the front door.

She shook her head, not knowing how she was ever going to get on even ground with him when he was always trying to take care of her, and feeling irritated at the part of her that wanted to give in and just let him.

Chapter Eighteen

Chase got home about two hours later than he'd hoped, but he guessed it was worth it. They'd had a good time at Alligator Alley, and Chase could tell that Bo felt most at home there. It was always the plan to end up there, but leaving Shayla looking the way she did was freaking torture.

He and Scott got out of the limo, the last to be dropped off. They managed to keep the conversation from Blake's place to Chase's focused on sports, mostly football and how the pro and college teams were looking this fall. They got out of the limo at Chase's house and Chase slipped the driver an extra bill past what he'd tipped on the app. He'd put up with a ton of shit from them that evening, and money always smoothed things over.

They started to head inside, but Scott stopped in the driveway. "Hey, thanks for letting me tag along with you guys tonight. I had a really good time. I liked everyone a lot."

Chase looked down at his keys, his chest filled with shame. "Even me?" He gave him a knowing smile. "I'm sorry if I've come off as a dick tonight."

"I totally get it, man. She's worth being a dick over."

Chase huffed a laugh, knowing he was busted.

"We talked earlier tonight," Scott said. "I'm gonna back off completely."

Chase thought about his conversation earlier with Felicity. "You can't stay friends with her?"

Scott shook his head, looking in the direction of the pool house. "No way. It'd be too hard."

Chase nodded understanding. "I guess I should feel bad, but I don't."

"I wouldn't. So, Felicity…" He trailed off with a question in his expression.

"She's fantastic," Chase said. "And she thinks you're *hot*, so there's that."

Scott huffed a laugh. "So the two of you aren't together in any way?"

"We have been, in full disclosure, but we're just friends now."

"Man, how can you do that?"

"She makes it really easy. But you may want to be careful with your heart. She's not one to be tied down."

"I can see that crystal clear," Scott said. "I'm not ready to dive into anything serious right now anyway."

Chase pointed at the house. "Then this is your lucky weekend."

Scott gave him a look.

Chase shook his head. "Sorry."

"I told Shayla I felt comfortable stepping away because I can see you're here to take care of her now."

Chase huffed a laugh. "Have you met Shayla?"

"I know. But I also know Brian. He's dangerous, man. I'm serious, and he's fucking lovesick about losing Shayla. He's been drinking at work. I smelled it on him the other day. He confronted me in the hallway."

"Does Shayla know this?"

"Fuck, no. I'm just keeping my eye on him at work. I really thought he might try to come here this weekend. That's why I'm here."

"Why this weekend?"

"He knows Bo and their whole family is occupied. When I got Shayla out of there, I brought a cop friend with me. We didn't hide the fact that she was coming home. Brian knows how close she is with her family and with Bo. Of course this would be the first place he'd look. We made sure he knew both her brothers were looking out for her, and that she'd be around them all the time at work and at home. This was before Bo took off for Indianapolis and left Shayla here unprotected." He held up a hand. "I know he had no clue. I'm not blaming him. But the cover was blown a few weeks ago when Bo was traveling home and stopped by to see Shayla's house. It was right after that he started getting crazy at work. He's still there, but I wouldn't be surprised if he got canned any day now."

The frustration welled up in Chase's chest. "How

could she want to be with a guy like this?" He hated that he said it, but he'd been thinking it for a while.

"I'm not making any excuses for either one of them, but I've known him a couple of years now at work, and before all this shit happened, I liked him. I respected him. Sounds crazy to say now, but he seemed like a good guy. Really tenacious at work, willing to pitch in. Fun guy, charismatic. The girls at work are fucking nuts about him, which makes me sick at my goddamned stomach. I can't say anything, but I'm paranoid, wondering who's gonna be the next victim. That's why Shayla feels so guilty about everything. She promised to stay with him if he'd go to this special two-month rehab that focused on rehabilitating domestic violence offenders in addition to the alcohol addiction. But she had no intention of that. She felt so bad coming out of the relationship, because that inevitably meant another woman would suffer next." He punched his fist into his other hand. "God I could just kill that son of a bitch." He shook his head, his face red as an apple. "I'm sure you know all this."

Chase didn't say anything, hoping he'd keep doling out the information he'd been trying so desperately to get these past weeks.

"Anyway," Scott said and started to head to the house.

"You can totally count on me, man. I'm in for whatever this asshole wants to bring."

Scott stopped and met his gaze. "Good. I heard you hired a security guard a couple of weeks ago when you were out of town."

Chase shrugged. "Of course. So, I'm just

curious, why do people at your work not know about him? I mean, they knew she was with him, and I assume she'd come to work banged up." He swallowed down the bile from his casual words, but he was trying to get information and he had to act as if he already knew.

Scott gauged him, his brow furrowed. Chase just stared back, hoping he wasn't going quiet. "Have you ever known anyone in a domestic abuse situation?"

Chase swallowed hard. "No, I guess not."

"It's not cut and dry. There's not always physical marks where people can see them. There's a lot of pushing, shoving against the wall, grabbing arms and shaking, holding the victim down, forced sex."

Chase's body went cold as he replayed her words from a couple of weeks ago. *A guy like you who could make me remember why I used to love sex.* Had she been raped by this motherfucker?

He took a step back, wondering if he might throw up.

Scott studied his face. "Are you okay?"

"Yeah, I'm fine," Chase said.

"Look, if you're in over your head here, you need to say something."

"I'm not. I'm in. I'm just…I'm fine."

Scott stood tall, gauging Chase. "I think I've said too much tonight. I apologize. Shayla would kill me if she knew I betrayed her trust."

"You didn't. She's told me about this," he lied, pretty much.

"Then what's gotten you looking like you're about to puke?"

He shook his head. "Just...too much to drink. It's been a long night."

"That it has," Scott said. "I'm gonna go to bed."

Chase nodded and headed to the door, unlocking it for them. When he got upstairs, he closed the door to his room and sat on his bed, his mind whirling. All of the things Scott had mentioned were scenarios that Chase had run through his brain, but now they'd become a reality. Shayla had been abused. She'd been thrown across a room and shoved like a ragdoll, held down against her will, violated.

What she'd done last night had been on her terms. She'd held him down by the wrists, but with the trust that he wouldn't overpower her. That was her way of allowing herself to have sex again.

Footsteps sounded, coming up the staircase, and he imagined Felicity heading to Scott's room, but the knock sounded at his door. He walked to it and opened it, finding Shayla standing in the doorway, makeup off, her leggings and T-shirt on, just like he'd known her for weeks now.

"Hey," she said quietly.

"Hey," he said, seeing her in a completely different light.

"I heard the limo pull up a while ago. I thought you'd already be changed for bed."

"Yeah, I was just getting ready to."

She nodded, glancing behind him to his room. He suddenly remembered Sam's picture lying on his bed. He'd never put it away. He turned back toward her, blocking the way in by resting his hand on the doorframe.

She furrowed her brow. "Do you have someone in there?"

"No, of course not," he said, meeting her gaze, imagining someone shoving her against the wall and then holding her down on the ground. He shuddered, physically.

Her frown deepened, and she backed up a step. "So, I wanted to come and apologize about last night."

He shook his head automatically. "No, I'm sorry."

"What are you sorry about?" she asked.

"For what I said to you earlier today. I had it all wrong."

She studied his face. "No you didn't. I was pretty much a bully. You wanted more and you deserved more. You still deserve more." She looked contrite, and he wanted to punch himself in the nose for getting all of this wrong with her. She pointed to his room. "Can we go inside to talk?"

He turned around again, eyeing the picture on the bed. He couldn't share Sam with her now. This timing was all wrong. Not on this already stressful wedding weekend. Not with Scott down the hall and Felicity downstairs. Not with him just now understanding what she'd been through.

He met her gaze wordlessly, the hurt in her eyes becoming palpable. She turned around. "That's fine. We'll just talk later." She walked away.

"Wait," he said, lunging for her, grabbing her by the arm, and then letting go like he'd stung himself on a hot burner.

She stopped and looked down at her arm and

then up at him. "What is wrong with you tonight?"

He stepped back. "Nothing, I just, I'm so sorry, Shayla."

Her expression went cold as she glanced at the room Scott was staying in, and then back at him. "You've been talking about me."

He started to shake his head, but it was a lie and he was sure it showed all over his face. She headed down the stairs, and he followed her into the kitchen. "Wait," he said.

She kept walking out the door. "I'm such an idiot."

"You're not an idiot."

She opened the door to the pool house and then tried to shut it in his face but he stood his ground. She walked away from him, to the far side of the room. "That was my story to tell, not something for the two of you to gossip about behind my back."

He shut the door, and then turned to her. "It wasn't gossip."

"Then what was it? And what was that upstairs with your room, by the way? Are we only allowed to *cuddle* here in the pool house where you don't have to share any other parts of you?"

"That's not fair, Shayla."

"Then what's up? Is there some reason you can't let me into your room?"

He rubbed his forehead, not ready for this, not now. "It's just, I was worried my sheets were dirty."

She put her hands on her hips. "The cleaning crew was here earlier. This whole place is immaculate."

"I forgot." He stared at her beautiful body,

imagining that asshole grabbing her and forcing himself into her. His stomach fumed like liquid nitrogen.

"Stop that. Stop looking at me like that," she said.

"How am I looking at you?"

"Like I'm some fragile flower that you can't touch."

He looked away. "That's not what I was doing."

She took a few steps toward him. "Yes you were."

He met her gaze, and then looked away again, wishing he had a manual that told him the right things to say and do.

"What is this? You can't even look at me now?"

He met her gaze, his neck hot. "Of course I can look at you."

She stared at him, and then huffed a laugh, shaking her head. "This is exactly why I didn't want you to know about any of this. The way you're acting right now. This was exactly what I was trying to avoid."

"I can't help it. I don't know what I'm doing here."

She tossed up her hands. "You think I'm some kind of expert?"

His frustration hit a boiling point. "I'm sick over it. I've been sick over it, but I haven't said anything about it because I know you don't want to talk about it, but I'm out of my mind here, Shayla, thinking about what you went through, worried that if I touch you it's going to be the wrong way. Then last night, it was finally happening, but I wasn't allowed to touch you, when it's all I've thought about doing for a month now, and I said all that to you earlier today because my ego couldn't take the fact that you'd gotten yourself off pretty much completely without my help, and then tonight, when I saw you looking the way you did, it was like you were a totally different person, and I almost forgot for a minute that…"

"Forgot what, Chase? Forgot that I was what?" She glared at him so hard his pupils hurt.

He scratched his forehead, his heartbeat pounding.

She got up in his face, stabbing a finger at him. "I'm not a goddamned victim."

He held her stare, his body trembling.

She took a step back from him, her gaze not leaving his, and then peeled her pants down her legs, stepping out of them. She pulled her shirt off and stood there in front of him, completely bare to him. She held her arms out to the sides. "Do you see any bruises on me? Any scars? I'm not frail or weak."

He swallowed hard, shaking his head. "No."

She stepped toward him, her gaze locked on his. She picked up his hands and placed them on her hips, and guiding them over her thighs and up the curve of her ass. She pressed her body against his, his cock coming to attention. She ran her hands up his chest and to either side of his face, her fingers threading through his hair. "Keep your promises. Make me feel sinful."

Chapter Nineteen

Something changed in Chase's eyes, and Shayla knew she needed to buckle up. She'd asked for this from him, insisted on it, and there was no backing down now.

He wrapped her leg around his, taking her down to the bed, his big body hovering over hers, face to face with her. He stood up and unbuttoned his shirt, while she scooted up on the bed and then lay back on her elbows, not wanting to miss the show.

He pulled back his belt and undid his pants, his cock springing out as they fell to the floor. He climbed on top of her, his knees between her legs, forcing them apart. He leaned down and opened her mouth with his, and her legs wrapped around him in response as he kissed her like she'd been dreaming of being kissed by him for weeks.

He moved on top of her, his cock flirting with her thigh and her belly. He was a big guy, in all ways, lucky for her. He kissed down her neck and over to her shoulder as he collapsed on top of her, rolling onto his side and taking her with him. She wrapped her leg around him and lay back again, her arm over her head, leaving her breast exposed to him. He took his time, trailing kisses over her chest, between her breasts and down to her stomach. Teasing her as he bypassed her breasts, he brought his hand up to cup one, and then finally took it into his mouth. She exhaled a breath, realizing she'd been holding it for a while, his touch on her body like water after a marathon.

His hand left her breast and moved lower, rounding her hip to her behind, and then over to her thigh. Her whole body thudded with anticipation as she silently begged him to touch her, squeezing him to her with her leg. His hand finally made its way to her warmth, and she gripped his shoulder as he teased her.

He slid down her body, spreading her legs as he positioned himself in front of her. She set her feet flat on the bed and moved to his mouth as he took her in. She gripped his arms as the sensations flew through her body like a hurricane.

"Chase," she whispered, because she wanted to say his name. He was the man her heart had been begging for every day and every night as he lay next to her in bed, his arm slung over her in the middle of the night.

He let out a hard breath as she gripped his arms and let herself go with moans, begging for him not to stop. It'd been so long since she'd wanted to be vocal during sex. But she wanted him to know what he was doing to her, and she also wanted to make sure he kept on doing exactly what he'd been doing, because he was doing it really right.

Her back arched off the bed, and then she fell backward as the release flowed through her body to him.

She rested back on the bed, her arms over her head as he kissed his way back up her body, slowly. She met his gaze, her hands rounding his back. "Come here," she said.

He moved to kiss her, but she guided him up farther, her hands sliding down to his ass. She pushed him up her body, sliding down between his legs, and then took him into her mouth. He inhaled a sharp breath as she moved up and down on him until she settled back, guiding him with her hands on his ass. He pulled away. "That feels too damn good."

"Then let's not stop," she said. "We've got time for more later."

"I want inside you now," he said.

She moved back up on the bed and reached over to her drawer, pulling out a row of condoms and handing them to him. He ripped one off and readied himself.

He stopped and met her gaze, moving her hair out of her face. "I'm so lucky."

She smiled, wordlessly. He sometimes knew the perfect thing to say.

As he pushed inside of her, she squeezed him with her thighs, the initial pain of his substantial girth turning quickly to pleasure. He dropped down to his elbows, propping himself up as he found a rhythm. Everything about him was right. Nothing he did felt wrong or bred any fear in her. She felt herself tensing for just a moment, and then released that tension, relaxing into the movements of this man she trusted with her body, and possibly with her heart.

She lay under him, letting him fill her up, the movement inside of her feeling so good she could let him do it all night. But she knew he hadn't had a release yet and she had, so it was time to set him free.

"Go ahead when you're ready," she said.

"Are you sure?" he asked, looking concerned.

She gave him a reassuring smile. "I'm positive."

He moved faster, and then finally collapsed down onto her, their chests melding together into one, the heat and dampness lying between them. "I'm sorry," he said into her neck. "I didn't last as long as I should have. I'm out of practice."

She smiled, those words not so bad to hear. "You did good. You're a lot of man. I couldn't take you for much longer."

He propped himself up, facing her with a grin. "You're a good liar."

"I'm serious," she said. "You feel really good inside of me."

He kissed her and then pulled back to look at her again. "You have no idea." He kissed her again. "I'll be right back."

His long, lean body made for delicious eye candy as he walked to the bathroom. She rolled over onto her side, waiting for him.

Walking back toward her, she admired his frame,

not too buff which was fine with her—she'd had enough of buff—but in good shape. He hopped into bed beside her and lay on his back staring at the ceiling. She ran her hand over his stomach and up his chest to his bicep. "You've got an attractive body." He flexed his muscle, and she ran her hand over it. It was bigger than she'd thought it'd be. "Nice," she said.

"I'm not ripped like your brother."

She winced. "You can't talk about my brother while we're naked."

"Sorry."

"So what was that talk about being out of practice?" she asked.

He put his arms behind his head. "It's been a while."

"How long's a while?" she asked. "Couple of days, couple of weeks?"

He gave her a look. "Couple of days? I've been in bed with you for the past two weeks."

She smiled at him. "I don't know what you do with your days."

He cut his eyes at her and then looked at the ceiling. "A few months."

"Since Felicity?"

He closed his eyes tightly. "Can we not talk about that?"

"I don't want to talk about you and Felicity. I'm just asking if she's the last person you slept with."

"Yeah." He turned to her. "Does that kill my reputation?"

"How long had it been before her?"

He squirmed. "I don't know."

"Yeah you do."

"A few months. I've been busy at work. I've been spending a lot of time with Seanna and Blake. That's a libido kill if there ever was one, watching the two of them be madly in love. Makes me want to eat whoopie pies and watch game shows or something."

She traced the hairs on his belly south and back up his chest again. "When you sleep with girls you don't know, do you use a condom?"

"I used one with you, didn't I?"

"Yeah, but I used one last night. I assume you were following my lead."

"I haven't had sex without a condom since I was married. I've damn near forgotten what it feels like."

She stilled. "Are you serious?"

He met her gaze. "Yeah. Why?"

"Every single time? You've never slipped up?"

"Hell no. I had a friend who was diagnosed with AIDS. He cheated on his wife. We were all friends. Scared the shit out of me. I was with this one woman a few years ago. I went to put the condom on and she told me not to. Said she didn't like the way they felt. I got up right then."

"You left?" she asked.

"Hell yeah. That shit's nothing to play with."

"Have you ever been tested?"

"I get tested every six months. It's on my calendar perpetually."

She lay back, relieved.

"What about you?" he asked.

"I hadn't in years, but I did when I got back here

to PCB a couple of months ago. I didn't think I had a reason to, but I just felt dirty all over. I don't know, I just wanted to be told I was clean, in some way. Now that I think about it, that's probably why I was always cleaning my brother's house."

He reached over and ran his hand across her belly, lovingly.

"I haven't really slept around since college and my early twenties. I'm usually in a relationship," she said.

"I bet you are. I can see where a guy wouldn't want to let you go."

A younger, more naïve version of her would take his words to heart, but he was talking in the abstract, as much as she realized she wished he wasn't. She wondered about his last relationship. "Does your ex-wife live here in town?"

"No, she's in San Antonio. That's where we met and lived."

"Is that where you grew up?"

"Partially. We moved there when I was twelve."

"From where?"

"Hawaii."

She furrowed her brow a little. "So, are you…"

"Polynesian?"

She gave a guilty smile. "Yeah."

"Partially. My grandmother was, but she was married to a white man. Both my grandparents on my dad's side were Irish, so I guess I'm more that than anything, despite the way I look. It's tough to put my family in a neat box when it comes to our heritage."

"So you lived in Hawaii?"

"Till I was twelve, yeah. My parents met at work. They were both stationed at Hickam Air Force Base."

"You're a military brat?" she asked.

He shrugged. "I've been called worse."

"So how did you get here?"

"When we divorced, I was looking for a change. My middle brother was based at Eglin so I moved to Fort Walton. I was in real estate, and the idea of coming to this area seemed to make sense. I was in town about five minutes before I heard about 30A and came over for a visit. Seemed like as good a place as any to start over."

She huffed a laugh. "I don't know why, but I just assumed you'd grown up here. You seem so much like a local."

"Good. I hope I do." He smiled at her.

"So do people here know you were married?" she asked.

"Nah. I wouldn't deny it, but I don't like to talk about it. My brother knows, of course. He's in Destin now. He's out of the military. Wasn't for him, to my father's disappointment. He's the only one of the three of us who even tried."

"Are you close with your brother?"

He shrugged. "We used to try to have dinner once every month or so. That's turned into six months. I need to reach out more, I guess."

"Any nieces or nephews yet?" she asked.

"No, neither of my brothers have settled with anyone yet, not that seriously."

"Is that something you want, a family?"

He rolled over onto his back, crossing his arms

over his chest, closing himself off to her, and she knew whatever fantasies she'd been kicking around in her brain about a life with him were just that, fantasies.

"No, not really."

She nodded, her heart heavy with disappointment. She was thirty-six years old. If she wanted to have a family, it was time to get started.

Chase looked at her. "Do you want that?"

She let out a heavy breath. "With the right person, maybe so."

He looked at her with curiosity. "You've never wanted kids before now?"

"I've been putting it off, I guess. I didn't want to have kids with the wrong guy and end up a single or divorced mom. There's a lot of that where I grew up. I'm kind of picky, I guess. Once I get married, I want it to be for good, but I don't want to get stuck in a marriage that I can't get out of." She thought about her mother defending her father's drunken behavior all the time. "It's more important for me to find the right guy than have kids, I guess."

He stared at her. "Makes sense."

She stared back at him, so many questions for him, but none she could ask.

"So the last guy, you knew he was the wrong guy?" he asked.

She exhaled, knowing he deserved some answers. He'd earned them. "I thought he might be the right one at first, before he started drinking."

"How long were things good between you two?" he asked.

"A long time. I thought he was a good guy. I

know that sounds ridiculous, but I wouldn't have dated him if I didn't think he was."

"I know that," he said, and his certainty of her gave her comfort.

She pressed her hand down on the mattress, running it back and forth. "Things were good until he started drinking, and somewhere down the line, I lost control."

He put his hand on her hip.

"Looking back, I know the exact point where I should have left. There were hints here and there, jealous comments that I tried to blow off as a phase. But the point I knew it was bad was the week Seanna came for a visit in March."

"I was there with her. We were at the Opryland Hotel for a convention."

Shayla met his gaze, thinking of Chase just down the interstate from her when Brian was losing it that night.

"What happened that night?" he asked.

She frowned and looked back down at the bed. "He lost it. He wanted to come with us, but I wanted to see her alone. He thought it was so I could talk about him, which wasn't the case. I think by then I knew that I wasn't going to stay with him, and I knew Seanna and I would primarily be talking about stuff going on back home because that was our connection. I didn't want him being a part of it."

"Did he show up anyway?" he asked.

"No, nothing like that. But when I got home, he'd been drinking whiskey, plenty of it. He was so mean when he drank that stuff. I tried to go to bed and he wanted to talk, but he wasn't being kind. He kept making jokes that weren't funny." She left out the part about him wanting to have sex, and her going along with it to keep the peace. "He apologized that next day, and things were okay for the next few weeks, until one night when we were out with some of his friends and a guy complimented my jacket." She huffed a laugh. "Such an idiotic nothing comment, but it meant everything."

He squeezed her hip, letting her know he was hearing her, which endeared her to him.

"When we got home, he did a couple of shots. I was unloading the dishwasher, and he kept making jabs at me. Did I think Andy was hot? Did I want to go home with Andy and not him? Did I have a clue how many girls he could go home with if he wanted to?"

"Do you think he ever cheated on you?"

She chuckled at the thought. "God no. I wished. I would have loved for him to have gotten with another girl…at that point at least, before I knew it was going to get worse."

"Did he lay hands on you that night?"

She reached her hand under his arm and threaded her fingers through his. "His violence was progressive. That night he grabbed me by my arms so hard that I had bruises the next day. He knelt on the floor in front of me, begging me to forgive him, apologizing, telling me he'd never drink a drop again." She huffed a laugh. "I'd walked in on my dad doing that same thing to my mom once. She'd forgiven him, and he still hasn't drank since. I was home from college at the time. I guess I thought that was how it worked." She shook her head at herself. "Such a silly girl."

He pushed her hair from her face with his free hand, wordlessly, but she felt his support, his nonjudgement.

"Things were better for a while," she said, "but then I started working with Scott on a project at work. Brian couldn't stand it, every night it was something different. He was drinking again, unapologetically. He started accusing me of cheating, which was ridiculous because I was always with him. I wouldn't engage with the drama, and that drove him crazy, so finally one night, he grabbed me and shoved me against a mirror we had hanging in the foyer. I was dumbfounded. He kept saying I was making him lose his mind. He couldn't take me to the hospital because he was too drunk, and I was afraid to drive myself, so I texted Scott to come take me. I didn't want any of my girlfriends asking questions. I hate that I had to involve him, but I didn't know what else to do."

She met his gaze, his face having turned white. She smiled at him to let him know she was okay now.

"I'm sure Scott's glad you called him," he said.

"It was just all so fucked up, Chase. I can't believe I'm telling this story about myself. It feels like someone else's story."

"Well it's not you, not anymore. You just got in over your head. What happened with your head, by the way?" He glanced at the top of her head like he was looking for a scar.

"It was fine. I had a mild concussion. It could

have been so much worse."

"Where did you go when you left the hospital?"

"To Scott's house. I wanted to come home, but I needed to give notice at my work. I didn't want to leave the company on bad terms since I thought I'd be needing them for a reference. I had no idea Bo was going to meet Maya and leave town at that point. Hell, he had no idea then. He hadn't even met her yet."

"So you stayed with Scott?" he asked, clearly wanting to know more about that.

She smiled. "Nothing happened, if that's what you're asking."

"No, of course not. Well, a little. Look I apologized to him earlier tonight. I don't want you to think I'm a jealous guy. I've never been one, and that's the God's honest truth." He ran his knuckle down her belly. "I've never felt like this before either."

Her heartbeat soared. She didn't have any reason to think he was bullshitting her, but she couldn't go crazy here, not before she was sure about him, sure he wasn't going to get bored in a few weeks and need to move on.

"Is there anything else you want me to know about what happened this past spring with you? Anything I need to know?" he asked.

She closed her eyes. She'd come so far with him. She really didn't want to tell him the full story, because she felt like such an idiot, such a naïve, silly girl, but she also didn't want to talk about it again. It felt like now or never to her.

"I did something really stupid." She opened her

eyes and kissed his knuckles, then let his hand go. "Brian had had a week to cool down. I'd seen him at work and he'd been apologetic. He'd heard I'd quit and he just wanted to talk. He seemed so calm and genuine. He said he'd been sober since that night, and he wanted to apologize for all the jealousy, for any blame he tried to put on me. He said all the right things. So I agreed to talk...meet him at a restaurant. The night went well and he even was fine for me to go back to Scott's house. It was like I had the guy back who I'd fallen for in the beginning. I started to wonder if I'd dreamed the past couple of months."

"You took him back," he said, as if helping her with the words.

"My boss offered me a large bonus if I would work out the end of the project I'd started with Scott. It was a new piece of software I'd helped develop and the woman I'd worked with on it had left the company, so without my expertise on that piece of software, they'd be set back quite a bit. So I agreed to stay till the project was over. I had lunch with Brian a couple of times, and his demeanor remained the same, contrite, apologetic, not at all jealous, never asked me a single thing about Scott. So I went home one night. For about a week, it felt like everything was falling back into place. I was even regretful I'd quit my job. I was considering asking if they'd take me back. I knew they were having a hard time finding someone with the skills needed who was a good fit." She shook her head in memory, feeling every bit the idiot she'd felt that night. "I had a late night at the office. We were up against the clock. We stayed there till like ten-thirty. The second I opened the door, I knew I needed to leave. But I didn't. I stood right there in that doorway, when all I had to do was turn around and run back to the car."

She closed her eyes tightly, images flashing through her brain.

"Shayla, you don't have to—"

"He stood up, and when he did he bumped into our glass coffee table which I'm sure hurt his leg, and that rage from the pain went straight to his head and he started in. Where had I been? I'd been fucking that asshole, he'd known I was a whore. Why wouldn't I fuck him? I hadn't for months." Her throat threatened to close. "He said he'd been patient enough."

Chase took in a sharp inhale. She closed her eyes, rubbing them with her forefinger and thumb. "It's so hard to justify why I went back, why I didn't run out. I don't know how to explain it."

"You don't have to, ever," he said.

She met his gaze. "I'm not a weak person."

"I've never once thought you were."

"I'm not stupid either," she said, her voice cracking.

Chase shook his head, staring into her eyes. "You're not."

She closed her eyes, done with the telling. Chase wrapped his arm around her while she buried her head into his chest. She didn't ever want to come out.

Chapter Twenty

Chase walked into the kitchen and found Felicity and Scott sitting at the kitchen table sipping coffee. "Morning," Felicity said.

"Morning," Chase said, feeling a little *walk of shame*, still wearing his clothes from last night.

Felicity put her finger to lips. "Wait, I'm confused. I thought your bedroom was upstairs."

Chase met Scott's gaze. He didn't look too broken up. "I've been swimming," Chase said. "I just came in to check on you two knuckleheads." He glanced at the white bags on the table. "Did you get breakfast?"

"Oh, yes," Felicity said. "Pastries from Seaside Sweets. And just in time. They're closing at noon today for the wedding."

He looked at the stove. "What time is it?"

"Eleven," Scott said.

"Damn," Chase said. "I've got to get my ass in

the shower."

"Dirty?" Felicity asked.

He shot her a look. "Takes one to know one."

She grinned, sipping coffee.

He took the stairs two at a time and shut himself in his room. The picture of Sam still sat there on his bed, face up. He picked up the frame and stared at his little boy, his heart breaking. Moving on with another woman, another family, another life had always seemed like a betrayal. He'd been living in limbo for six years, but somehow feeling like he was honoring his son by doing so.

"I love you, buddy," he said, and then kissed the frame. He thought about Shayla and all she'd shared with him last night, how hard it must have been for her to utter those words to him. It was time for him to go all-in with her. Bo would be married today, and every weekend couldn't be dedicated to him. He'd get over it as soon as he saw Chase's devotion to his sister…as soon as he saw that Chase wasn't going anywhere, ever again. But there was one thing he needed to do first.

He pulled up Rachel's contact in his phone. He had no idea if she'd changed her number or not. He didn't see a reason why she would have. It wasn't like he ever bothered her. He typed a text message.

Rachel, it's Chase. Is this still your number?

A moment later, he got her reply.

Yes. What's up with you?

Can you talk?

Another moment passed and then his phone rang. "Hey," he said. "Thanks for calling."

"It's good to hear your voice. How are you?"

Her voice took him back to another life. "I'm good. How are you?"

"I was glad to get your friend request on Facebook a while back. But you never post. You make it hard for a girl to spy on her ex."

He smiled a little at the idea of Rachel looking him up. He'd always imagined her plowing forward through a new life, never giving him another thought. "Not been too much to post about."

"Well, I know that's not true. I keep up with you, ya know. My friend Raleigh has a sister who lives in Blue Mountain. She says you can't throw a rock without seeing a sign with your picture on it down 30A."

He rolled his eyes at himself.

"I'm so glad you've found that kind of success, Chase. But I'm not surprised. You were always driven."

"That means a lot coming from you," he said. Rachel was one of the hardest workers he knew. "I see you have a family," he said, his heart cinching.

"Yeah, Devon's four and Midas is nineteen months."

"They're beautiful kids. Your daughter looks just like you."

"Thanks. I think they're pretty wonderful, but I may be biased. Are you…with anyone?"

He paused, gathering his courage. "I hope so. I'm headed in that direction, I think."

"Does she live there in South Walton?"

"Yeah," he said, not needing to get into the fact that she was renting his pool house. "She grew up in the Panama City Beach area."

"Oh, okay. Well, that's great, Chase."

He scratched his forehead, wincing. "I was wondering about something."

"Mmm hmm," Rachel said, with patience and kindness like when they first got together, before life and their marriage beat them down.

"Do you think of Sam?" he asked.

"Of course I think of Sam."

"I mean, it's hard to tell. Your Facebook page is full of pictures of your new family and stuff about your kids." He knew he sounded like a dick, but he needed to get to the point.

She let out a heavy breath. "Chase, that's Facebook. Everything on Facebook is the best of our lives. Do you think I'm going to post on Facebook on the anniversary of Sam's death, about how I spent the day at a hotel by myself because I needed time to grieve on my own? Do you think I'm going to post about how I can't buy applesauce for my kids because it was Sam's favorite? I know other people post like that, but does that seem anything like me?"

He swallowed hard, realizing he had it all wrong, once again.

"Every single morning I wake up and I talk to Sam without ever opening my mouth. I lay in bed and I tell him how much I miss him. I tell him when I win a case or when Devon eats her green beans at dinner. I tell him when I watch an episode of Dora and that I love him more with every day, not less. I tell him I will never forget him, not for a moment, and I don't."

Chase's throat threatened to close. He couldn't

believe Rachel was saying all of this. He'd never dreamed she felt this way.

"Chase," she said, "It's okay to move on. You're not moving on from Sam. You're moving forward for you. Just bring Sam with you."

A pressure built in Chase's forehead. "Thank you," he choked out. "I need to go."

"Can I call you back, check in sometimes?"

"Yeah," he said.

"Take care of yourself," she said, and he disconnected the call.

Shayla sifted through the coat hangers in her closet one more time for the handkerchief she'd brought back from her mom's house a couple of weeks ago. She'd draped it across one. She was sure of it. Where was the silly thing? She couldn't leave without it. Maya was counting on it for her *something old*.

She peered at the bottom of the closet to see if it had fallen down there somewhere. That was the only explanation. She pulled the boxes out, but nothing was there. She let out an exhausted breath, standing in the middle of the room, palm against her forehead, in her lavender bridesmaid dress thinking, which was doing her no good.

When she went to shove the boxes back in, her box on top of Chase's toppled over, taking the lid from Chase's box with it. "Dammit," she said, more frustrated than ever.

She knelt down and loaded the stuff back in her box, and then went to put the lid back on Chase's box. Her gaze was drawn to a picture of a little boy with dark hair. He looked around two or three years old. She flipped it over and read the writing on the back that said, "Sam, 2 years, 9 months."

She flipped it over, zoning in on the face. The child looked like Chase. Knowing she shouldn't, but unable to resist, she looked at the next pic. It was of Chase with this same boy at the bottom of a big bouncy slide, smiles covering his face and the boy's. She kept going to find one of Chase with a woman with sandy brown hair and the same boy, all huddled up, family-style, smiling with a carousel as their backdrop.

Did Chase have a child? That made absolutely no sense. He would have mentioned that by now. And she remembered asking him if he had kids and he'd said no. Was he hiding this kid for some reason?

She dug further into the box, checking to make sure the blinds were closed and feeling like a total heel, but she had to know. The box had a toy frog in it with rubber hands and feet for teething, the book *Brown Bear, Brown Bear, What Do You See?*, a dump trunk with a little toy man driving it, and a tiny T-shirt that said "Daddy's Twin."

A knock sounded at her door, sending her heart into overdrive. "Shayla? No rush, but we're all ready," Chase said.

"Okay," she said, putting the box back exactly like she'd found it. "I'll be right there. I'm just looking for something I promised to bring to Maya."

"You need help looking?"

"No. I'll be out in a minute. Why don't you all

go ahead and start the car. I'll be right there."

She shoved the box back into the closet and lowered the other box on top, her mind in a frenzy over what might possibly be going on. A child? Why would he not have told her this, especially last night when he was talking about his life? What kind of man would disown a child? Did his ex-wife have him in San Antonio? How could he have just moved away from him like that?

She caught a glimpse of the purse she'd bought to match her dress, and remembered that she'd put the handkerchief in there a week and a half ago so she wouldn't forget it. She pulled herself together, gathering her bag for the day, and then headed toward the car.

Scott and Felicity sat in the backseat talking in low voices, smiling and picking at one another like lovers did. Shayla would be happy for them if she wasn't freaking out.

She got into the front seat. "Hello, stranger," Felicity said. "You missed cinnamon rolls from Seaside Sweets."

"I saved her one," Chase said with a smile.

She forced a smile back, and then looked down at her purse. Why was this happening right now? Right before Bo's wedding?

When they got to the venue in PCB, a botanical garden that belonged to a client of Harrison Pool Supply, they all piled out of the car. Shayla headed straight inside without waiting for anyone. She found Maya in the small dressing room in the back of the venue. She stood with a girl who looked a lot like her, but with curves and boobs that Maya didn't have.

Maya smiled, and started to tear up. "Shayla."

"Oh my God, you've got to stop this. She's been at it all day." The girl held out a hand. "I'm Meade, Maya's sister."

"I'm Shayla, Bo's sister."

"Well, I guess that makes us family of some sort." She pulled Shayla in for a hug. Right off the bat, Shayla could tell this girl was Maya's polar opposite in demeanor.

Shayla hugged Maya. "You ready to get married?"

Maya pulled away, wiping at her eyes. "I can't believe any of this. I feel like I'm in the middle of someone else's dream."

That was ironic. Shayla had felt like she was in the middle of someone else's nightmare for the past months. After last night, she had started to feel like the nightmare was coming to an end, but then seeing those pictures had changed everything. Did Bo know about Chase's child? Did Maya know? She could not ask. Jesus.

Maya's mother came out of a bathroom and discarded a paper towel in a waste basket with a repugnant wince.

"Hello, Mrs. Forbes," Shayla said. She'd been seated near her at dinner last night and had spoken with her briefly.

"Oh, hello, Sheila."

"It's Shayla, Mom," Maya said.

"Oh," the lady said, looking mortified. "I'm so sorry."

"It's no problem, ma'am."

"Bo was asking if you were in here earlier. I think he was anxious to see you."

"Okay, I'll go see him." She set her bag down in a corner, and then remembered the handkerchief. She pulled it out and took it over to Maya. "Before I forget, I want to go ahead and give this to you. I mentioned I had your *something old*. It was my grandmother's."

Maya took the handkerchief like it was a precious jewel. "Shayla, I can't take this."

"I want you to have it," Shayla said.

"But you'll want it for your own wedding."

Shayla huffed a laugh. "Let's not all hold our breath. Seriously, she left us a few of them. I'll carry another one if the day ever comes."

The door opened, and Felicity came in.

"Maya," Mrs. Forbes said. "You already have your *something old*. Aunt Mimi's earrings?" Her mother indicated Maya's ears and she grabbed for them.

"Oh, well, this handkerchief can be my *something borrowed*."

"You're borrowing my pearls," the woman said with a raised eyebrow.

Maya's eyebrows furrowed in stress.

"Mother," Meade said with a warning glance.

Felicity held up a blue garter belt, stretching it out between her pointer fingers. "I've got your *something blue*."

Maya's mother's face drew up in a pinched expression, and she held up a hand as she turned around and collapsed into a chair, arms folded over her chest. "Don't forget you're thirty-five years old,

278

Maya."

"Yes, you've reminded me of that fact a few times recently."

"Mother," Meade said. "Have you seen the back room of the garden where they have the tropical plants?"

"No," her mother said with attitude.

"Let me show you."

"I hear it's so breathtaking it brings women to their knees," Felicity said, and Maya's face went beet red. There was a reason this place was so special to Maya and Bo, and Shayla could take three guesses as to why.

Meade and her mother left, and Maya clenched her fists. "Why did I let her come?"

Felicity rubbed her back. "She's your mother. Either you invite her or you kill her."

Maya rubbed her temple. "Okay, I'm going to use the restroom one more time, then I'm going to let you two help me into my dress."

"Do you think Meade will want to help with that?" Shayla asked.

"No, we have this plan in place specifically so my mom won't be here for that. I can't take the criticism of my body."

Shayla looked at Felicity in confusion. Maya's body was as toned and fit as they came. Felicity rolled her eyes discreetly with a small shake of her head, a warning for Shayla not to go there.

Maya headed for the bathroom. "I may be in here a second. My stomach is a little upset."

"Should we leave?" Shayla asked.

"Please don't go far," Maya said.

"Just turn on the fan in there if they have one and we'll close our ears," Felicity said.

Maya glanced inside and located a switch. She flipped it on, and a loud fan came on. She gave a thumbs-up sign and headed inside.

Shayla eyed Felicity. Maybe she knew something. "Did you have fun last night?"

Felicity lifted an eyebrow. "As much fun as you had."

Shayla looked down at her hands.

"Everything okay with you today?" Felicity asked.

"Yeah, just a big day."

Felicity nodded.

Shayla racked her brain. "So, is there a flower girl or ring bearer?"

"Oh, God no. I hope not. She's not mentioned one, and Meade doesn't have any kids, so I'm assuming."

Shayla nodded. "Not a fan of kids?"

"I don't mind them being on the planet. I just don't want them near me."

"Ever dated a guy with kids?"

"Not more than once. I get that out of the way on the first date. Why? Does Scott have kids?"

"No, not that I know of."

"Oh, shew. Not that we're turning this into a double wedding or anything, But I do like to know these things."

So it didn't seem like she knew anything either.

A knock sounded on the door. "Ladies, I need Shayla Harrison please," came Sebastian's voice.

"She ran off and joined the circus this morning,"

Felicity said.

"Then please go retrieve her from the trapeze."

"I'll be back," Shayla said. Sebastian stood on the other side of the door in a gray tailored suit that looked like it came off a red carpet. "I thought you weren't supposed to upstage the bride," Shayla said.

He lifted his eyebrows. "Like you're one to talk."

"Maya picked out this dress, not me."

"I know, and I advised against it. You and Felicity could at least darken a tooth or give yourself a quick perm to try not to look so fabulous."

Shayla smiled. "What's up?"

"Your brother. He's so freaking cute. He's all nervous about stuff. Does he get this way? I've never seen him like this."

"Neither one of us have ever seen him on his wedding day. Where is he?"

"Back here. He wants to talk to you, but he wanted to make sure Maya wasn't out."

"She's tucked away."

"All right, come on." Sebastian led her to the other dressing room, and Shayla waited outside. In a second, Bo came out.

"Hey," he said, his face flushed.

She smiled. "Who knew you could look handsome."

He looked her up and down. "You, too, but pretty."

"Aww, thanks for the heartfelt words, Lord Byron."

Bo glanced around. "Have you seen Maya?"

"Just a minute ago."

He smiled. "What does she look like in her dress?"

"She's getting it on now. But I wouldn't tell you if I did know."

"Traitor."

Shayla rolled her eyes. She guessed he was kind of cute, all happy like he was. She would not cry.

His expression turned serious. "So, listen, I haven't really talked to you much about the wedding, about where you're gonna stand."

"I was here for the rehearsal last night, you know."

"I know. You know what I mean. I always assumed when I got married, you'd stand up for me, but Maya was so excited and nervous about asking you to stand up for her that I didn't want to take that from her."

She pinched his arm through his white shirt. "Quit worrying about all this. I don't care where I'm standing as long as you're getting married to the woman you love and you're happy. That's all that matters."

He smiled, letting out an exhale. "Thanks for understanding."

"Nothing to be understanding about."

"It goes without saying that you're my best friend in the world. You know that, right?"

She nodded. "I do, baby brother. Come here." She wrapped her arms around him and hugged him tightly to her, the pressure building behind her eyes. She was so lucky to have had him by her side all these years. Just knowing he was there when she needed him, if she ever chose to call on him, was more of a comfort than he'd ever know.

She pulled away and swallowed hard when she saw how red his eyes were. "Don't do something stupid like ruin your mascara," she said.

He shook his head, the backs of his fingers to his eyes. "Shut up."

"Shayla," Sebastian said from the altar, standing next to Ashe, who was holding a camera. "Can you stand in for light? Bo, send out Blake or Chase to stand here. I've got to go check on Maya."

She turned to Bo to let him know to send Blake, but he was already headed back to the dressing room. Shayla stepped up to the altar and stood, her heart spinning when Chase came out of the dressing room, decked out in his tux. She'd barely noticed it in the car in her frenzied state.

"Is the height going to be a problem?" Sebastian asked Ashe. "We've got like a six-inch difference between Chase and Bo."

"It's fine," Ashe said, already working.

Chase stepped up to the altar, and Sebastian was off. Ashe started snapping pictures and then stepped around them to adjust.

"Hey," Chase said.

"Hey," she replied, forcing a smile.

"What's going on? Something's been off with you since we left home."

She shook her head, wishing she were a better liar. She let her emotions sit too close to her chest when it came to people she loved. She cringed at herself for even thinking that word.

"I'm fine," she said.

283

"Hold hands and act like you love each other," Ashe said.

Shayla gave him a look. "Is that necessary?"

He put a hand on his hip. "If I say it is." He backed halfway down the aisle and kept snapping.

Chase took her hands, which she knew were clammy to match her nerves. He squeezed them. "I need you to talk to me. Did I do something wrong last night?"

"No, you didn't. Nothing like that."

"Then you've got to tell me."

"We'll talk after the wedding, okay?" she said, glancing around at the flowers surrounding them from all sides, realizing she was in no state to take in the moment like she should be doing.

"You've got to clue me in here. Is it about Brian? Has he contacted you?"

"No, nothing with Brian."

"Scott?" he asked.

"No, of course not. It's nothing."

"Stay put," Ashe said. "I've got to go grab something from the car."

Shayla let go of Chase's hands, and he ran them through his hair. "This is making me nuts, Shayla. What is wrong? I need to know."

She met his gaze, her mind swirling into a tornado that was spinning out of her control, words sitting on her tongue ready to leap off. "Do you have a child, Chase?"

His features morphed, his eyes a world of anguish and betrayal at her words. "What are you talking about?"

She swallowed hard, realizing how badly she'd

screwed up, but there was no turning back. "I found a picture in a box in the bottom of the closet. I wasn't snooping. I was just looking for something, and I saw it."

Blake walked up. "Chase, I wanted..." He paused. "Are you okay?"

Chase met Blake's gaze, looking like he was trying to find himself again. "Yeah. What's up?"

"I wanted to talk to you about the toast. I think what I've got is too sappy. I need some humor." He pulled a piece of paper out of his pocket and handed it to Chase.

Shayla inwardly slapped herself around for not being able to keep her mouth shut. She pointed at the women's dressing room. "I'm going to see about Maya." She walked away, feeling two inches tall.

She opened the door to the dressing room where Felicity, Meade, and Mrs. Forbes were all fussing over Maya, trying to get her into her dress, Meade and her mother bickering.

"Mother, it is not too tight. It fits perfectly. I'm telling you, there's something caught on one of these little hooks that's causing this."

"Some brides gain weight right before the wedding due to all the stress. I'm not judging, I'm just suggesting that she should have been refitted yesterday."

"How is that in any way helpful right this minute?" Meade asked.

Shayla backed out of the room and shut the door behind her. She let out a deep breath as she glanced around at everyone busying themselves, prepping for the wedding. Chase was scribbling notes on Blake's toast. Sebastian was directing the women who were delivering the cakes. Ashe was snapping photos.

Scott was talking to Shayla's dad. She realized that as of last night, Bo thought Shayla was dating Scott, and she'd let him keep thinking that. As far as she knew, her dad was over there welcoming him to the family. Her mother was nodding and smiling as Maya's father looked to be droning on about one of the many fascinating topics he'd been talking about last night at dinner which included the stock market, the hoax of climate change, and the rise and fall of the GDP.

A pressure built at her temple that she could not tamp down. She turned around and headed to the patio for some air. She stood out there breathing deeply, feeling like she was possibly on the verge of a panic attack. She'd never had one, but she wondered if rapid heartbeat and chest pains were signs.

Guests were arriving in the parking lot, people getting out of their cars and heading inside. She squinted as she noticed an all too familiar SUV at the back of the parking lot. The driver got out of the car, and her heartbeat went nuts. It was Brian.

Chapter Twenty-One

"Will that work?" Chase asked.

Blake grinned. "Thank God for you. I was afraid I would single-handedly end the reception early."

"Mmm hmm," Chase said, glancing around for Shayla.

"Are you all right, man?" Blake asked. "You're definitely not yourself this afternoon."

"I'm fine. Just weddings. I've been in about ten of them. You'd think I would have it down by now."

"You want to hear something funny?" Blake asked. "This is the first wedding I've been in besides my own."

Chase smiled at him, wishing he had the time to focus on his friend right now, but his mind was all over the place after the bomb Shayla dropped on him. He was planning on telling her as soon as everyone left for the weekend. The timing couldn't

MELISSA CHAMBERS

possibly be worse. "You're gonna do really well. If you flub over your words, people will forgive you because you're so damn handsome. I know from experience." Chase flashed him a reassuring smile.

Blake smiled back. "Thanks."

Sebastian walked with purpose through the venue clapping his hands. "All right I need my groomsmen by the front door for usher duty. Guests are pulling up. It's go-time people."

Chase looked around again. "Did you see where Shayla went?"

"She said she was going to check on Maya, remember?"

"Oh," Chase said. He'd been so freaked out that he'd spaced out. He looked at the door of the women's dressing room. It's not like he could go in there and grab her and explain everything, could he?

He felt hands on his arms and a gentle shove. "Door, please," Sebastian said.

Brian stood by his SUV, staring at her, letting his presence be known. But he didn't walk toward her, thank God. Still, the thing she'd feared since the day she found out Bo was getting married was happening.

She turned around and slid open the door, closing it behind her. What was Brian going to do? Would he come inside? Surely, he knew better than to do that. He'd let her know he was there. He'd put the ball in her court. She just had no idea what to do with it.

The door opened to the dressing room and

Felicity made eye contact with her. She waved her over. "Maya's asking about you."

"Sorry, I was just getting some air."

"Everything okay?"

"Yeah. I'm great. Just got a little stuffy in here with the humidity."

When Maya saw Shayla, she smiled. "Hey, is everything good?"

"It's great. Just helping Ashe a minute. Chase and I were standing in for you and Bo while he checked the lighting."

"Ah," she said with a smile, and then took a deep breath, resting against the table.

"Don't do that, dear," her mom said. "You'll snag that dress. That fabric you picked is beautiful but I'm seeing little snags all over."

Meade shook her head at Maya, rolling her eyes a little.

The door opened. "We've got five minutes before show time, ladies," Sebastian said.

Maya nodded her thanks, and Sebastian put his hand over his heart. "I've never seen a more beautiful bride."

Her mother pursed her lips, but kept her mouth shut, thankfully.

Sebastian left and Meade put her arm around her sister. "He's right about that."

Maya's mother glanced around at the group. "You all look stunning. Gosh, Maya, you could have picked at least one unattractive bridesmaid."

The room stayed dead silent, the comment not going over well, coming from her.

Felicity inspected her nails while Meade closed

her eyes like she was calming herself. Shayla wasn't sure if she'd ever had a more miserable day, then she remembered she had.

"What?" Mrs. Forbes said. "It's true. The bride needs to be the most special one on her day, am I right?"

They sat in uncomfortable silence mostly for the next five minutes, with an occasional joke from Felicity and bicker between Meade and her mother. Shayla could think of nothing other than Brian standing outside by his vehicle.

"Shayla," Mrs. Forbes said, "do you always bite your nails?"

The door opened to reveal Sebastian's smiling face. "It's time," he sang. "I'll take all the ladies except for Maya, and I'll replace them with your father. So I need Mrs. Forbes first, Meade second, Felicity third, and Shayla fourth please."

They lined up and Sebastian marched them to the end of the aisle where the guys were waiting. Maya winced as she saw Chase waiting in the back of the line, her escort up the aisle.

They took their places, and Chase glanced down at her, forcing a smile that didn't get near his eyes. They stood silently by one another, staring forward as the mothers were seated by Bo and Dale. Shayla's mind whirled around with everything that was bearing down on her. She couldn't believe she'd asked Chase about his child. She couldn't believe Brian was there.

Bo and Dale took their places in line, and then Sebastian nudged Bo down the aisle. Sebastian peered down the line, and then leaned in where

Chase and Shayla could both hear. "Arm and arm please," he said pointing.

Chase offered his arm, and Shayla took it, closing her eyes, pumping herself up to smile as they walked down the aisle, or at least some version of a smile. With each couple that took off down the aisle, Shayla's heartbeat accelerated. When Dale and Felicity were almost to the end of the short aisle, Shayla squeezed Chase's arm. "I'm sorry," she whispered.

He glanced down at her, and then Sebastian nudged them along, Shayla taking off with a small trip over her own two feet, Chase steadying her.

Shayla stood near the front door, glancing around the room, one eye on the parking lot. Brian was waiting for her out there. She couldn't go. Of course she couldn't.

What was the end game here? Was she just going to continue to pretend like he wasn't there? Was she going to throw birdseed at her brother and his new wife and then hop in Chase's car and let Brian follow them back to where she lived? Had he already been there?

She glanced around the room, taking stock of everyone. Bo and Maya were totally caught up in one another on the dance floor. Felicity and Scott were cheek to cheek as well. Blake and Seanna, Sebastian and Desiree, and Marigold and Chase were all in a circle laughing and drinking beer and wine. The cake had been cut and eaten, the bouquet thrown, and the food and the crowd were dwindling. If there was going to be a time to sneak out, this was it.

What could he possibly do to her here? If she stepped outside, she'd stay right by the front door. With people leaving, it's not like he could knock her out and drag her to his car.

She wanted this to be over. He came to say something. She'd let him say it and tell him if he tried to follow her she'd call the police. She'd get a restraining order against him. Neither of them wanted that. If anything at all happened, all she'd have to do was yell, and someone would be outside instantly.

She snuck out the front door and stood on the sidewalk, just out of sight of the windows behind some heavy greenery obstructing the view.

Brian stepped out of his SUV and shut the door, walking her way. She closed her arms over her chest, erecting a wall around her. Brian walked up, hands in his pockets, no doubt a peace offering.

"Hey," he said.

She just stared at him wordlessly.

"Look, I know this is a big day and I don't want to ruin it. But I needed to talk to you, and this is the only way I know how since you've cut me off, which I'm not blaming you for." He shifted back and forth in his stance. "First off, I've moved out. That's your house. I don't want anything from it. Last time we talked I was hurt and pissed and I spoke completely out of turn. Of course you don't owe me any part of it." He bit the side of his lip. "Next, I've been thinking a lot after what you said to me on the phone the last time we talked."

She rubbed her forehead. "Brian, I don't want

to—"

"I'm so sorry, Shayla."

She met his earnest gaze.

"I don't remember doing that, but I believe you...that I did that. I can't believe myself. I know it sounds disingenuous, but I really have learned a lot about myself, not only through that program, but through my sponsor who would kill me if he knew I was here right now, actually. But I couldn't just let this go. I love you more than anything on this earth, more than I've ever loved anything, and the idea of hurting you, especially that way...you have no idea how sick I am over it." He shook his head, his eyes bloodshot and watery. "I don't need your forgiveness, but I need you to know I'm sorry from the depths of my soul, Shayla."

She blinked, her guard still very much intact, but her heart opening for him just a tiny bit, not to let him back in, but to accept what he was telling her. She didn't nod or say anything. She just stared at him, letting him know silently that she wasn't up for a reconciliation.

He nodded. "Okay. That's what I came to say, so I'll leave you now."

"Leave me for how long?" she asked.

He frowned, his mouth open, but no words coming out.

"I've been living in fear of you, Brian. I've been looking over my shoulder every day. I've been paranoid that you were going to be waiting in the bed of my truck or behind a tree at my house. I've been afraid you were going to pop up out of nowhere and attack me...shove me against a mirror or bend me over a table. Do I need to keep worrying about that? Or are you going to let me have my life back?"

He shut his eyes tightly, and then wiped at them with the back of his hand, shaking his head. "You don't have to worry about any of that. Not anymore."

She stared at him, so contrite, and a wave of anger rose in her so strong that overcame her with a force that was so much bigger than she was. She shoved him as hard as she could, and he stumbled backward, his eyes wide. "Fuck you!" she screamed. She slammed her palms into his chest again. "Fuck you for taking everything from me. You took my dignity from me. You made me feel embarrassed and ashamed for falling for a guy who would hit me and rape me. I made excuses for you and lied to my family and friends. That's not who I am." She shoved him one last time, with strength she didn't even recognize. "I'm not your goddamned victim."

The door opened, and Chase walked out followed by Scott and Felicity, and maybe a few others. She was so out of her own mind she wasn't even sure of where she was anymore.

Chase made eye contact with Brian, barely even hesitating before swinging at him, the crack of his fist against Brian's face sending a shock through Shayla's core that woke her back to reality. Brian stumbled around from the impact, his confused expression quickly turning furious.

Scott stepped between Chase and him. "Get the fuck out of here."

Shayla's stomach sank to the ground as Bo stepped outside with Maya behind him. "What the fuck?" he asked, his expression registering Brian. "What's going on?"

Everyone clammed up, like this whole situation was going to somehow evaporate before their very own eyes.

Shayla tucked her arms around her stomach. "Leave, Brian."

Brian glanced around at everyone, his gaze landing on Shayla. "I'm sorry," he said, his voice in a whisper, meant just for her.

Everyone stood stone still as he walked to the parking lot and got in his SUV.

Bo glanced around from person to person, presumably looking for answers that nobody was willing to give. "What the fuck just happened?"

Shayla looked at Chase, who looked at his bloody hand.

"Shayla," Bo said, a command for a response, which he no doubt deserved.

She met his gaze, her whole body coming down from the adrenaline of the moment. "Let's just go back inside."

Bo lifted his eyebrows. "Are you fucking kidding me? Chase, who has never so much as killed a bug, just punched your ex. What the fuck?" He looked at Chase. "Are you that fucking jealous?"

Chase looked quickly at Scott and then at Shayla, and then nodded. "Yeah. I'm jealous."

"And the worst fucking liar on the planet," Bo said. He pointed at the ground beside him, his face turning beet red. "What the fuck is going on?"

As people poured out, Maya's expression became more panicked. Felicity scratched her forehead. "You know what? We haven't done the electric slide yet. I'm fixing this now. Maya, come on. Everyone, let's dance. Come on."

Felicity herded the group inside, touching the back of anyone who hesitated and nudging them along until everyone was inside except for Shayla and Bo.

Shayla scratched her forehead, her eyes closed tightly.

"Come here," Bo said, pulling her in for a hug. She kept her arms close to his chest, her brother, doing all the hugging, which despite its intention was making her feel ten times worse.

She pulled away. "I'm sorry for all that."

"Want to start by telling me what Brian was doing here? Did you invite him to the wedding?"

She shook her head, pressure building behind her forehead.

"Do you want to get back together with him?" he asked.

"No, God no."

"Oh," he said, looking relieved. "What's he doing then, stalking you?"

"He just wanted to talk."

"At my wedding? Couldn't he have picked a better time than this?"

"I've cut him off. That's why I changed my number. I didn't lose my phone."

"Well," he said, lifting his chin, "I was wondering about that. Didn't sound like you."

"He's here this weekend because he didn't know where to find me otherwise."

"He doesn't know you work at the shop?"

She scratched her cheek, wishing her lying skills were better. "He does know I work there, obviously, or I'm sure he could figure it out. But he wouldn't come there, knowing you were there."

"Why would that stop him?"

She shrugged. "I don't know. Maybe because he knows you don't want us together."

He narrowed his gaze, and she tried to put on her best poker face, but if anyone on earth could see past that, it was her brother. "What the fuck's really going on here, Shayla? I've already deduced that Scott's not here as your date, based on the way he can't keep his hands off Chase's date, or fake date, or whatever. So you're with Chase. Is that what this is about? I had no idea he was so jealous."

She let out a resigned breath. "He's not jealous."

"Okay?"

She met his gaze, her chest hot. "He's being protective. Brian is...dangerous. Or he was, I guess, but I think it's over."

He stepped back from her, looking her up and down, and she shut her eyes tightly, not believing she'd just told him, but not sure how else to proceed at this point.

"Dangerous? Like a threat, to you?"

She looked off to the parking lot at the empty space left from his exit. "Yeah."

"Fuck, Shayla. Since when?"

She glanced down at his shiny tux shoes, not able to believe that her actions had ruined this day for him, the worst possible result of weeks of worry. "Just…let's just go inside."

"Shayla, for how long?" he said, his voice unwavering.

She met his gaze with pursed lips. "For a while, okay? It's over now though. Can we please go inside?"

"What's over?"

She just stared at him, watching the color drain from his face. "Holy fuck," he said.

"I'm fine," she said, her voice a shaky mess. "It's over. He just came to apologize. The rehab he's been in has been helpful. The one he went to wasn't only about the alcohol, it was for…" She couldn't finish the sentence.

"Abusers?" Bo asked, his eyes wide. "Fucking shit, Shayla. Why are you just now telling me this?"

"I've got it under control," she said through clenched teeth.

"How? How did this even happen?"

She watched as his expression revealed what his mind was conjuring. Every worry she ever had about what her brother would think of her if he found out was coming to fruition. The humiliation and dread of the past six months pounded down on her.

"Did he hit you?" he asked, his voice weak, as if the words pained his throat.

"Just fucking leave me alone, okay?" she shouted and pushed past him to the door of the church. She walked to the dressing room as inconspicuously as she could but feeling eyes on her. She found her purse and pulled out her phone to dial up an Uber, but she had no service down this wooded road. "Fuck," she said, tossing her phone back in her purse. "Fuck it. I'll walk," she said aloud and opened the door to find Chase standing just outside of it.

"Wanna go home?" he asked.

She pulled him into the room, shutting the door behind him, and wrapped her arms around him so tightly they'd have to get the Jaws of Life to get her loose.

Chapter Twenty-Two

The car ride home was spent in utter silence. Felicity and Scott said they would catch a ride with Sebastian, so it was just Chase and Shayla. Chase didn't know what to say or how to say it, so he said nothing for once in his life. Shayla just peered out the window, her brow furrowed in thought. He wished he could kiss that frown line and make her worries vanish, but everything she'd been anticipating for months had just played out, so no amount of kissing was going to relieve her stress at this point.

They got out of the car, and he followed her through the house. He hesitated before the stairs up to his room, but she headed to her own space.

Collapsing on his bed, he stared at his bloody hand. He'd never hit a man in anger before. He'd evaded bar fights most his life, assuming guys thought twice before messing with him because he was so big. Besides that, Chase had used humor to get out of most unwanted situations throughout his life.

But when he'd laid eyes on the guy who had made Shayla's life hell, there was nothing in him that could stop his fist from flying without permission, like someone else had taken control of his body.

It had felt great.

He hadn't anticipated his own hand hurting so badly as a result, but that was a small price to pay to get that kind of satisfaction.

He washed his hand and bandaged it up the best he could with the other one, got out of his penguin suit and into some sweats, and then headed downstairs. He needed a beer. He'd refrained from drinking at the wedding reception, not in the mood after what Shayla had asked him, standing there on that altar.

How had he been so stupid as to leave that box in that closet? He'd completely forgotten it was out there. He remembered now. He'd put it out there years ago when he'd come across it after the move and wanted it as far away from him as possible, though not ready to rid himself of Sam's favorite books and toys.

He stuck a handful of beers into a bucket, covered them with ice, and then headed out by the pool. He sat in a chair and popped the cap. It wasn't long before Shayla joined him wearing a tank top and shorts that covered way too much of her luscious thighs.

"Pilsner?" he asked.

She sat beside him. "Thanks. How's your hand?"

He looked at it. "Satisfied."

She gave him half a smile, and then stared down at her beer bottle. "Didn't you say you weren't a fighter?"

"I'm still not. That was an isolated incident."

She gave him a curious look. "How did you know that was Brian?"

"I took one look at your face."

She looked down at her beer again, a humorless smile crossing her lips.

He picked up the picture of Sam he'd brought downstairs with him and took a deep breath. He handed it to her as he exhaled. "This is Sam. I know you've already seen other pictures, but this one's my favorite. It was taken right before he died."

She met his gaze, her expression worried.

He smiled at the picture. As many times as he looked at it, he never tired of it. "Kids grow so fast and their faces change so quickly. When I think of what this picture looks like compared to his baby pictures, it doesn't even seem like the same little boy. I try to imagine what he'd look like now. He'd be ten years old, a fifth-grader. It's crazy to think of this little boy who I held and fed and changed sitting at a desk taking standardized tests or learning about what causes tornadoes and hurricanes…whatever fifth-graders learn." He swatted a hand through the air. "Anyway, I'm sorry I kept him from you."

"Chase, I—"

He held up a hand. "I was going tell you. I promise I was. I'd gathered up my nerve earlier today, but I wanted to wait until the madness died down. I wanted it to be just the two of us when I told you." He gauged her, making sure she believed him, and by the look on her face he was sure she did.

She squeezed his arm. "Of course. I'm so sorry I sprung that on you today. I think my nerves have just been shot from everything. I saw the pictures and it was all I could focus on. Honestly, I think it was a way for me to focus on something other than Brian and Bo and the wedding." She turned her body toward his. "Tell me about Sam."

He smiled, thinking about where to start. He told her about how curious he was all the time, all the questions he'd ask. He told her about how much Sam loved the movie *Cars* and how he himself could recite it to her verbatim if she'd like, which she didn't take him up on. He told her about how Sam smiled when he slept and how much he loved the beach. He told her about the first time he watched Sam eat an ice cream cone and about the time he ran and jumped into the water their first time at a swimming pool before Chase could get his arm floats on him.

"I'm sorry," he said. "I didn't mean to get carried away."

She just smiled at him, her head resting on the back of the chair. "I like hearing you talk about him."

He frowned, knowing if he was going to do this honestly, he had one more story to tell. "Sam died alongside my mother."

Shayla closed her eyes, her brow furrowed as she

let it sink in. She took his hand in hers.

"I needed a night alone with my wife. Just one night. Our marriage was falling apart. As much as we both adored Sam, he changed everything in our lives, and we had a hard time adjusting. We were both driven at work and trying to focus on our careers and be good parents. Keeping our marriage cohesive became a distant third on the priority list. She'd tossed out the word divorce more than once. I couldn't stand the idea of Sam growing up in a broken home, not that young. I asked my mother to take him so I could be with Rachel. We hadn't been intimate in months...hell, probably a year if I'm being honest. I wanted so badly to make it work. She just wanted out. We were arguing when my brother showed up at the front door that night with the news." He huffed a humorless laugh. "If I just would have given her the goddamned divorce."

Shayla didn't say anything to try to make him feel better, which was one of the reasons he loved her.

"Anyway," he said, facing her, "that's it. That's everything."

"Does anyone else know about Sam?"

"Nah, not in our circles."

"That's a lot to keep in."

He nodded. "Mmm hmm."

"Thank you for trusting me."

He met her gaze. "I've trusted you since the day I met you. Even when you were swinging a bat at me."

She smiled. "I never swung."

"Well, close enough. What happened with

Brian?"

She shook her head. "Nothing. He came in peace. I was the one who got violent. He said he wanted to apologize. The last time we talked, I told him what he'd done. He didn't act like he believed me. I think he realized he was wrong, and he felt sick over it."

"As he should."

"I know. He said he wasn't going to bother me anymore. I might believe him."

"I'm not taking any chances, not with the woman I love."

She met his gaze, a smile tugging at her lips. He stuck his beer in the ice and then took hers from her and put it beside his. He stood and held out his hand, and she took it, standing with him.

He put his hands on her hips. "I love you, Shayla. The past few weeks with you have done more to heal my heart than anything else these past six years. I'll always have a huge hole there, but my heart's bigger now than it's ever been. I've never known love like this that I have with you. I don't want to ever let it go."

She kept her expression impassive, but her glassy eyes gave her away. She dabbed at a tear with her knuckle and sniffed. "I don't want to let go either."

He closed his eyes, bringing her to his chest, feeling the universe shift around him. This was his woman…his person to be with and share life with, and she didn't want to let go either. He inhaled the perfume of her hair, still curly and pulled halfway up from the wedding. She'd blown him away when he'd seen her in her bridesmaid dress with her hair and makeup all fancy, but standing here in front of him in sweat shorts and a tank, he couldn't want her more.

She pulled away and tugged him toward her pool house. He stopped and tugged back. She met his gaze with confusion.

"Let's go to my room."

Walking across the threshold into Chase's room felt like a step into a new life. They were together now. He'd told her he loved her, and she couldn't see a way to stop herself from saying it back. She just needed a moment to process the craziest day of her life.

He pulled the tank top over her head. She hadn't bothered with a bra. He cupped the back of her neck and kissed her, his soft lips filling her soul like a warm breeze off the ocean on a summer day.

He tugged her shorts down. She'd left the underwear in the drawer as well, and she stood there before him completely bare.

"I can't believe you're mine," he said, gazing over her body. He picked her up, literally sweeping her off her feet, and then set her on his unmade bed, ripping the covers to the floor with his good hand.

"Was all that necessary?" she asked.

"Oh yeah," he said.

He knelt on the bed with his knees between her legs, lifting one leg to the ceiling and resting it on his shoulder, kissing her ankle. He pulled the other leg up and did the same thing, sort of hugging her legs to his chest. "Fuck, I love your body."

She smiled. Her body wasn't anything to write home about, and she knew it. Her thighs were too big, her boobs were too small, and gravity was starting to take hold of her almost-late-thirties skin. But she loved that he appreciated it nonetheless.

He moved both his hands, even the bandaged one, up and down her legs, and then let them go as he worked his way toward her center. "And there's nothing on the planet better than this." He tossed each of her legs over his shoulders and sank into her in a way that had her lifting herself off the bed and likely smothering him to death.

She grabbed onto his shoulders for the ride, which was shorter than it should have been because she was so ready for him. His touch on her freed her body like a bird being let out of its cage.

"Chase," she whispered, which made him work harder, finding the spot inside her that was a guaranteed smash hit.

She arched her back, letting the sensations rush through her, reaching all the way down to the tips of her toes. She nudged him away as soon as she'd had more than she could take, eager to let him keep going because she was pretty damn sure she could go again, but she wanted him inside her as much as she wanted his mouth on her.

She sat up. "Get out of those clothes," she said, and he obeyed, standing off the bed and undressing. She stood off the bed as well and ran her hand through his hair, kissing his mouth, tasting herself on his lips. His cock pressed against her belly, hard as a rock, and she pressed on his shoulders, instructing him to sit on the bed.

She knelt down in front of him, spreading his legs, wanting to show him that she trusted him in the power position. She took him into her mouth, and the power shifted to her as she watched his head tilt backward, his eyes closing with the pleasure of her mouth.

She pushed him backward with a single finger to his chest and then spread his legs even farther as she explored him.

"Fuck, Shayla," he said. "I'm not gonna last."

"Let yourself go," she said, and he did, onto his own stomach, which she couldn't help but find a little hot.

"Stay put," she said, standing and then heading to his bathroom, which was three times the size of hers. She came back with a wet, warm towel that she used to wipe off his stomach.

"That was hot as fuck, Shayla."

She smiled at his stomach. "I know."

She started to stand to return the towel, but he took it from her and tossed it on the floor. "I'll get it later. Come here."

She ran her hand over his chest, settling in next to him. "I don't know what to make of this room. I think it's bigger than the whole pool house."

"It might be. Wanna trade?" he asked. She kept her smile closed-mouth, not wanting to show any cards. He smoothed the hair away from her face. "Where does a relationship like this go? You've already moved in."

"I didn't *move in.* I rented a pool house from you."

"Well, I can't let you stay down there anymore.

That'd just be too freaking weird."

"Then I'll stay down the hall," she said.

He pulled her over on top of him. "You'll stay right here."

She kissed him and then pulled away, her hair draping over his chest and shoulders. "We'll take it one day at a time."

He played with one of her curls. "We'll take it any way you want it, my love."

"You're sure free with that word," she said.

"I've been wanting to say it for a week now. I can't say it enough."

She let out a breath, feeling love for him like a tidal wave. "I'm a lucky girl."

"I'm the lucky one."

She felt something nudge her down below and furrowed her brow as she took a look. "Are you ready to go again?"

"Getting there. It doesn't take much, sweetheart. Not with you."

She smiled and pulled his length between them, straddling him and pressing her pelvic bone against him. "Fuck," he said, closing his eyes. She moved a little more until he was at full attention. He met her gaze. "Damn, you're good."

She pointed to the drawer. "Condoms in there?"

"Are you on the pill?" he asked.

"I'm on birth control," she said, because she didn't take an actual pill, but she was covered. She made sure of that every three months.

"Fuck it, then."

She narrowed her gaze. "Are you sure? You've been so diligent all these years. I hate to break your no-condom streak."

"I'm totally sure."

She smiled. "You seriously haven't had unprotected sex since your wife?"

"Nope. Not once." He had her on her back in seconds flat. "And I can't think of anyone I'd rather break that seal with."

He pushed inside her, and she gasped at how good it felt to have his skin directly on her...in her.

"Oh, fuck," he said, sinking down to bury his face in her neck. "You feel fucking amazing."

He pumped into her, and the part of her that begged for that second orgasm earlier came alive quickly. She wrapped her arms around his shoulders and held on tight as he pushed into her, their chests melded together, every part of them possible, touching one another. Her heart beat against his chest, the rhythm of their hearts moving into sync with one another. She wrapped her legs around his back, and he pushed until she let out a howl from the sensations flowing through her. He pushed one last time, hard, collapsing on her.

"Fuck," he said again, into her neck, their bodies, wet with sweat, tangled together.

He balanced himself on top of her, letting his weight rest in his arms on either side of her. "I fucking love you, Shayla Harrison."

She smiled. "You say fuck a lot in bed."

He smiled and went back in for kisses that went on and on and on...

Chapter Twenty-Three

The ding-dong of a doorbell had Shayla opening her eyes. She was sprawled out on Chase's chest. "Do you think Felicity and Scott both forgot the code?" she asked a naked Chase beneath her.

"I texted it to her so she wouldn't forget. Besides, it's morning time. These are black-out blinds." He pointed to the blinds on the window that faced the front of the house.

She sat up. "Really?"

He showed her his phone. "Yep."

Knocking sounded now. She stood and tiptoed to the window, getting a glimpse of her brother's truck, her heart sinking. "It's Bo."

"Aren't they leaving for a honeymoon?"

"No, they aren't doing one right now since they just moved back."

Chase got out of bed and grabbed his shorts. "Take your time getting dressed. I'll go talk to him first." He put his shorts on and then headed downstairs.

She cleaned herself up a bit before dressing. Nothing like talking to her brother when she was fresh from a night of hot sex. But it needed to be done.

She walked downstairs, her hand sliding down the bannister as her brother came into view in the foyer. Maya was with him, his new wife. They would be Bo and Maya from here on out. Shayla was happy for him, but there was a part of her that understood that their practical twin bond was a little bit weaker now. But she was okay with it.

Bo scrubbed his hand over his head, his eyes wide, looking contrite and reasonable. Seeing the encouraging look on Maya's face, Shayla inwardly thanked her for Bo's calm demeanor.

"Hey," he said.

"Hey."

"I tried calling and texting, but you didn't answer."

"My phone's in the pool house. I stayed here last night."

He nodded, glancing between Chase and her. "Good. I mean, if you want to do that, that's good."

She almost grinned at his attempt to be agreeable.

"Can we go somewhere and talk?" he asked.

She looked around the room at Chase, her new relationship, and Maya, her new family.

"Let's all talk together," she said, and headed into the kitchen.

Maya hesitated before pulling a chair back from

the kitchen table. "Are you sure, Shayla? I don't mind waiting in the truck or outside by the pool."

"It's fine, Maya. Welcome to the family," she said with a smile.

They all sat, and Bo scrubbed his hands together, setting them on the kitchen table. "Look, Shayla, I had a completely wrong reaction to what you told me last night. Maya helped me understand that."

Shayla gave Maya a grateful look, and Maya smiled at her in return.

"I hope you don't mind that I talked to her about this," he said.

Shayla shook her head.

He looked down at his hands, brow furrowed like he was prepping for an exam. "Look, Shayla, what happened back in Nashville is none of my business. But I'm your brother, and I can't help but feel protective of you." His knuckles were turning white. "And the idea of some son-of-a-bitch—" Maya put her hand on his arm, and he stopped mid-sentence, meeting her serious gaze. He looked off to the side, gathering himself, then he met Shayla's gaze. "I'm here to listen, not to judge you or ask you for answers. I'm here to see if you're okay."

Maya squeezed his arm, giving him a nod.

Chase set his arm on the table and held out his hand. Shayla took it and squeezed it, smiling at him in return. She looked back at Bo. "I'm sorry I kept it from you. I was embarrassed and ashamed of what had happened, and I didn't know how to talk about it. I still don't, but I'm trying." She squeezed Chase's hand again, thankful beyond words for his presence in her life.

Bo nodded slowly, his eyes scanning hers fiercely. "I want you to know that if I'd had a clue that you were going through this I never would have left to go to Indianapolis, and I'll say that right here in front of Maya."

"I know you wouldn't have you, dum-dum. Why do you think I kept it from you? Besides, Brian was headed to a two-month rehab when I came home, so I knew I'd be okay."

"Physically, maybe. But what about letting your brother be there to help you out with the rest?" He made a vague motion toward her head.

She couldn't help a little chuckle. Bless his heart. "I'm sorry," she said, leaving it at that. She wasn't sure he could ever understand the loss of pride, the shattering of the idea of her as the big sister he looked up to.

He ran his hand over the top of his head and then let out a resigned sigh. "Okay." He turned to Chase. "You knew about this?"

"Not until last night, not really. But I suspected." He glanced at Shayla, and she digested what he must have been going through the past few weeks trying to figure her out, knowing how he felt about her now.

Bo glanced at Chase's bandage. "How'd that feel?"

"Fucking satisfying," Chase said.

Bo huffed. "Wish I knew what that felt like," he said, his lip curling up.

"I'm so sorry you didn't get to pound somebody on your wedding day," Shayla said. "I know Maya would have loved some stray blood on her white dress."

He let out a resigned breath. "All right. I guess we'll let you all get back to…whatever you were doing," he said through pursed lips.

Shayla gave him a look. "Seriously? You still have a problem with this?" She pointed between Chase and her.

He looked between the two of them. "I don't guess so, as long as this asshole doesn't go back to his old ways."

Chase locked gazes with Shayla. "No fucking way."

She grinned at the goofy bastard who she adored.

Chase frowned, looking at Maya and Bo, scratching his forehead with his bandaged hand. "Hey, so I need to tell you all something about me."

Shayla squeezed his hand and gave him an '*Are you sure?*' look.

He nodded and then turned back to Bo.

Chapter Twenty-Four

Shayla ended the call and grinned over at Chase in the driver's seat. "They lifted the inspection contingency. I'm closing on the 8th."

"This is cause to celebrate. We should go to dinner somewhere," he said. She lifted an eyebrow, waiting for him to look over at her. "Oh, yeah. I guess not tonight, huh?"

"Another night, maybe in a week or two?"

"It's gonna take a week or two before we can leave the house again?"

"Not at nighttime. We'll need time to get settled…all of us."

He pulled into a parking space up front and exhaled a deep breath. "Okay."

"Are you sure you're ready for this? It's a major life decision."

"I'm the one who suggested it, aren't I?" he said.

"We could wait until after your dad's visit next

week."

He took her hand and kissed it. "No, I don't want to wait a second longer."

She grinned at him, happier than she'd ever been in her life. "I love you," she said, the words coming out more naturally than she'd ever dreamed they would.

He smiled so wide. "You do?"

She nodded. "Of course I do. But you knew that."

"Well, I hoped."

She reached over and kissed him. "It's hard for me to believe that you're real sometimes." She bit her lip, feeling giddier than a twelve-year-old with a crush.

He nodded at the building. "Things are about to get really real up in here. Are you in?"

"Let's do this." She opened the door, and they headed into the animal shelter.

The Next Chapter...

Marigold sat on a beach chair, her toes digging into the sand, her pedicure going to hell. She took a sip of her water, wondering if it'd turn into a cocktail if she wiggled her nose. She'd had to seriously take a look at her life choices after she drunkenly slipped off Sebastian's diving board and hit her head last fall. She still imbibed, she just had to pace herself. One drink per hour for a max of three drinks. Boring. But this way she didn't have to go to the hospital, which was better, she supposed.

Chase stood on the other side of the bonfire with his hands on Shayla's ample hips, wandering around to her curvaceous ass, the two of them glowing in the firelight like they were planted there for a professional photo shoot. Marigold pointed with her water bottle. "That's absolutely disgusting."

"Leave them alone," Sebastian said. "His dad's

up at the bathroom. Chase is copping a feel while he can."

"His dad's kind of hot for an old guy," Marigold said.

Sebastian shrugged. "What do you expect? Look at his son."

"Do you think he'd do me?"

"Chase's dad?" Sebastian asked.

"I doubt it," she said, answering her own question. "No other hot guys in this town are interested."

Sebastian patted her arm. "Your turn's coming, sweetie."

"When?"

"Give it time."

She pursed her lips at him. "What time is it?"

He looked at his phone. "Eight forty-five."

"That's close enough. I'm getting another cocktail," she said, but didn't stand. She glanced around at their group of friends, loving and hating each and every one of them, but mostly loving them. They were just all so dang in love. "Look at all these assholes," she said, motioning to their group.

"Mmm hmm," Sebastian said, unfazed as usual.

"Blake's about to lay Seanna out on this sand and do her, Chase can't keep his hands off Shayla's ass, and Bo just whispered something into Maya's ear that has her cheeks redder than the flame from the bonfire. Hell, even Desiree and Ashe are over there cuddled up in that blanket watching the waves and probably pontificating on the depth of the ocean and their helplessness in surrendering themselves to it. They're all so goddamned happy, coupled up," she said. "And they're all so damned beautiful."

"Sweetie, you are beautiful."

"Well, duh. But I don't have that thing."

"What thing?"

"I don't know. That thing that attracts men. I don't have Shayla's cool, hot molten lava sexy confidence, or Seanna's mouthwatering rack mixed with her candid charm, or Maya's got-it-together but so sweet and demure appeal, or Desiree's artistic, interesting, earthy vibe."

Sebastian kicked some sand onto her foot. "You've got your own thing."

"What is it?" she asked.

He thought about it. "You're honest, fun, sincere, up for anything."

"These are not character traits that reel in a man."

"I'm trying here. You've put me on the spot. Let me think."

"Oh, Jesus Christ," she said, wiggling in her chair, wishing a cocktail would appear in her plastic cup.

"Oh, hang on. Look at this." Sebastian nodded at Seanna's Aunt Cassidy intercepting Chase's dad with a smile and a beer, which he took with appreciation.

"Well, there went that," Marigold said.

"You were not going to screw Chase's father."

"Why not?" Marigold asked.

"Because he's like fifty-seven years old."

"You know his exact age?" Marigold said.

"I listen. He told me he was twenty when Chase

was born, and I know Chase is thirty-seven. I can do math."

"Damn. I didn't know Chase was thirty-seven. I thought he was younger than that."

"He's got excellent genes. He's part Hawaiian. I'd kill to be part something interesting like that, have some color on these sad, white arms."

Cassidy brushed his arm as he said something funny to her. "Oh, look at her now, making her move," Marigold said.

"She's into older guys. Bo's going to be so jealous." He looked over at him laying one on Maya. "Scratch that."

Marigold took Sebastian's hand and held it between them. "Will you marry me?"

"I won't rule it out."

She let go of his hand. "Sadly, that's the most promising offer I've had."

A guy walked up to Chase and they did that cool guy handshake thing, the half hug the extra step that indicated they really were happy to see each other and not faking it. The guy shook Shayla's hand.

"Who is this?" Marigold asked.

"I don't know, but his physique looks yummy through the firelight."

He turned for a second, and she got a quick view of his face. "Mmm, he's got a little Alex Pettyfer thing going on."

"Who?" Sebastian asked.

"The scrub from *Magic Mike*."

"Hmm. I'm thinking more Chris Hemsworth."

"Ha! He wishes."

"No, I'm serious," Sebastian said.

"Maybe."

"Let's get a better look." Sebastian waved. "Yoo-hoo, Chase. Who's your friend?"

"I see you took the subtle approach."

"You'd have done it differently?" Sebastian asked, and she shrugged concession.

Chase nudged the guy and they walked around the bonfire over to them. Marigold should have stood, but she was really comfortable in her beach chair, and she was tired of standing up for guys who walked away.

"Howdy." She held a hand out. "Marigold."

The guy took her hand. "Dane." She mentally rolled R's through her head. Definitely Chris Hemsworth.

"Hello, Dane," she said, with plenty of innuendo. What the hell did she have to lose?

His mouth tipped upward in an amused grin, and she let go of his hand first, though she was really enjoying holding it.

"That's Sebastian," Chase said.

"Hello," Sebastian said, holding out his hand. "How do you know the Jolly Green Giant here?" Dane smiled at Chase, who shrugged, used to being teased by this group.

He considered Chase. "I'm not sure. Was it the tough man contest?"

Chase shut one eye like he was thinking hard. "MMA championships?"

Dane pointed at Chase and snapped. "It was the heavyweight boxing tournament. It was a tough match, but Chase knocked me out in the ninth round."

Marigold lazily stared at Chase. "In your wet dreams."

He looked back over at Dane. "He's good looking, but not my type."

She rolled her eyes, but she adored Chase. She teased Chase, Bo, and Blake and flirted shamelessly, but she'd never really fallen for any of the three of them. She'd come close with Blake before Seanna came on the scene, but she was really more interested in the idea of these three big, hot guys who would do anything for her. They really did make her feel like a princess, although, all three had princesses of their own now. She supposed it was time to find a new prince or three.

"How do you know him?" Dane asked Marigold.

"I was his dominatrix, before he met Shayla, of course."

The guy smiled, scratching at the side of his mouth, his eyes curious. Good. Keep 'em curious. Maybe that was the way to work it. She held out her hand to him. "Help me up?" He took her hand, his strong and a little rough. Maybe he wasn't a total pretty boy. She stood, and they were face to face, kissing distance, for sure. "It's cocktail time for me. Nice to meet you."

She made her exit and headed toward Sebastian's cabana where the bar was set up. She shouldn't turn around. She'd done so well so far. Turning around would undo her good work.

Maybe he'd be there when she got back. *Don't turn. Don't turn.* She took a few more steps...and then she turned.

He wasn't there. Of course he wasn't there. Oh

well. Easy come.

She used the community restroom before heading to Sebastian's cabana where she fixed herself another vodka cranberry with a splash of seltzer and another half a shot for good measure. She was way too sober for the couples' retreat going on out there. She stepped back into the sand and found Dane walking toward another cabana where a handful of people gathered. He held up a hand in a wave. "Good meeting you."

She lifted her cup. "Likewise."

She held his stare a moment longer than she should have, but she never claimed to know how to hook a guy.

"Marigold," he said, and she turned to meet his moonlit gaze across the beach. Maybe she did know how to reel 'em in.

He motioned toward his ass. What the hell? That was forward. He pointed to her, and she turned around to find her flowy skirt somehow tucked up in her underwear. Goddammit. She'd thought she felt a breeze back there.

She freed the material and then gave him an embarrassed wave. "Thanks for the heads-up."

"No problem." He smiled and then walked up to the group where a beautiful girl put her arm around him.

Peachy. Just freaking peachy.

To stay informed of all Melissa's new releases, bonus content, and giveaways, sign up for her newsletter at melissachambers.com.

If you enjoyed this story, please consider leaving a review on Amazon. Your words are so valuable to authors, and even a really short review is very much appreciated!

Marigold and Dane's story coming soon!

SEASIDE SWEETS and SEACREST SUNSETS now available on Amazon

About the Author

Melissa Chambers writes contemporary novels for young, new, and actual adults. A Nashville native, she spends her days working in the music industry and her nights tapping away at her keyboard. While she's slightly obsessed with alt rock, she leaves the guitar playing to her husband and kid. She never misses a chance to play a tennis match, listen to an audiobook, or eat a bowl of ice cream. (Rocky road, please!) She's a member of RWA and serves as the president for the Music City Romance Writers. In addition to the Love Along Hwy 30A series, she is the author of The Summer Before Forever and Falling for Forever (Entangled Teen).

CPSIA information can be obtained
at www.ICGtesting.com
Printed in the USA
LVHW092252220919
631915LV00001B/7/P